"Do you think you could pretend to be my fiancée?"

Violet turned and skipped the rock over the surface of the lake. Jordan didn't count, but it had to skip at least thirty-five times. A record-setter. But he doubted Violet had even counted.

"You want me to pretend we're engaged?" Violet asked, not looking at him.

"That throw," he said, pointing to where ripples still spread from the rock's final sinking. "You shattered our record."

"Seriously," Violet said, turning to him. "You know I have no poker face. I'm terrible at keeping secrets. I tell you what your Christmas gift is as soon as I buy it because I can't wait to give it to you."

It suddenly occurred to Jordan that, if he got the job, he wouldn't be there the next Christmas. Wouldn't see Violet's face when he opened her gift or gave her one. He felt his heart sinking like that rock in the lake, but he pushed the worry away. This was a once-in-a-lifetime chance.

Dear Reader,

Welcome back to Christmas Island for the fourth book in the series!

Christmas Island is in the Great Lakes region of the United States. Just off the Michigan shoreline, it has warm summers and snowy winters. It's a beautiful area with clear water, trees and rocky shores. Several hundred people live on the island all year, but Christmas Island really comes alive for the summer tourist crowd and the holidays. Day visitors travel aboard the ferry to the island where they bike, rent golf carts, shop in downtown boutiques, enjoy the scenery and buy souvenirs of their excursion.

In *Last Summer on Christmas Island*, Violet Brookstone agrees to a surprising request when her best friend asks her to masquerade as his fiancée. Jordan Frome wants a big promotion that will take him away from Christmas Island, and the more Violet tries to help him, the more they both realize what they could be sacrificing.

I hope you'll love your visit to Christmas Island and come back for the rest of the series!

Happy reading,

Amie Denman

HEARTWARMING

Last Summer on Christmas Island

—

Amie Denman

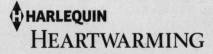

HARLEQUIN
HEARTWARMING

HARLEQUIN®
HEARTWARMING™

Recycling programs
for this product may
not exist in your area.

ISBN-13: 978-1-335-49092-6

Last Summer on Christmas Island

Harlequin Enterprises ULC
22 Adelaide St. West, 41st Floor
Toronto, Ontario M5H 4E3, Canada
www.Harlequin.com

Printed in U.S.A.

Amie Denman is the author of fifty contemporary romances full of humor and heart. A devoted traveler whose parents always kept a suitcase packed, she loves reading and writing books you could take on vacation. Amie believes everything is fun, especially wedding cake, roller coasters and falling in love.

Books by Amie Denman

Harlequin Heartwarming

Return to Christmas Island

I'll Be Home for Christmas
Home for the Holidays
A Merry Little Christmas

Cape Pursuit Firefighters

In Love with the Firefighter
The Firefighter's Vow
A Home for the Firefighter

Starlight Point Stories

Under the Boardwalk
Carousel Nights
Meet Me on the Midway
Until the Ride Stops
Back to the Lake Breeze Hotel

Visit the Author Profile page
at Harlequin.com for more titles.

This book is dedicated to my amazing editor, Dana Grimaldi. You've been my rock, a source of inspiration and a caring and kind guiding hand for over fifteen books. I appreciate you, and I love having you by my side on my wonderful journey as a Harlequin author.

CHAPTER ONE

MORNING SUN STREAMED through the front windows as Violet Brookstone hurried to the front door of her Island Boutique when she saw her friends Camille and Rebecca standing outside. Camille straightened her pink-and-white-striped apron in her reflection in the shop window and Rebecca tapped quietly on the front door. It was only eight in the morning, and the first ferries to Christmas Island wouldn't arrive with visitors and shoppers for at least thirty minutes. Violet had planned to unpack yesterday's shipment of new clothing, but friend time was precious.

"Can I try it on again?" Rebecca asked as soon as Violet pulled open the original leaded-glass door.

Violet laughed. The wedding dress had arrived the day before, and Rebecca had already visited it twice. "It's still too long, remember?

I didn't magically alter it overnight, and your wedding is still months away."

"I'll just admire myself in it, even if I have to hold up the bottom."

Violet twirled a finger and directed Rebecca and Camille to the back room of the boutique where a wedding dress shimmered in the morning light. In the style of Princess Grace, the dress had a white lace bodice and sleeves and a long white silk skirt. Violet had ordered it especially for her friend's November wedding, and she had only disagreed with Rebecca on one point.

"It would be even better with a train," Violet teased. "More drama that way."

Rebecca smiled as she touched the lace sleeve. "Look at the sparkle from these tiny sequins. I don't need any more drama. And I don't want any trip hazards on the way to the altar. Plus, I want to dance freely at my reception."

"I could bustle a train for you with fabulous tiny silk-covered buttons. I love little buttons," Violet said. Details that seemed small to other people—an embroidered flower on a cuff, a narrow ribbon on a hat, an extra flounce on a skirt—sparked Violet's imagination.

"You love everything about clothes. I can't imagine how fabulous your wedding dress will be," Camille said. "Someday."

Violet took the dress off the hanger and draped it over her arms. She nodded her head toward a fitting room door. "Let's see. I'm already twenty-eight, I haven't had any proposals yet and we live on an island. But I can always hope an eligible bachelor will parachute in and land on the roof of the Island Boutique."

Rebecca took the dress and went into the fitting room, leaving Camille and Violet in the quiet back room of the shop. "I'm pretty sure you'll make it to the altar before I do," she added, grinning at Camille.

Camille flopped into one of the pink velvet chairs in the fitting-room area. She already wore her uniform for working in her family's candy shop, which she'd taken over the previous year. "No time right now, not with the summer fudge business going warp speed. Besides, I've known Maddox all my life, so we don't have to rush into anything."

"Every time I see you, I check for a ring," Violet said.

Camille smiled. "Officially, I'm being patient. But I wouldn't turn down a ring either."

"Fair enough," Violet said. "In the meantime, you could occupy your time shopping for new summer clothes from my latest shipment." She pointed through an open door to a small storage area tacked on to the back of the store. Like the other businesses lining Holly Street in downtown Christmas Island, her shop was a century old with aged wood, a tin ceiling and big glass windows facing the street. In addition to the holiday spirit year-round, the Northern Michigan island drew tourists in for the cute shops, candy and fudge and miles of biking and hiking trails. The Holiday Hotel downtown offered overnight guests an elegant room, but they could also stay at the Great Island Hotel where five-course dinners and velvet curtains were luxury with an exclamation point.

"Need help with the zipper?" Camille called through the dressing room door.

"Please," Rebecca said.

Camille propped open the door with her foot and zipped Rebecca into the bridal gown.

Violet's phone pinged and she glanced at the name on the text.

"Anything important?" Camille asked.

"It's just Jordan." She read the message. "He says he needs to ask me for a favor and wants me to meet him at our spot."

"Sounds mysterious," Camille commented.

"Hardly," Violet said. "Careful not to catch the lace in the zipper at the top."

Violet responded with a time that evening after her shop closed, and then she slipped the phone into her pocket.

Rebecca held up the skirt that was several inches too long and walked into the room where a three-way mirror stood between two pink velvet chairs.

"Gorgeous," Camille and Violet said at the same time. Violet put her hand over her heart. She loved almost all clothing, with the notable exceptions of rain parkas and fishing vests, but formal gowns were her favorites. Wedding gowns were even one rung higher, and seeing her friend glowing in the white gown was even better in the morning light than it had been the previous day.

Rebecca covered her mouth with both hands. "I can't believe it's really happening. I came to this island a year ago to keep a sweet old lady out of trouble, and now I'm marrying her honorary nephew. If this is a dream, I hope I never wake up."

"The freezing winter we had would have woken you up if it was a dream," Camille said.

Violet retrieved a sturdy box covered in green fabric and put it in front of Rebecca. "If you have a few minutes, I can go ahead and pin the skirt." She pointed to the box. "Up you go."

Rebecca stepped onto the box and let the hem of the wedding gown fall around her. "I love this," she breathed, admiring her reflection in the mirror. "I look so tall."

Violet knelt with her pin holder and began measuring and pinning around the full length of the white satin skirt. Camille sat and watched for a few minutes before saying, "So, what favor do you think Jordan wants?"

Violet sighed. "I'm afraid I know, and I've been trying to avoid it."

"What?" Rebecca asked.

"I can't be sure, but he's seemed restless lately, like there's something missing in his life. Although he's always been that way to an extent, always thinking there's a better life for him outside of Christmas Island." She carefully inserted a pin. "I've heard him hinting around about getting a pet."

"Dogs are nice," Rebecca said. "Griffin and I may get one."

"I think Jordan is going to ask me to go to the shelter on the mainland and pick one out, and I'm not sure I want to," Violet said.

She paused with a pin in her hand just long enough to notice a strange look pass between Camille and Rebecca. She'd known Camille all her life, and Rebecca had become like a sister to her throughout the last year. The glance they exchanged was so brief most people would have missed it, but Violet didn't.

"Why not?" Camille asked. "You like dogs and you certainly like Jordan."

Violet went back to pinning the soft satin, creasing it carefully between her fingers and catching the barest hint of fabric on the back side so there wouldn't be pinholes left in the elegant gown. She loved getting the chance to do alterations on a good friend's wedding gown. It saved Rebecca the trouble of going to the mainland, and it made being part of the wedding even more special. She and Camille and Camille's sister Cara would be bridesmaids, and Violet couldn't wait for the wedding. Any reason to dress up was a good reason, although they hadn't selected their gowns yet.

"Sadly, I know myself too well, and I know my own limits," Violet said.

In the mirror, she caught a glimpse of another look exchanged between her friends. Why were they being so odd and mysterious?

"Limits?" Rebecca asked, leaning forward so her hem dipped lower.

"Stand up straight," Violet said, "unless you want an uneven hem ruining your wedding day. And I'm talking about the limits of my power of resistance. I'm afraid I'll get to the shelter and absolutely fall in love."

"With…a dog?" Camille asked.

Violet shrugged. "Or a cat, or a hamster looking for a home. I'd love a shop cat, but I'm afraid shedding and upscale clothing are a bad mix. And a dog… I don't know. I'm afraid he'd be lonely while I'm at work."

"Which of those do you think Jordan will want?" Camille asked.

Jordan Frome, the goofy, lovable friend of her entire life, had worked his way from bellhop to front desk manager at the Great Island Hotel. "He can get a dog or a cat or a hamster if he wants to, although he works a lot of hours at the hotel during the summer. Winters, though," she said. She cocked her head, studying the hem of the gown before her. "I guess it could work."

"Well," Rebecca said. "You'll have to let us know what the mystery favor is, and if you want someone else to go pet shopping, maybe Maddox or Griffin would do it."

Violet smiled. "Jordan may surprise me and ask me to design new uniforms for the desk clerks at the hotel. Maybe it's not at all what I'm expecting."

Either way, it was something to look forward to. He was asking her to meet him at their spot. The patch of beach on the far side of the island they'd biked to a thousand times. The best skipping rocks were piled up there and never seemed to run out. Violet held the current record of thirty countable skips. She'd set it the previous summer on a calm night when the sun had lingered forever in the sky.

"I'd bet you're right about the dog. You know Jordan better than anyone else on the island does."

Violet had to admit that was true. They'd confided in each other since grade school, and she knew the message behind his smile, depending on its width, the size of the dimple created and whether or not his eyes were fully included. She also knew his own particular scent of Dial soap and hotel air-conditioning. *Rats.* She was sure she was right about the dog thing, and she couldn't let him down. He needed her help, and she'd have to use all her powers of resistance.

JORDAN COULDN'T REMEMBER the last time he'd been so nervous, but he knew Violet would soothe his feelings as soon as he saw her. It had always been that way for them. They sought each other out back in school in the lunchroom or at recess. Picked each other up on the way to community events so they wouldn't have to walk in alone, even though they knew every other year-round resident on Christmas Island. They always danced together at parties, just so they wouldn't feel awkward.

Yes, this would go okay because it was Violet. Not some stranger, not someone he needed to impress or explain himself to. She already knew everything about him.

He picked up a smooth black stone, got

the feel of it in his hand, crouched along the water's edge and waited for the perfect moment before he let it fly across the surface. He counted the wide skips that eventually narrowed and sped up until he lost count at thirty-one. *Thirty-one.* A new record and he had no witnesses. He straightened and looked across the clear calm water. He was going to miss Christmas Island.

Gravel crunched on the path behind him, and he turned. Violet's long brown hair streamed out behind her as she approached on her bike, and she wore a white shirt that flowed and rippled in the mild breeze off the lake. The shirt was probably the height of fashion, something that Violet had a knack for even if he didn't know the first thing about it. She skidded to a stop right in front of him, testing him as she usually did to see if he'd jump out of the way, but he didn't budge. He trusted her. She smiled at him as she put her feet down, and something happened inside his chest.

She'd always been pretty. Everyone said so. Lovely Violet who ran the Island Boutique and advised people on clothing. She'd outfitted most of the island women and some of the men for the annual formal party at the Great Island Hotel, and she always had a fabulous gown herself. He was used to her physical beauty.

But there was something in her smile that knocked him a little sideways as if he was the one balancing on a bicycle, not her. He tried to shake it off. This was Violet, the one person in the world who made him feel comfortable in his own skin. He was just nervous about what he was going to ask her.

"You look happy, like you had an amazing day and sold every dress in your shop and accessories to go with them," he said.

"It was a busy day," she replied. "I finally found the perfect woman for a red dress that's been hanging around my store forever."

"You sold the red dress!" he exclaimed. It had been a joke between them that someday she was going to find the right person for it.

"Turns out there's a mate for everything," she said. "A tall lady with the perfect shade of chestnut hair and just the right amount of sass in her walk. She's going to love it."

"We should celebrate," Jordan said. He reached down and scooped up a skipping rock. He bowed and handed it to her with a flourish. "I bequeath unto you, the next record-setting rock." He didn't mention that he'd just broken the record because he knew it wouldn't count since Violet hadn't been there to see it. "I believe the number is thirty-one."

Violet took the rock from his outstretched hand and gave him a curious look. He knew why. He'd told her in his message that he had something important to ask her, a favor. Why was he stalling? She approached the water's edge, preparing to skip the rock, but she didn't bother with any of her usual setup. She didn't rub the rock between both hands, do three mock throws as a test, roll her shoulders, plant her right foot in front of her. She just bent and tossed it out there, and it sank after a measly four skips.

Something was definitely off. Violet never bothered to hide her feelings.

"Okay, I'm killing us both with suspense," Jordan said. They stood side by side, watching the place in the water where the perfect skipping stone had sunk ingloriously. "I have to tell you why I needed to see you tonight."

He turned and put both hands on her upper arms. She looked up at him with expectation, as if there was no one else on the planet. She always made him feel that way.

And it was nice.

He counted on her.

"You know you're my best friend and you've always been there for me, no matter what," he said.

She nodded.

"I love…this island and all the people on it, but there's no one else who I…"

"Just say it," she whispered. "It's okay."

There she was again, smoothing his way. He took a breath and felt more confident. "I need to ask a huge favor."

She tilted her head and pressed her lips together. She'd never refused him anything, and he'd never refused her anything. She was just thinking. That was her thinking face. He knew she pressed her lips together so she would have to listen instead of talking. She'd revealed that strategy to him back in high school when he needed advice on an awkward dating situation.

"I have an amazing opportunity for advancement," he blurted. "General manager."

"At the Great Island Hotel?" she asked, a smile replacing her look of concentration.

"That's wonderful. You deserve it. You'll be fantastic."

He shook his head. This was the hard part. "It's not at the Great Island. It's at their sister property in Virginia. The Great Valley Hotel."

Her smile disappeared. Went out like a light.

"You'd leave the island?"

He let out a long breath. "You know I've been thinking about it for a long time."

Which was an understatement. A sad string of events had kept him on the island, but he finally had a chance to change that.

"Yes," she said, her voice a whisper. Her eyes were wide and her lips formed a perfect circle as if she was trying to formulate a word.

"But I want to…get ahead. Be successful. This could be my only chance," he said gently. If she was this shocked about his potential exit from the island, his request was really going to upset her. Maybe he should reconsider. Was it too much to ask of a friend? Worse, was he making a mistake? The thought occurred to him for the first time since he'd heard about the job. He'd only thought of the benefits and the opportunity, even though his first impulse had been to tell Violet.

"But…" she began, and then she stopped and swallowed. Paused a few seconds. "Tell me about this job. You must be so excited."

"I am. It's a huge promotion, honestly more money than I ever thought I'd make in my lifetime. More than I'd ever make here because there are so many people ahead of me in line at the Great Island."

Violet knew his backstory. How his parents had died when he was young and his grandparents had moved to the island to raise him so he wouldn't have to leave the only home he remembered. They were gone now, too. He had only himself.

And Violet.

She smiled. "What an amazing opportunity."

"It is, but I don't have it yet. The owner of the Great Valley Hotel wants to meet me, and he's coming to the island. He arrives next week with his wife."

"That's terrific," Violet said, her tone encouraging. Her expression had brightened. Jordan hoped the shock had worn off and she was truly happy for him. He was counting on it. "When he sees you in action at the hotel," Violet continued, "he'll see you're the perfect person for a promotion. It's your chance to prove yourself, and I know you will."

Jordan gave her a quick hug, but he noticed she wasn't quite as quick to wrap her arms around him as he expected. Maybe he'd caught her off guard. He released her and stepped back, giving her a little bit of room. He knew he was throwing a lot at her, and he hadn't even gotten to the big question yet.

"The owner's name is Quentin Shelley, and Mr. Shelley is a devoted family man. His wife is his equal partner, and he thinks that's... well, he thinks married people are better employees and better managers and the other two candidates are married."

Violet rubbed a finger over her bottom lip. He'd seen her do that a hundred times when there was something bothering her. She bent and sorted through some rocks at her feet, and she picked up one smooth flat stone and squeezed it between her hands as she stood and faced him.

"Okay," she said.

"He'll be more likely to hire me if he thinks I'm married or at least engaged."

"But you're not."

"No, but... I really need this chance, Violet. I know this is asking way too much from a friend, but for the next month or however long it takes for them to hire the position, do you think you could pretend to be my fiancée?"

Violet turned and skipped the rock over the surface of the lake. Jordan didn't count, but it had to skip at least thirty-five times. A record-setter. Incredible. But he doubted Violet had even counted.

"You want me to pretend we're engaged?" Violet asked, not looking at him.

"That throw," he said, pointing to the spot way out in the water where ripples still spread from the rock's final sinking. "You shattered our record."

"Seriously," Violet said, turning to him. "You know I have no poker face. I'm terrible at keeping secrets. I'm awful at pretending. I tell you what your Christmas gift is as soon as I buy it because I can't wait to give it to you."

It suddenly occurred to Jordan that, if he got the job, he wouldn't be there the next Christmas. Wouldn't see Violet's face when he opened her gift or gave her one. He felt his heart sinking like that rock in the lake, but he pushed that worry away. This was a once-in-a-lifetime chance. How many opportunities would he have to get off the island and be more successful than his parents and grandparents? He didn't want to grow old and die in his inherited house with sagging floors and creaky windows.

He swallowed. "Would you do this for me?" he asked softly.

"You're my best friend," Violet said, her cheeks pink.

Jordan was sure she was going to say no. And she was right. It was a ridiculous request. He regretted asking her and even the waves quietly swishing on the beach next to them didn't take away the tension of the moment as he waited for her answer.

She blinked rapidly and drew her eyebrows together as if something was physically painful, but then she swallowed and looked up at him. Her shoulders lowered and she brushed back her hair, leaving a faint trail of sand across her temple.

"If I can't pretend to be in love with you," she said. "I don't know who else could."

CHAPTER TWO

VIOLET HAD NEVER given herself credit for having any acting skill. She'd never needed it. She was genuinely glad when customers came in her store, so greeting them with a smile and an offer of help was the easy truth. She never needed to pretend with the people she'd spent her entire life with. Her brother Ryan was just as much an open book as she was, and Violet was glad he was off the island working. She wouldn't be able to fool him, and she wasn't sure she could fool anyone else.

She wasn't going to try fooling Camille, especially when she saw her just hours after Jordan's bombshell question.

"Dog?" Camille asked, peering closely at Violet. They stood on the sidewalk in front of Violet's boutique. She'd hoped to escape upstairs to her apartment where she'd have some comfort food while trying to digest the uncomfortable request Jordan had made. "You don't look happy, so I'm guessing you folded like a house of cards and you're getting a cat. Two cats."

Violet took Camille's arm and pulled her into the interior stairwell that led up to her apartment. She and Jordan had agreed on secrecy, and they'd also agreed on a dinner the next night to discuss the terms and details. One detail Violet had secured was permission to let Camille and Rebecca know the truth so they didn't think she'd gone off the deep end by dating her best friend. That would be ridiculous.

"No cat," Violet said. She swallowed. "They might try to climb up the skirts of fabulous dresses, and then we'd really be in trouble."

"So, what did Jordan want?" Camille asked.

Violet sighed. "Come upstairs. You're not going to believe it."

For the next hour, Violet shared her comfort food—leftover macaroni and cheese paired with diet soda—and spilled the whole scheme to Camille. Camille was shocked, but contemplative, as if she needed to think about the unusual request for a while before formulating words. She was halfway through her drink before she'd uttered the fatal statement that played through Violet's mind later that night.

"I can't imagine this island without Jordan," Camille had said, and Violet had swallowed back tears at the thought of her lifelong friend leaving. She'd feel that way about Camille and her sisters Cara and Chloe, Rebecca, the May brothers. Any of the group she'd grown up with, but especially Jordan. She could only tell a few people the truth about the fake engagement because the fewer people who knew, the lesser the chance of a slipup that would jeopardize Jordan's plans. She'd chosen Camille and Rebecca, and he'd chosen Griffin and Maddox. They were couples anyway, so it was practically keeping the secret in the family.

"I know," Violet responded to Camille's statement. "I can't either, but this is his big chance. I have to help him grab it."

THE FOLLOWING DAY, just twenty-four hours after Jordan's question on the beach, Violet met him outside the Holiday Hotel for a practice date. So much had changed in one day, and she needed ground rules to steady her. She'd made Jordan promise they'd discuss details during their dinner date, but she already felt trapped into playing a role that was going to break her heart by providing a sure exit for her best friend. What would Christmas Island be like without Jordan next to her singing at Christmas and over campfires? Who would skip rocks with her and make her laugh?

"There's my beautiful fiancée," Jordan said as he strode down the street toward her with a bouquet.

"You didn't need to bring me flowers," Violet said, trying to smile. She didn't want to ruin his excitement over a potential new job, and he really *did* look happy. But the flowers were over-the-top.

"Not just any flowers," Jordan said. "I had them mix in some violets, especially for you."

She peered at the bouquet and saw there were tiny purple violets scattered among the white carnations and lilies. "Very thoughtful," she said. "And hard to find."

Jordan leaned down and kissed her on the cheek. They'd hugged plenty of times, but a kiss on the cheek? He'd never done that before. The unfamiliar sensation sent nervous shivers down her jaw and neck. She didn't dislike it, but everything was so new and happening so fast.

"I'm buying dinner and you can't argue or offer to go halves since we're engaged now."

She laughed nervously. "Then I'm going to order something very expensive."

He slid an arm around her and whispered in her ear. "I'm perfectly willing to drain my checking account if it helps finance my promotion." His lips so close to her ear—also new and somewhat electrifying—was like a warning bell that they were playing a dangerous game. They should go inside and eat before anything else unexpected happened. She'd dined with Jordan too many times to count. How hard could it be to bluff her way through a date with him?

As soon as they entered the piano bar, and Violet saw some islanders she knew at the bar, she sensed it was going to be very hard. Nothing was as it should be. How did she think they could get away with fooling people…and should they?

"Is it really true?" Hadley, the front desk manager who sometimes filled in for the bartender, approached them. She wore a loose maternity top and a big smile. "Finally you two lovebirds realized you were made for each other, and now the rest of the island can stop worrying that you're never going to figure it out."

Violet's breath caught and she paused mid-step. Just what on earth did Hadley mean by that? Lovebirds? Finally? Violet wanted to tell Hadley it was all a temporary game, but instead she gave a one-shoulder shrug and put on a big smile. "Yep, we're engaged. Totally crazy in love."

"I want to hear all about the proposal when I come over and get your drink orders in a few minutes," Hadley said.

She led them to a round table between the front windows and near the piano where Rebecca played several nights a week. Violet held up a menu as a shield and leaned close to Jordan. She couldn't look at his face. He'd heard what Hadley had said. What did he think of Hadley's assertion about what islanders thought of them? Violet forced herself to be practical. She was in this now. "We need a proposal story," she said quietly so only Jordan would hear her.

"That's easy," he said. "We were skipping rocks on our favorite beach, and I asked you a very important question. It's even partly true."

Violet nodded as she processed that thought. His question hadn't been a real proposal. She felt a bubble rise up her chest, tension escaping from the absurd situation she was in. Of course Jordan was never going to propose to her. They were friends. If they were the last people on the island, she would never have expected a declaration from him. Of course she'd also never expected he'd ask her to fake an engagement so he could leave forever.

Hadley was back in less than a minute with a vase filled with water. "For your flowers. And he even got violets. Romantic," she said, nodding. "What'll you have to drink?"

They placed their orders for fruity cocktails and soft pretzels with golden mustard, and Violet settled back in her chair to listen to Rebecca at the piano. She'd heard show tunes when they first sat down, but Rebecca had switched to romantic music. Slow songs, themes from movies, the classic "I Will Always Love You."

Jordan gave a nod toward the piano and smiled. "Think she's doing that for us?"

"Maybe a little."

"She knows, right?"

Violet gave a short nod of assent. "I told Camille she could tell Rebecca and Maddox and Griffin." Everyone else would get the fake story, but would they all find it… believable? Hadley's reaction told Violet that people had been talking about her and Jordan for a long time. How hadn't she known? Had Jordan known?

"I'm sorry to put you in this position," Jordan said. He reached across the table and squeezed her hand. "When our charade is over, you can tell everyone you were the one to break it off with me. And whatever reason you make up, I'll acknowledge I was in the wrong."

Violet tried to let the tight knot of tension in her chest unwind. This was Jordan who she cared about, and she knew he cared about her. She could do this. She just had to find the joy in spending time with him before he left. Was he really going to leave?

"That gives me something fun to think about over dinner. What shall I tell people when you finally break my heart and call off our engagement?" She smiled at him and tapped her chin with one finger. "Should I say you're a bad dancer? A messy eater? A bad kisser?"

She thought it was going pretty well, having some fun banter, but his expression turned serious. "About that kissing," he said.

"Is this where you confess to me that all your previous girlfriends have left negative reviews?"

Jordan sipped his drink. "I don't have any former girlfriends, as you well know."

She shrugged. "You could have hidden them from me."

"Not a chance."

She almost hated to ask, but facing the situation head-on was the only way. "So...what did you want to say about kissing?"

"I think we should do it," Jordan said.

Oh, no. That would be putting her toe over a line she wasn't ready to cross, even with fabulous new sandals that complemented her pink dress. "Now?" she asked, grinning and hoping to convey a casual tone.

"Sometime soon," Jordan said. "We have to see if we can pull it off and appear believable."

"Oh," Violet said.

"For the sake of the scheme, in case we

ever end up kissing in front of people who don't know we're not really together," Jordan added. "And thank you in advance."

Violet glanced over the dance floor where a few couples were slow dancing to Rebecca's piano playing. She could have lived with a practice kiss, but the way he said "thank you in advance" made it sound as if she were a bank teller helping him count all the change he'd stored in a pickle jar since he was eleven.

"You're thinking about dancing," Jordan said.

Violet turned her attention back to him. "Absolutely." She'd actually been thinking about kissing, but dancing was a safer subject. She'd danced with Jordan plenty of times. It wouldn't mean a thing, and they both had decent rhythm. "Let's eat first, and then we'll demonstrate how madly in love we are by slow dancing to whatever Rebecca is playing."

She wanted to treat it all like a game. It was the only way she would get through the pretense and help her friend get the life he thought he wanted.

JORDAN HELD VIOLET in his arms and moved slowly around the floor to a familiar song.

The first few steps had been strained, even awkward, which was unusual for them. Had Violet forgotten how well they'd always moved together now that a fake engagement had come between them…or had he? Their relationship had a new name—a false one—but they could certainly carry on just as they always had. It didn't have to change.

"How about singing one for us?" Rebecca asked when the song ended and Jordan and Violet were near the piano. "You won't even need a microphone because it's not loud in here tonight. Your choice, but I've heard you do some pretty terrific duets."

Jordan and Violet had been stepping cautiously, almost questioningly, around the floor, but singing was something they could handle. At the annual Christmas sing, campfires, parties, weddings of friends and going clear back to school days, they had always meshed their singing voices. His low tenor, her high alto, and a perfect sense of each other's timing had made them seem almost like one singer.

"I don't know," Violet said. "I'm sure everyone is perfectly happy listening to your playing."

"Variety," Rebecca said. "Never hurts to mix it up, especially when I have no worries about the quality. What do you want me to play?"

"Maybe something cheerful like 'Happy Birthday,'" Violet suggested. "It's probably somebody's birthday right here in this room."

Rebecca laughed. "I mean something romantic. How about 'A Thousand Years'? Everyone likes that song, and I've heard you sing it before." She whispered, "Just in case anyone doubts you, it'll cement the fact that you're together."

There it was again, Jordan thought. When he'd started spreading the news of his engagement with Violet, he hadn't surprised a single person. Everyone said the same thing, usually along the lines of "finally" or "about time." What was with people? Did they not understand that Violet was his best friend? If he had any romantic ideas about her, he wouldn't destroy a potential real relationship by proposing a false one. It was a small island where people saw what they wanted to see and made assumptions, and those were good reasons why he was trying to find a way off Christmas Island and start fresh where no one knew him.

"Sounds great," he said, mustering enthusiasm. "We'll grab a sip of water and then sing 'A Thousand Years' for anyone who wants to listen."

He noticed Violet hadn't said anything. Her face was flushed, but he was sure his was, too. It was the dancing. He went to their table and brought back water for himself and Violet. "B-flat," he told Rebecca who nodded and began playing the notes of the introduction. Violet still hadn't said anything, and her expression was pensive, serious. Was it a mistake to sing together when they were trying to put on a show of another kind? Up until the first word in the lyrics, he wasn't sure Violet would sing or that their voices would melt and blend together as they'd always done.

His fears were unfounded. The sound was sweet and full, and they were only a few lines into the achingly lovely words when Jordan took Violet's hand and they sang together, fingers joined, as they always had. His idea for a fake fiancée to help his job prospects wasn't a disaster. As he harmonized with Violet, he was sure she wasn't upset about it, and everything was going to be just fine.

When they left the Holiday Hotel and he walked her back to her store where a flight of steps would take her to her apartment, he wished he hadn't already declared they should kiss. The evening had smoothed out and turned into just another night out with Violet in a long string of things they'd done together. The singing had reharmonized them, but a kiss might derail their evening.

"About that kiss," he said as they paused outside her door. "You don't have to. I don't think anyone is going to require us to kiss to prove our love. That would be weird and archaic. It's not like we're going to actually get married and have to kiss at the altar."

"So you don't want to," Violet said.

Was she relieved?

"I'm saying we don't have to."

"Okay. Good night." Violet put her key in her door's lock.

"Unless you think it would help us look like the real deal," Jordan said.

Violet turned and sighed. "I think we're not having trouble persuading anyone."

They were both silent a moment. Jordan

hadn't told her about the lack of surprise he'd encountered from people when he told them about their engagement—just like Hadley. Had Violet experienced the same thing? What did she think about it?

Jordan touched her arm. "I'm sorry to drag you into this. I know it's a pain, but at least we'll have a good dinner at the hotel when the Great Valley's owner comes. I'll text you the date as soon as I find out."

She nodded, but she didn't say anything. Night sounds of insects were all around them in the quiet street downtown. Distant music and laughter from restaurants and bars reached them, but the air felt heavy. Jordan had said good-night to Violet a thousand times. Why did it feel so strange tonight? Maybe it was the pressure of having his dream right in front of him and knowing he was taking huge risks to grab it. If he failed, what would he do?

The thought hit him like a punch. If he didn't get the job, and he'd used Violet like this...would they be able to return to their easy friendship? What would other people say?

That kiss would be a horrible idea, and Jordan resolved to avoid it as long as he could, just in case it was the kind of thing that would be too hard to forget if he failed and stayed on Christmas Island.

While he stalled and tried to think of something to say, Violet took the matter into her own hands. "Good night, Jordan," she said. She patted his arm and slipped through her door, leaving him alone.

As he walked home along the quiet streets of Christmas Island, Jordan remembered playing the lead in the school musical and kissing a girl who was two years older than he was. It hadn't meant a thing, just acting. He'd have to make sure he kept his truth and fiction carefully separated as he navigated an uncomfortably deceptive route to the better life he knew was waiting for him outside Christmas Island.

CHAPTER THREE

JORDAN LISTENED TO a guest complain about the shower in his room, nodded and took the usual steps of sending maintenance immediately. He offered the man a tray of refreshments in the lobby or on the porch, and put a discount in his folio.

"And if there's anything else I can do to make your stay more comfortable, please ask for me. My name's Jordan."

The guest tilted his head. "Were you here last year?"

"Yes," Jordan said. The guest looked familiar, but he'd seen a lot of people come and go.

"My wife left her shawl on the ferry, and I believe you went and retrieved it for us."

Jordan smiled. "Was it white lace with little violets on it?" He remembered the little violets and had looked online for a similar one for Violet's birthday, but had given up, concluding that it must have been handmade.

The man laughed. "I can't believe you remembered that. My wife was so happy to have it back."

This was the kind of thing that made Jordan's day. The loss of the cherished item could have ruined the guest's stay the previous year, but it hadn't. And now they were back again patronizing the Great Island Hotel.

"My friends own the ferry line, so they helped me out," Jordan said. "Believe me, you're not the first guest to lose something on the ferry."

Quentin Shelley stood nearby, and although he was talking with the operations manager of the Great Island Hotel, Jordan was sure Quentin was listening closely to his exchange with the guest. He knew Quentin would like what he heard. Doing the job of the front desk manager was something Jordan had been preparing for since he was a teenager working as a bellman.

He loved the world of the hotel with its plush lobby, the constant influx of new people, the shiny old-fashioned keys the hotel still used and the embossed seal on the guest welcome packets. There was even a bell on the counter he could ding when a bellman's services were needed, and from the desk he could hear the chime of the elevator as it announced the lobby floor. Down the hallway ahead of him with its black-and-white tile floor came the constant aroma of fresh flowers from the flower shop and fresh coffee from the bakery. A fancy boutique selling men's and women's clothing and accessories and a jewelry store with items he could never afford anchored the end of the hallway.

This was a world he'd only dreamed about as a kid in a run-down house on a back road of the island. It was a world he never wanted to give up. He'd never seen the Great Valley Hotel where he hoped to get the general manager position, a huge step up from front desk manager. But the Great Valley was the sister hotel of the Great Island, and he'd seen pictures. It was spacious and elegant, and instead of lake views, it had mountain views all around. Quite a change from his life on the island. He'd be making twice the salary and enjoying the success he'd always longed for. He wouldn't be the poor kid, and no one there would know how his parents had died far too young and his grandparents had struggled to provide for him.

He was determined to have a different life, even if he had to leave Christmas Island to do it.

"Is our dinner tonight still on?" Quentin Shelley asked when the guest had left, satisfied for the moment with the accommodations Jordan had offered.

"Absolutely. Violet and I are looking forward to meeting your wife."

Quentin Shelley smiled. Jordan's impression of him so far was that of a genuinely nice guy. He could see it in the way Quentin interacted with guests and, then, more importantly, what he said about the interaction when the guest had walked away. Jordan had seen other managers roll their eyes and criticize picky hotel guests in private, but Quentin didn't. The older man's attitude about service matched Jordan's, and Jordan wanted the chance to work for him at the Great Valley.

"My wife, Jillian, says you can tell a lot about a man by the woman he chooses to marry," Quentin said. "This isn't a very big island, but you seem like the kind of person who would find a perfect fiancée anyway."

"Thank you," Jordan said, not sure what

the compliment conveyed for certain, but recognizing that his remark was complimentary.

"I mean your silver-lining approach," Quentin said. "I've overheard you talking to guests and behind the desk to your coworkers. I like your positive attitude."

"Then you're going to love Violet," Jordan said.

Hours later when Violet walked up the steps to the grand front porch of the hotel, Jordan was certain he'd found the best woman on Christmas Island to marry. If their engagement wasn't a scam, he reminded himself. She was beautiful, friendly and she cared about him. He'd choose her over anyone else on the island to spend a day with skipping rocks, hiking or just lying in the grass watching the clouds.

He stood and greeted her, kissed her cheek, and put a hand on the small of her back as he introduced her to Quentin and Jillian Shelley. "This is Violet Brookstone," he said, her last name sounding odd to him. All the Christmas Island residents were on a first-name basis, and even though his name tag at the front desk said Jordan Frome, he didn't usually need a last name anywhere else. His last name came with baggage anyway. *That poor Frome kid who lost his parents in an accident when he was in first grade.*

"It's a pleasure to meet you," Violet said after Quentin introduced himself and his wife.

"Jordan tells us you own a boutique on the island," Jillian said.

Violet nodded. "I'm the third-generation owner, but I've taken it in a slightly fancier direction than my parents and grandparents. I love sparkle, and I was admiring your dress as soon as I walked onto the porch. The shimmer right at the hemline is genius."

Jillian smiled. "I like you already, but how are you going to leave your boutique if Jordan comes to work for us at the Great Valley?"

Jordan held his breath. He hadn't worried about difficult questions, tests of their relationship, because no one on earth knew him better than Violet. She knew his favorite foods, color, movies, music, even what kind of shaving cream he used because they shopped together. But they hadn't discussed in advance what story they would tell about her leaving her island store. Because she wasn't actually going to leave it. They weren't getting married.

Violet slipped an arm around him and smiled up into his face. "The things we do for love, right?" she said.

Jordan kissed her temple. "I'm a lucky man."

VIOLET WALKED THROUGH the familiar doors of the Great Island Hotel dining room. She wore an emerald-green sleeveless dress with white trim at the waist and around the hem. It was one of her favorite dresses to come through her boutique and she also had it in white with black trim. She wore high-heeled sandals that brought her closer to Jordan's height, but also made her feel as if she needed to step carefully.

Jordan took her hand as they followed Quentin and Jillian Shelley down the center aisle of the dining room toward a banquette in the back corner where they could view the entire room but also have a window onto the porch and the lake beyond. Glasses of ice water and a bread basket were already on the table and a waiter stood nearby. Violet had expected the royal treatment because they were dining with the owner of the hotel chain, but she hadn't expected to like Quentin and Jillian quite so much. From their first greeting, they seemed like nice, sincere people.

Was it wrong of her and Jordan to play a trick on them? Jordan was an excellent front desk manager and would be a wonderful general manager at the hotel in Virginia. He'd told her there were other candidates for the position, but Violet was certain he would get the job. He deserved it. But when he arrived there without her, what would happen? She was free to invent a story about their breakup when he left Christmas Island, but what was he going to say to the Shelleys and everyone else? Would he claim Violet had broken his heart?

She never wanted to break his heart, but she had to protect her own, too. Sure, she would be Jordan's best friend just as she always had. If she had to kiss him or pretend they were more than that, she would just go along and ignore her unsupportive wish that he would just stay on the island. Lock it away as if she was locking the door of her boutique for the night. And pretend that the thought of her best friend leaving was not gut-wrenching.

"I love hearing stories about how people

met," Jillian said as they sat and picked up their menus. "As soon as we order, I want to hear about your Christmas Island love affair."

Violet met Jordan's eyes across the table and they smiled at each other, both, she imagined, remembering the end of their first day in kindergarten. They had a lifetime of memories together, all of them good. She could pretend they were engaged a little longer to give her best friend the opportunity of a lifetime. He would do it for her.

They placed their order for all five courses and settled back. Instead of waiting for Jillian to ask, Violet decided to tell the story so they could move on to other topics—safer topics—like the Great Valley Hotel and how it compared to the Great Island Hotel.

"I think we might have seen each other a few times before our first day of kindergarten," Violet said. "It's a small island, and people are scarce in the off season."

"My father had gotten a job at the Great Island and we'd moved to the island a year before I started kindergarten," Jordan told them.

"But we really met that first day of school," Violet continued. "We rode our bikes to the island school because it was a short ride for both of us. My parents trusted my big brother Ryan to make sure I got there without pedaling into the lake, and I suspect Jordan's parents were watching him from a distance but letting him be independent."

Jordan smiled. "I'd like to think they were."

"Me, too," Violet said. "Anyway, I came from downtown, and Jordan from a road just outside of downtown. We parked our bikes on the rack outside the Christmas Island school, but when we came out after the first day, our bikes were hopelessly tangled together."

"My pedal was through her spokes and somehow her seat got lodged under my handlebars," Jordan added. "We tugged at them for a while."

"Jordan got a big scrape on his knee," Violet said.

"And I think I poked you in the eye accidentally with my elbow," Jordan said.

"And then we gave up—" Violet said.

"And started laughing," Jordan interrupted. "We laughed until our bellies hurt and then we lay down on the grass by the bike rack and watched the clouds go by overhead. I remember it like it was yesterday."

"Me, too," Violet said, looking at Jordan's

smile and remembering how much he'd been part of her life. How was she ever going to let him go?

"My heart," Jillian said, placing her hand on her chest. "What a wonderful story. And you've been friends ever since?"

Violet nodded, but she didn't speak because there was such a lump in her throat. That had also been before Jordan's parents died, when their lives had been simple.

"A teacher eventually came out and separated our bikes and told us we better get home before our parents got worried," Jordan said. "I accidentally took Violet's backpack home and she took mine."

"Even better," Jillian added. "That's adorable, and I just love a story of best friends who fall in love. That's how it was for Quentin and me. He was my brother's best friend growing up, and he was always nice to me and insisted my brother let me go along on their adventures to the stream behind their house. We went our separate ways in college, but then Quentin came home with my brother for spring break one year, and suddenly we discovered our friendship was more than we'd realized. We've been together ever since."

"That's wonderful," Violet said.

"Having someone to share your past and future with is the most important thing," Jillian continued. "Right, honey?"

Quentin put a hand over his wife's and turned his gaze on Jordan. "Absolutely. That's why I was thrilled to hear you were getting married. Living at the Great Valley is a little bit like living on an island because we're in the middle of the mountains, and it's nice to have someone to go home to. We've had some young single managers over the years, and they never seem to stick around."

Their soup arrived, and Violet was glad the conversation turned to the quality of the food and then to talk about the Great Valley Hotel. She hated fooling such nice people as the Shelleys, and when she glanced across the table at Jordan, she suspected he felt the same way. His polite smile might have fooled other people, but Violet knew him too well. The lies they were telling were weighing on him, too.

After dinner and dessert, both couples made their way toward the ballroom where a live orchestra played every night during the summer season. Violet had danced there many times, often with Jordan, so she felt her equilibrium returning. She could manage dancing, especially if she was alone with Jordan and they didn't have to pretend for other people.

"Do you mind if I have the first dance?" Quentin asked Violet as the music began.

Violet smiled automatically. "I'd love it." She hoped Quentin was a man who concentrated on his steps instead of moving smoothly and taking the opportunity for conversation. She could handle polite silence. Years of patiently waiting for shoppers in her boutique to choose an item without being pushy or interrupting their conversations with friends had been good training.

Quentin, however, was not a silent dancer. He moved easily from the first step. "Jillian and I dance all the time at the Great Valley," he said. "And we spent two weeks here last year. One of the perks of being involved with hotels."

"You're an excellent dancer," Violet said.

"Thank you. Now, I want you to tell me what's on your mind. You and Jordan seem so happy, but my wife says she thinks there's something bothering you. Is it the idea of leaving the island and moving several states away?"

Violet was quick on her feet as a dancer, and she was also glad she could think fast. "You caught us," she said with a smile. "I love my boutique here, and I've never lived anywhere else."

"The things you do for love, though, right?" he said, using her words from earlier in the evening.

"Yes."

"And you might be interested to know we have a boutique at the Great Valley, but there are plenty of retail opportunities in the immediate area for someone talented like you."

"You're putting my mind at rest and we're not even halfway through this dance," Violet said in what she hoped was a convincing tone. Jordan was a lucky man if he was going to have the chance to work for such nice people.

CHAPTER FOUR

ON SUNDAY MORNING, Jordan shoved aside his frayed bedroom curtain and groaned. It was a perfect day. There would be no getting out of a round of golf with Violet and the Shelleys. Violet had cheerfully agreed to ask her friend Cara to open her boutique at noon so she could get on the golf course early as a favor to Jordan and get back to work by the afternoon.

Through his open windows—he'd never installed air-conditioning and didn't need it anyway most of the time—he heard a car in his gravel driveway. He went into the kitchen and pushed aside a curtain that felt dusty in his hand. How old were those curtains? In the hatchback running in his driveway, he recognized Hadley Pierce's sister Wendy at the wheel and saw the heads of her three kids bobbing in the back seat. Wendy and Hadley had both been several years ahead of him at the island school and he remembered them being nice to him, almost as if he was a lost little brother.

A lot of people had treated him like that.

An elderly lady got out of the front seat carrying a large plastic bag. Jordan opened his front door and stepped out. Hadley and Wendy's grandmother strode toward the house as if she was on a mission, and Jordan, despite his surprise, quickly went down the porch steps so the older woman wouldn't have to climb them—especially since they were in as poor condition as the rest of the place. He didn't know why she was there, but he didn't want a sweet old lady falling through his porch floorboards.

"We're on the way to church where they're collecting donated raffle items. I made a dozen afghans last winter and finally put the decorative edges on them," the elderly lady said. She shivered as if remembering the cold winter. "The church certainly doesn't need all twelve blankets for the fundraiser. I thought of you, alone up here on this little hill in the cold, and I wanted to bring you one that I'm keeping out of the raffle."

"That's very…nice," Jordan said. "But it's

summer." He hadn't had coffee yet, and the unexpected visit threw him off.

"Winter comes every year," she said. "This will help keep you from freezing."

Jordan swallowed. This wasn't the time to tell the sweet old lady that he hoped to be in a warmer climate before winter, far away from the drafty old house with poor insulation and ancient windows. She meant well. And it wasn't the first time some nice islander had brought something to his house as a gesture of kindness. His mind flashed to casserole dishes. Lots of them. They'd shown up after his parents had died, and then they'd shown up again after the deaths of each of his grandparents.

Casseroles, hand-me-downs and now a handmade blanket.

He knew Penny, of course, just as he knew all the year-round residents of Christmas Island. But he didn't know she'd thought of him on cold winter nights. He'd assumed Violet was the only person who did that.

"It's two shades of blue," Penny said, holding out the bag. "So it will go with your couch if you still have the same one your grandparents used to have."

She remembered what the couch looked like? She was probably five or ten years older than his grandparents had been, but he didn't remember her visiting. Maybe he hadn't paid attention to his grandparents' visitors, or maybe Penny had just dropped something off occasionally, like a casserole or something from the church.

Jordan tried to push down that old feeling of being the island charity case. People intended to be nice. And he wasn't a little kid anymore. He had a great job and a chance at an even better one.

"Thank you," he said. He took the bag and looked inside and then forced a smile. "It's perfect and it looks really warm."

The elderly lady smiled and patted his arm. "I have to get going now, but if you're feeling lucky, you could come to church today and buy some raffle tickets afterward."

Lucky. That was a quality Jordan was pretty sure he didn't have. His advancement at the hotel wasn't based on luck. It was entirely from his ability to be friendly and hospitable to people and his love of the job.

He mustered a genuine smile. "I don't need a raffle ticket because I'm already holding the best prize right here." He hoisted the bag with his new blue afghan. "Nothing else could compete with this."

"You're a dear," she said. "And you can wash it on cold if you spill anything on it."

"Thank you," Jordan said. He tucked the bag under one arm and waved to Wendy and her kids with the other hand.

The car backed out of his driveway, and he went inside where he left the bag on his couch and returned to his bedroom to get dressed for a hot day of chasing a golf ball.

THE GREAT ISLAND GOLF COURSE, in Jordan's opinion, was eighteen holes of utter misery. Every day, he watched guests arrive with their luggage, which included expensive sets of golf clubs in pricey bags that cost as much as the used car he drove. Those guests had grown up golfing, had parents who took them on golf vacations, had golf teams at their high schools and colleges.

Jordan had about two dozen rounds of golf spread over ten years on days when it was free or discounted for Great Island Hotel employees. He was an off-time and off-season golfer, always using rented clubs. Still, the course rolled along the lakeshore with lush green grass, shade trees and flower beds. He could enjoy the view even though he'd probably be the worst golfer in the party.

Violet's family golfed. Her parents and grandparents, her brother Ryan. Their modest success with the downtown clothing store that eventually evolved into a boutique had allowed them spare money for clubs and a golf membership.

"I'm letting you win," Violet said as she biked into the parking lot next to the golf shop and Jordan secured her bike to the rack.

"Don't you dare," he said. "I can handle a loss, especially when it's fair and square. You never cheat, and even if you did, I'd know it because you're good at everything except hiding your feelings."

"But this is your big day out with your future employers. I want them to be impressed with you."

"They're hiring me to manage a hotel, not to be a golf pro," Jordan said. "I packed a cooler with drinks. Lemonade for you and a variety for the Shelleys since I don't know what they like."

"Maybe they'll bring flasks and imbibe on

the front nine too much so we can both beat them on the back nine," Violet said.

Jordan laughed. "Somehow, that doesn't seem like something they would do."

"I do like them, and I enjoyed dinner a few nights ago," Violet said. "If I were really going to marry you and go bury myself in the hills of Virginia, I wouldn't mind spending time with Jillian and Quentin."

"But you'd have to put up with me," Jordan said. His tone was light, but an image of him married to Violet, working away in the shadow of green mountains somehow robbed that lightness. It wouldn't be right. Something about the image didn't fit.

"I can't believe you haven't noticed," Violet said. She spread her arms and stood in front of him.

"Did you get taller?" Jordan said, smiling.

Violet swatted his arm. "New outfit. I ordered some athleisure items for the store, and I decided my own testimonial would be valuable. This is from the golf club line."

She wore a blue top that was almost a perfect match for her eyes. The top was sleeveless and had a skirt in a complementary shade of blue. Two tones of blue, just like that afghan still in its bag on his couch.

"The shoes, too?" Jordan asked, keeping his focus on Violet instead of the charity gift.

"You're hopeless," Violet said. "I've had these golf shoes for three years at least."

"Lucky guess," Jordan said.

They were both laughing when Quentin and Jillian joined them. "You two are so cute together," Jillian said. "But sometimes the links and fairways cause some unexpected drama. There's a couple we used to golf with," she said, shaking her head. "We had to stop because it was awful watching them have near-divorce experiences all over the course."

"Are they still together?" Violet said.

Quentin nodded. "They took up bowling. There's a nice bowling alley at the Great Valley Hotel, and I gave them a free pass to use it all they want. You can't put a price on happiness."

They walked toward the back of the pro shop where golf carts were lined up, waiting. "I reserved two carts and they already loaded four sets of clubs for us," Jordan said. "I also have a cooler, and of course there's drink service throughout the course."

"We'll follow you to the first tee since this is your home course," Quentin said.

Jordan gave him a thumbs-up and got in the first cart with Violet. While the Great Island Hotel was technically Jordan's home territory, he had no responsibility for overseeing the golf course. Besides, Quentin was the owner of the two hotels, so it was far more his home course than Jordan's.

"Stop feeling like an imposter," Violet said. "I know that look. You're just as good as all the golfers with expensive sunglasses and solid-gold-divot-repair tools."

"Do they make those?"

"Sure. I have five of them."

Jordan elbowed her. "I'm glad you're along today so I remember not to take myself so seriously."

"Save your seriousness for your game. We can't laugh so hard we fall into the pond again."

"We could, but it wouldn't impress my potential new employer."

"You never know," Violet said as Jordan parked at the first tee.

Jordan met Violet at the back of the cart and they worked together to unbuckle the strap that held their golf bags. Violet's long brown ponytail brushed over his arm and he smelled her familiar namesake fragrance. Did they have violets growing wild all over Virginia? It was eight hundred miles south of Christmas Island. What did he even know about that climate? Were there snowy winters and frozen ponds where he could ice-skate?

Who would he ice-skate with?

He grabbed a set of clubs and started toward the tee, but Violet stopped him by putting a hand on his arm. "Those are the ladies' clubs," she said.

Jordan smiled. "All part of my plan. If you have to use clubs too long for you, I might not come in last."

Violet stood back and shook her head, smiling, while Jordan slung his clubs over his shoulder and also carried hers to the set of ladies' tees.

"Ladies first," Jillian said. Jordan noticed her husband also carried her clubs for her and set the bag near the tee.

"When they start beating us, then they have to carry their own bags," Quentin said, leaning close and whispering.

Jillian adjusted her sun visor and said, "I heard that."

A squirrel dashed across the tee, paused and perched on its back legs, and then took off again. Like the other squirrels on Christmas Island, it was accustomed to being around people and didn't appear concerned that four humans were wielding shiny silver sticks.

"Those little pests eat all my birdseed in the winter," Jillian said.

"What are the winters like in Virginia?" Violet asked. Jordan had been about to ask the same thing, and he was grateful Violet had jumped in with the question. It would help convince the Shelleys that she planned to be there for the next winter.

"Icy," Quentin said. "The mountains hem us in, and there's snow, but the ice on the highways is the tricky part for traveling."

"We have plenty of days when the roads are fine," Jillian said. "Thank goodness. Half of the rooms at the Great Valley are filled with skiers from December until March."

"That's a big change from here where we shut this place down for the winter," Jordan said. What would it be like to accommodate guests trooping through the lobby with snow boots and to make sure the driveway, parking lot and sidewalks got cleared every time it snowed? On Christmas Island, winter was a long, deep, refreshing breath after the busy summer tourist season. Could he adjust to a hectic pace year-round?

"Good for revenue," Quentin said. "Shutting down a massive place like this is a lost opportunity."

Violet shot Jordan a sympathetic glance, and he could guess she was thinking about all the opportunities a quiet winter on an island offered. Friendship, starry skies, ice-skating, snowmobiling. Time with people they loved.

"That's wonderful news for the Great Valley," Violet said, recovering her place in the conversation more quickly than Jordan. She was always more confident in conversations than he was. What was he going to do when he was hundreds of miles away?

But that was the point, wasn't it? On Christmas Island, he'd always be Jordan Frome, the quiet man who was the best thing to come out of a struggling family. In another state, he could stride up to the front desk with confidence, even if he had to fake it for the first year.

"I'm sure you've considered keeping the Great Island open longer into the winter," Violet said. "My boutique used to close when the last tourist left, but recently, I've discovered it's worth keeping open, even with limited hours. Christmas Island slows down a lot, but it doesn't stop like it used to."

Quentin and his wife regarded Violet seriously as if she'd just said something very interesting. It was time for Jordan to jump in or they'd think he didn't have anything in his head.

"There's a big difference between a hotel with two hundred rooms and a clothing store," he said.

All three of his golf companions turned a surprised look on him, and he realized he'd blundered. Suddenly, though, Violet laughed and put a hand on his arm. "Don't listen to him. He loves to tease me about my little shop, but he's the first one to recommend it to guests who can't find what they want in the shop at the hotel."

Her cheerful way of passing off his remark lightened the entire mood again, and Jillian stood over the tee to line up her shot. Behind Quentin's and Jillian's backs, Violet gave Jordan a reassuring smile—just what he needed. As always.

VIOLET MUSTERED ALL the pleasantness she'd usually need when helping a customer who couldn't be talked out of trying on a dress that didn't suit her. She'd seen plenty of mistakes made in her shop and tried to prevent all of them, but some people just couldn't get out of their own way.

Today, Jordan was in his own way. She could practically see the tension in his jaw and his shoulders, and she wanted to make him laugh. If they could just jump on a bicycle and take a breathless ride around the island, dodging tourists on rented bikes, Jordan would be okay. His smile would be the real thing, the one she'd grown accustomed to and loved.

This man clearly trying to impress people who were practically strangers was not someone she'd want to skip rocks or race across an ice-skating pond with. Still, she was there to play a role and she'd do it, even if her own fake smile broke her face.

"Excellent shot," Violet said when Jillian sent her ball flying straight down the fairway where it landed in an advantageous spot.

"Thank you," Jillian said. "I took lessons from the golf pro at the Great Valley last fall when Quentin was gone every single day pouring himself into an expansion of the convention center."

Violet had been operating under the assumption that Jillian helped Quentin with running the hotel, but her comment suggested otherwise.

"I was so glad when they cut the ribbon on that place and I got my dinner partner back," Jillian continued. "Although my golf lessons are paying off. I used to have a wicked slice."

Violet smiled. "My brother has a wicked slice, but we all pretend it's a gust of wind with terrible timing."

"Does your brother live here on the island?" Quentin asked.

Violet shook her head. "He visits, but Ryan's work in construction projects keeps him busy on the mainland."

"He's a carpenter?"

"More of a developer," she said. "Real estate deals and housing developments. Not the kind of thing we have or need on Christmas Island."

"What about the rest of your family?" Jillian asked.

"My parents moved to Florida for the warmer climate, so it's just me."

A loneliness she'd never felt before crept over her like a big shadowy cloud. On nights when she didn't feel like eating alone, she'd call Jordan. If she wanted to go for a walk or a bike ride or take a kayak out at sunset... there'd always been Jordan.

"That's good," Jillian said. "You won't be leaving anyone behind if you move to Virginia."

Violet sucked in a breath and forced a smile. "You're right." She gave her ball a solid whack and had the pleasure of watching it soar down the fairway. Quentin and Jordan teed off—Quentin's shot getting a lot closer to the green than Jordan's—and they all got in the carts and moved along.

"This isn't going to work," Jordan said as soon as he and Violet pulled away from the other cart. "I thought it would, but—"

Violet turned to look at him as he drove, both hands gripping the wheel. "It's going fine. We just have to get through seventeen and a half more holes."

"Would you be willing to invent a reason why we should all stop at nine today?"

"No. I'm inventing enough. Just be yourself. It'll be fine."

Jordan let out a long sigh. "If you ever need me to pretend to be your boyfriend or husband or tax accountant, I doubt I'd do as good a job as you're doing. I owe you, Violet. And I feel lousy for putting you through this, but I just…want this promotion so bad."

"I know," she said softly as he parked by his golf ball, which was the farthest from the hole. "The safest way for you to get through the rest of the day is to ask them lots of questions. Let them talk about the Great Valley Hotel, themselves, their pets, anything. If they're talking, you can just smile and nod."

"Good strategy," Jordan said.

"Tried and true. I used it already, and now I know the winter roads are icy in Virginia, so you're going to need new tires, maybe even snow tires."

"Maybe I can live at the hotel and I won't have to drive anywhere."

"That's your next topic of conversation. Affordable housing near the Great Valley."

Three holes later, Violet was way behind the other players due to some wild shots she'd made intentionally. It was harder than it looked, purposely whiffing a ball at the tee and then sending it skidding a measly twenty yards.

It was hard work pretending to be lousy at something, and Jordan had sent her several looks that said he knew what she was doing and didn't like it. She sent her next ball into the pond anyway. It was Jordan's big day on the links, and she was along for the ride—not along to compete or show off.

Even though Jordan didn't look happy with her performance, Violet was pleased to see that he was taking her advice about making easy conversation. He'd asked broad, leading questions, and Quentin and Jillian were natural talkers. Especially when it came to their little farm with horses and chickens and even a goat.

On hole number six, Jordan, who was in last place on the scorecard, hit a perfect drive down the fairway. Violet wanted to applaud because she'd seldom seen him make such a solid shot, but she didn't want to act as if it was anything out of the ordinary. She settled instead for a playful kiss on the cheek. "Uh-oh," she said. "I was afraid you were just getting warmed up and you'd been holding back."

Quentin teed off and then got in a cart with Jordan, leaving Violet and Jillian to ride together.

"I'm onto you," Jillian said. She gave Violet's shoulder a gentle nudge as she drove.

Violet froze, but she kept her gaze straight ahead.

"I see what you're doing," the older woman continued. "And it's sweet, but it will only lead to trouble in the end."

"I...don't know what you mean," Violet said.

"You've been holding back. Anyone can see you've got a better swing than Jordan and your short game is good, too. Letting him win is nice, but I say don't do it. He seems like a gracious loser, and you must have beaten him before, right?"

Violet relaxed and smiled. "Every time."

Jillian laughed. "I know he wants to impress us, but we're not hiring him for his golf skills. You, however, will make an excellent addition to my golf league and I'm already looking forward to having you on my team."

Violet walked to her ball and took a long

time lining it up. Things had been easier for her than they had been for Jordan. Her family had a successful business and a solid name on the island. She'd walked into Brookstone's and had the luxury of renaming it Island Boutique and turning it into exactly what she wanted.

She didn't have Jordan's baggage. She wasn't desperate to find success. It had been right there waiting for her. She took a steady swing and put her ball squarely on the green. She'd come close to walking in Jordan's shoes because of their long friendship, but she still hadn't squeezed her feet into the hand-me-downs he'd worn until he was old enough to get a job.

He had a reason for his journey.

CHAPTER FIVE

JORDAN SELDOM ASKED any favors. He was a self-made man who'd fought his way up by his own efforts. However, the possibility and promise of a new job had scrambled his head. He had Violet pretending to be in love with him and attempting to throw a golf match, and now he stood in the Great Island Hotel kitchen waiting to make a personal request of the catering manager.

"Yes?" Destiny asked. "Is there some problem at the front desk you need tea sandwiches or boxed lunches to solve?"

Destiny had managed the catering department at the Great Island Hotel since before Jordan had started working there, and even after ten years, he still felt like the new kid compared to her. She wasn't unkind or mean, but she moved with total assurance, as if she was accustomed to her ducks falling neatly into rows wherever she went. The catering department at the hotel provided food for special events both on the grounds and elsewhere on the island, and it had a reputation for high quality and excellent presentation.

He needed both those things for the statement he wanted to make.

"There's not a problem at the desk," he said. "I'm here to place an order for a private event."

"A personal event?" she asked. She cocked her head and looked interested—or was she dubious? Jordan had never catered a personal event and his lack of experience was about to show.

"Sort of. I guess." He took a deep breath and tried to quell his nervousness. "It's a party with a group of my friends from the island."

"I've heard the rumors about you," Destiny said. "So this is either an engagement party for you and Violet or a bon voyage party as you trade an island for mountains."

Should he have thrown an engagement party? Whose responsibility was that? Probably friends of the engaged…and their closest friends knew it was a scam. No. An engagement party would be way too much. Too much potential for being outed, too many reminders of the game he was playing. And a bon voyage party? He briefly pictured himself getting on the ferry and waving farewell—perhaps permanently—to the island where he'd spent almost every single day of his life.

"Neither one," Jordan said quickly. "It's something else."

"Well, you've got a lot going on this summer," Destiny said.

She took off her apron and motioned for Jordan to sit down in front of her desk. She claimed her own chair and sat, waiting for him, her hands poised over her computer keyboard.

"Go ahead when you're ready," she said. "Date, time, number of people, diet restrictions and theme of the event."

Jordan hadn't been prepared to answer detailed questions. Violet would be so much better at that, but she was having a sidewalk sale to make way for new inventory and she was busy. He couldn't monopolize every moment of her time, and he was going to have to get used to doing things without her help and input.

"It's June twenty-first, the summer solstice."

Destiny raised an eyebrow. "I didn't know you celebrated that holiday."

Jordan laughed. "We're going to celebrate the longest day of summer," he said. "Just like we do every year. Our group—"

"How many?" Destiny interrupted.

"Oh," Jordan said. He ticked off names on his fingers. Griffin and Maddox, Rebecca, Camille and Cara, Violet and maybe her brother Ryan if he was in town, Mike and Hadley, and a few other friends. "Maybe twelve or fifteen."

"Location?"

"The Winter Palace. Flora Winter used to host a party every year, and now Griffin and Reb—"

"Will there be desserts and alcohol?"

"Uh, yes? Maybe?"

"That influences how much people eat," Destiny said. "And what are you thinking for food?"

"I was going to ask you that."

"What did you serve last year?"

Jordan sat in the chair she'd offered two minutes earlier. "This is harder than I thought. Can you reserve a spot in your catering calendar and I'll get back to you with details?"

"It's only a few days away," Destiny said. "So it's a bit late to reserve a spot. And I'm assuming you haven't been involved in the food in the past, so why this year?"

Jordan swallowed. "It may be my last chance, and I wanted to do something nice for my friends. If I really do leave."

Destiny's expression softened. "You're in a spot, aren't you? Excited but nervous, thrilled to get away, afraid of what you'll find. I felt the same way when I left the hotel in Dallas and came way the heck up here to an island."

"Are you glad you did?"

"It was twenty years ago, but I'm still glad I did it. Almost every day," she said. "And you'll be fine. Tell you what—I'm going to put together three sample menus and prices for your group, and I'll email them to you. Pick one by the end of the day tomorrow and I'll make it happen for your longest-day, engagement, bon voyage party."

Jordan smiled. "Thanks. I'll tell my friends not to worry about bringing potluck or anything else."

"You might want to wait until you see the prices," Destiny said. "This could be very expensive."

There it was again, people reminding him of his poor childhood—even people who hadn't been on the island when he was a little kid.

"Don't look so serious," Destiny said. "I warn everyone about the bill. I'm going to give you the special employee discount, but I want my trays back the next morning. Clean."

"You got it," Jordan said. "Thanks."

"My pleasure," Destiny told him. "Even though every day of summer is long in this business and I have no idea why you'd want to celebrate the longest one."

"Tradition," he said. A tradition he was going to miss.

Destiny waved a hand and turned her attention to her computer.

Jordan went back up to his office behind the front desk, double checked to make sure housekeeping had cleared all the rooms for the rest of the day's check-ins and then stood looking out his office window. His view was a narrow sliver of lake framed by two porch columns. In the winter, the strip of sunshine that came through the window barely illuminated the flower pattern in the carpet. On summer days, the late afternoon sun lit up the dust particles in the air and glanced off his shiny laptop screen.

From the general manager's office at the Great Valley Hotel, would he see mountains? Would there be a strip of sunshine, predictable in its patterns depending on the time of year?

He pulled out his phone and texted Rebecca Browne who had taken up residence on one floor of the Winter Palace as she helped the May brothers manage their ferry line, their Holiday Hotel and the expansion of their dock.

Don't worry about food for the solstice party. I'm having it catered from the hotel.

Really? Is this payment for my silence?

Jordan sent back a smiley face emoji and then closed his laptop for the day. He didn't make it to the parking lot before his phone pinged. He pulled it from his pocket and saw Violet's name.

Nice.

Just one word, but he knew Violet had already heard about his catering plan.

May need your help with menus.

Of course. Just don't spend all your money. You need to save up for those snow tires.

Violet considered calm seas an incredible blessing for her sidewalk sale. Even tourists who weren't stalwart sailors were brave enough for the short crossing on the fresh, beautiful days in June. All the downtown merchants set up sales inside their stores and on the sidewalks out front. The annual event thrived or failed based on the weather, and the stores were open late in honor of the long hours of daylight.

The second day of the sidewalk sale had already been spectacular, so much so that, for the first time, Violet was considering hiring part-time help. If only they could start in five minutes. All morning, she had shoppers consistently browsing the racks and lining up at her cash register.

She almost didn't answer her phone because she was busy helping a woman find her size in a bright pink sleeveless dress, but it was Jordan calling. What if he needed something?

"How's business?" he asked as soon as she picked up.

"Busy," she said.

"Need a hand?"

"I need five hands," Violet replied.

"It's my day off, and I can offer you two hands and a decade of customer service experience. I can also run a cash register and cheerfully handle complaints."

"You're hired."

"I'll be right there."

Jordan showed up ten minutes later wearing a Great Island Hotel polo shirt and khaki cargo shorts.

"I thought you weren't working?"

He did a one-shoulder shrug. "It's my only short-sleeve shirt that isn't a T-shirt. I didn't want to look like a slob working in your boutique."

Violet smiled. "You're engaged to the island's fashion expert, and you have one choice for clothing. Something's not right."

Joking about their fake engagement made it seem less awkward.

"Before I move away for good, I'll have to ask for your help building a non-Christmas-Island wardrobe. What do normal people wear out there?" he asked.

"I'll think about it. Right now, can you get behind the register?"

Jordan had helped in her shop a few times before, usually when he was hanging out on his day off or waiting for her to close up so they could go for a bike ride or to dinner. He already knew how to scan price tags and credit cards, so Violet flashed him an appreciative smile and went to the front of the store where she could assist customers inside and on the sidewalk.

Across the street, the souvenir shop was also doing a brisk business, and there was a line out the door at Camille's family-owned candy and fudge store. Good weather combined with island-wide sidewalk sales was clearly a winner.

Violet didn't have to think about what Jordan was doing because she trusted him. Instead, she took a moment to appreciate the sunshine while she offered assistance to a mother and daughter who already had several shopping bags from downtown businesses. The items Violet had selected for clearance were dwindling, and she was considering marking down some of the newer summer dresses, skirts and shoes she'd recently gotten. If she waited to discount them until later in the summer, who knew if they would sell?

Jordan waved at her from inside the store and Violet ducked inside. "Food for thought," he said. "Jalapeño poppers or meatball sliders?"

"Is it already lunchtime?"

He laughed and shook his head. "For the solstice party. Appetizers."

"Poppers," Violet said.

"That's what I thought."

She went back to the front of the store. A few minutes later during a lull in the business, Jordan walked over and leaned on a rack of bathing suit cover-ups.

"Lasagna or mac and cheese with bacon?"

"You're making me hungry."

"I could go get lunch."

"In a minute," Violet answered. "Are we talking about the main course now?"

He nodded. "What kind of pasta dish says *longest day of the year* party?"

Violet considered the question as she straightened pairs of shoes on a table. She ducked under the table to find a sunshine-yellow loafer than had fallen off the end.

"I need to see the whole menu laid out.

Appetizers, main course and sides before I can make a good decision. Some things don't mix well."

"Destiny, our catering manager, needs to know by the end of the day today," Jordan said. "Sorry to rush you on a busy shopping day. I feel like I'm asking the world of you this summer."

Violet smiled. "You're my best friend. You can ask anything. Besides, I know you'd do anything for me, even untangle the massive pile of empty clothing hangers I tucked behind the counter. I'd rather clean the toilet than do that."

"I can untangle," he said. "But first, I'll read you the list of food choices while we have a minute." He scrolled through screens on his phone and read off four appetizer choices, four main course choices and four choices for side dishes. "Destiny actually put together some suggested combinations," he said. "Do you want to hear those?"

"Absolutely," Violet said. "She's a professional at food whereas I'm a frozen-dinner person. Now, if Destiny wanted my advice on shoes and accessories to go with an outfit, I'd be all over that."

Jordan read three sample menus and finished reeling off the last one just as a group of three women came into the shop.

"Is that handsome man offering to pick up lunch?" one of them asked. "That all sounded good to me."

"He's planning a party and needs advice," Violet said.

"I love a man who isn't afraid to ask for help," one of the other women replied.

Violet grinned. "He's available."

All three women laughed and started browsing.

"I'm not really available," Jordan said in a low voice. "I'm officially off the market, ensnared by the most beautiful woman on the island."

Violet had joked about their engagement just minutes earlier, so she played along and laughed, but a strange thought got stuck in her mind. Would Jordan be ensnared by a beautiful woman at the Great Valley Hotel? He deserved someone funny and kind who understood him and wanted the best for him. Would he find someone like that and be happy?

She swallowed. "Definitely menu number three," she said. "That one sounded just right."

Violet wasn't sure what she'd just told Jordan to order, but it didn't matter. She trusted Destiny to put together excellent choices, and she needed to get Jordan out of her shop so she could keep her mind on her business.

CHAPTER SIX

Four days later, Jordan surveyed the dwindling food trays on the dining room table at the Winter Palace, and he knew Violet had chosen the menu well. The grilled corn on the cob, whitefish bites, honey chicken wings and picnic burritos were perfect tastes of summer complemented by mini key lime pies and homemade whoopie pies for dessert.

The desserts were untouched because the group was saving them until almost dark when they would get on their bikes for a twilight loop around the island culminating in a bonfire at the ruined winery. They did it every year, but this year felt special to Jordan.

"You didn't have to do all this," Camille Peterson said. "Especially the desserts. I would have been happy to supply those like I usually do."

"Which is why I wanted to cater it," Jordan said. "You and other people always do the food, and this may be my last chance to contribute."

"They have the summer solstice in Virginia, too, you know," Maddox said.

"But there's no island to bike around and all of you won't be there."

Maddox laughed. "You must be counting your blessings already. You get to go where no one knows way too darn much about you."

Camille elbowed him.

"Unless you like that sort of thing, of course," Maddox added. "Like I do."

"Is everything okay?" Rebecca asked as she and Violet came into the dining room. "We were watching the water from the porch because we were too stuffed to move. I should have come in and offered to do dishes or put food in the fridge."

"Everything's perfect," Jordan said. "There's not much food left, and I'll wash the trays later. I love that you're continuing the summer and winter solstice parties in this old mansion."

"Traditions," Rebecca said. "I'm loving them."

Having grown up in foster care, Rebecca had taken to the family atmosphere of the island like a struggling swimmer grabs a life ring. Jordan could empathize a bit with her because his childhood had also been parentless and rocky. His grandparents had loved him, but as he grew older, he understood how much they had sacrificed by moving to the island and raising him there. They could have made an easier choice, and it took a toll on their health.

Jordan followed his friends into the front parlor of the Winter Palace. The mansion still had most of the formal furnishings left over from Flora Winter's lifetime ownership of the three-story Victorian home. Flowery wallpaper still covered the walls, but the whole space looked lighter to Jordan as if it had shed a few years.

"What's different?" he asked. He was accustomed to the formality of the Great Island Hotel lobby and seating areas, so accustomed he would notice if a lamp or an ottoman was missing.

"Curtains," Rebecca said. "I took down some of the velvet ones and replaced them with sheers. I love the light and the view too much to block it, and Flora gave us her blessing to do anything we want since she handed over ownership and doesn't want us to feel like we have to honor her legacy in any way."

"Even though we do," Griffin said as he got up from a winged chair and put an arm around Rebecca. "We folded the old curtains carefully and stored them in the attic, just in case we want to put them back up when we're eighty."

"Or in case Aunt Flora comes to visit," Maddox said.

Rebecca shook her head. "She doesn't expect this place to be a museum, and I don't know if her health will allow her too many trips. She's coming for our wedding this fall if the weather cooperates, and that will be so nice."

The light coming through the large windows was fading fast, and Jordan was considering breaking out the dessert trays stored in the massive fridge in the Winter Palace's kitchen, but the doorbell rang.

"I thought everyone was already here," Rebecca said. She stepped out on the porch and leaned over the railing to get a view of the lower door by the driveway. "Come in," she called, and then she strode into the parlor.

"It's your brother," she said to Violet. Everyone in the room froze and looked from Jordan to Violet.

"He doesn't know," Violet said.

Everyone else did. Camille and Cara, Griffin and Maddox, and Rebecca. Hadley and Mike Martin had come earlier in the evening, but they went home, skipping the twilight bike ride because of Hadley's pregnancy.

"He texted me earlier and said he might make it tonight, but it would be late and he's only staying one night and going back on the first ferry," Violet said. "I wondered why he was coming at all if he was only staying such a short time."

They heard footsteps on the stairs.

"So, we either tell him the whole story," Jordan whispered, "Or we act like there's nothing going on."

"Nothing going on," Violet said quickly.

"Hey, everyone," Ryan Brookstone said as he entered the room. He gave his sister a hug and then did the same with Rebecca, Camille and Cara. "You smell like horses as always," he said to Cara.

"You smell like—"

"Hey," Ryan interrupted her. "Be nice to a guy who flew over with a family of seventeen children who were all crying because it's past their bedtime."

"Were you crying, too, when you landed at the airport?" Cara asked.

"Inconsolably. I hope you've all saved me some food."

"Come on," Violet said. "I'll help you make a plate. We haven't started in on the desserts yet, so you're lucky." She looped an arm through her brother's. "And I'm glad you're here."

Violet and Ryan left the parlor, and the rest of the group exchanged guilty looks. "It feels weird not to tell him his sister is fake engaged," Camille said. "What if he hears about it somehow? Won't that be worse?"

"You're assuming he'll be unhappy," Jordan said.

"Yes," Griffin and Maddox replied at the same time.

"Would I be such a bad choice for Violet?" Jordan asked.

"No," Cara said. "It's just the fake thing. Ryan is pretty protective and he might worry that…"

"What?" Jordan asked. Why did it seem like everyone knew something he didn't? Couldn't people see that his best friend was helping him out temporarily? Even if the whole thing fell through, it would hurt him, not Violet.

"Let's just all act like we always do. A close-knit group."

"With a lot of pairs in it," Cara grumbled.

"We're all friends," Griffin said. "I say we grab the desserts and load up the bikes for our ride and our stop at the ruins. Maddox and I already checked on the firewood supply and stashed some party supplies where we hope no one else will find them."

"Who else would be brave enough to go to those haunted ruins at night?" Rebecca asked.

"Plenty of people." Griffin kissed her temple. "You're still new here, but we're not the only people who use it as a gathering spot."

"And Griffin's not brave," Maddox said. "Just foolish."

"Be nice or I'll put up ancient velvet curtains in your living room when you're not home," Griffin said.

VIOLET WATCHED HER brother choose two white-fish bites, one burrito, and three wings. His plate had plenty of room left.

"Saving room for dessert?" she asked.

"I don't want to hold you all up by eating a three-course meal," Ryan said. "I wanted to come earlier, but I couldn't get away from the job site."

"The multimillion-dollar mansion project?"

He nodded, his expression grim. "It's worth a lot of money to my company, too, but there are days I wish I hadn't bid on it."

"Why?"

"You ever get that creepy feeling that something's just not right?"

Violet picked up a napkin that had fallen under the table. Was her brother talking about his life or hers? They'd always been close, even though they'd chosen different paths in life. His path took him off the island for college and then kept him on the mainland for his building projects. Christmas Island seldom had new construction. Its historic downtown, hotels and island homes had remained unchanged most of her life—and that was how islanders liked it. She couldn't imagine a big commercial project or a housing development, although an expensive private home was certainly not out of the question. Would Ryan come back to the island for an extended project if given the chance?

"What's bothering you?" she asked. If Ryan had heard about her and Jordan, she wasn't going to stall or evade his questions. She'd tell him she was willingly playing the part to help Jordan.

"The millionaire I'm working for didn't get to be a millionaire by rescuing stray cats and being nice to the elderly and downtrodden."

"Have you rescued any stray cats?" Violet asked.

"Only the ones you brought home and I helped you conceal in the garage."

"Well," Violet said, adding a piece of grilled corn on the cob to Ryan's plate. "I know you're nice to the elderly and downtrodden. So that makes up for the cats."

"Thanks," he said. "I shouldn't worry about the guy I'm working for. He's happy with our work and the people who work for me are treated well on site and paid well for sure."

"Maybe you just needed some island air," Violet said. "You should visit more often."

As she said the words, she silently added *but not for a few weeks*. For better or worse, though, even when the charade with Jordan ended, people on the island would still know about it and remember. She should have thought of this. Her parents lived far away, but they had island friends. What were the chances they'd accidentally hear the news that, oh, by the way, their only daughter was engaged? It was a good thing they were on an extended camping trip with little access to phone and internet, or they would probably have heard already.

She sighed. What a mess. Maybe she should come clean with Ryan and her family and tell them it was all an act and they should ignore any rumors they might hear. Why hadn't she thought of that already? Probably because she'd been focused on her own role in the theatrics.

"Maybe later in the summer," Ryan said. "I'm too busy right now."

He was busy, her parents were busy, everyone had plenty going on without fussing over her fake engagement. She was sparing them the worry by keeping it as quiet as possible until it was over.

And it would end. Probably with Jordan leaving the home where he'd grown up and the people who'd known him every step of the way. He'd find new people in another state.

"I'll eat and then we'll do the bike thing.

I've hardly ridden all summer. I was lucky to grab a loaner bike from Mike as I came through downtown on my way out here. I only saw him for a minute because he wanted to get Hadley home, but he said you had some big news. What did he mean?"

Violet swallowed. Was she really going to lie to her big brother? "Business. I had a huge sidewalk-and-clearance sale. All the downtown merchants did well. A real boost to my bank account."

"Okay," Ryan said. He didn't look impressed, and he was clearly waiting for something more interesting than a sales report. Should she just tell him now?

"Brookstone, are you in there finishing all the food or can we get going?" Maddox's voice reached them from the living room, and she and her brother laughed.

"Told you I didn't want to hold up the group," he said. He shoved two whitefish bites into his mouth and then set the plate aside. "Let's go before I get kicked out of the summer solstice group."

"No chance of that," Violet said. "We're all stuck together for life."

Except Jordan who wanted to leave. How

long had he been serious about leaving Christmas Island? Sure he'd mentioned it a time or two, always in the context of wanting a better life than his parents and grandparents had enjoyed. But had he been serious all along, more than she'd realized?

Maybe she didn't know him as well as she'd thought.

"The desserts can go in a box in my big bike basket," Camille said. Like other islanders, she had outfitted her bike for her daily needs. As an owner of the candy shop, that meant occasional deliveries that required cargo space. "I won't even sneak any on the way."

"I made the secret Winter family punch recipe Flora shared with me," Rebecca said. "That's going in my basket, but the container is heavy."

"It'll be lighter on the way back," Griffin said. "I could try to carry it with one hand."

"Or you could trade and ride my bike," Rebecca replied.

"It's a bit short for me," Griffin began, but Rebecca cut him off with a laugh.

"I'm kidding. I can handle a basket filled with your family's secret recipe."

"Our family," Griffin said as he reached out

and touched Rebecca's arm. Camille sighed and Cara groaned.

"I have a new bike light, so I'll lead," Cara said.

In five minutes, their bikes were loaded, and the group kicked off from the Winter Palace. They rode down the hill to the main road that circled the island and began the trip. Although it was late, there was still a glimmer in the sky thanks to the summer solstice. Lights on the mainland shimmered and there were some green-and-red marker lights from boats. Violet had made this trip so many times that she could guess what they'd talk about on the way, who would end up in the front and the back of the pack and what songs they would sing after the May brothers got the fire going and they passed around drinks and desserts.

She rode next to Jordan. Her brother and Cara were in the lead and the other two couples were behind them.

"I wonder what you'll be doing next year on June twenty-first," Violet said. "Arranging concierge service for wealthy patrons or movie stars at the Great Valley or having champagne on the porch with Quentin and Jillian Shelley?"

"Maybe I'll be taking advantage of the daylight by attempting to get through eighteen holes of golf without embarrassing myself," Jordan said.

"No chance," Violet said. "The day isn't that long."

Jordan laughed and Violet tried to forget the shadow hanging over all of them. She should savor the night instead of worrying about Jordan leaving and her brother being irritated that she'd kept him out of the loop about the fake engagement.

After several miles of camaraderie and a few spiderwebs hanging in the air and wrapping themselves around the group members, they arrived at the ruins of the old winery. Having burned decades ago, it was never rebuilt. Instead, the stone walls that didn't fall victim to the fire loomed over them. The windows were long gone and the holes looked like empty eyes. Griffin and Maddox had a fire going in just minutes, and the orange light danced off the walls, making them seem eerie.

Camille opened the box of desserts. "Whoopie pies or key lime pies?" she asked.

"I even have napkins and forks if anyone wants to be civilized."

"Can I have both?" Cara asked.

"I ordered two desserts for everyone, so yes," Jordan said.

"Thanks," Cara replied. "But I'm still mad at you for deserting Christmas Island. I don't see how anyone can be happy anywhere else."

"I'm happy," Ryan said as he sat next to Cara on a log facing the fire.

"Are you?" Cara asked.

Ryan didn't answer and an awkward silence fell until Griffin declared it was song time.

"Do the one about the shipwreck, 'Safe Upon the Shore,'" Camille said. "It's creepy and sad and it only sounds good in the dark. I tried listening to it with my earbuds one day while I was riding my bike and it didn't have any mystery at all."

"Maybe it only sounds good when Jordan and Violet sing it," Rebecca suggested. She turned to them. "You make everything sound good."

"Even 'The Wheels on the Bus'?" Violet asked.

Rebecca laughed and held up a hand. "Don't. I beg you."

"Okay, sad shipwreck pining for lost love song coming right up," Violet said. "But if the ghosts from actual wrecks come out of the lake and scare the whoopie pies out of us, I'm not responsible."

"All the verses?" Jordan asked. "Even the sad ones?"

"We've got all night," Violet said. She hummed a key and counted to three and they launched into the sad shipwreck song they had harmonized on many times before. Camille passed around desserts, Griffin filled drinks and the rest of the group kicked back, watching the fire.

It was a perfect night and the song rolled off Violet's tongue. It began with the story of a ship leaving port on a long-awaited journey but with a promise to return. The joyous mood of the parting ended with the first verse, and the second verse was all about expecting and watching. A lover roamed the shore, waiting, despite fair winds that should have brought the ship back.

The mood of the third verse shifted along with a key change that Violet had never missed before, but her mind was on that lover watching from the shore and wondering. Would that be her? Would she always wonder what happened to Jordan or would there be frequent texts and calls, perhaps a visit. But it could never be the same.

She glanced at him in the firelight and a realization hit her like a raging forest fire. She would be that lover. She would be sorry to see Jordan go. Not just because he was her friend, but because she was in love with him.

Her lips parted but no sound came out.

"Violet?" Jordan asked. "Did you forget the lyrics?"

She couldn't tell him. Not now, not ever. She loved him. How long had that been the case? Had it happened so gradually that she never noticed? Was she only aware now because of the threat of his leaving? If it was not for the ruse and the Great Valley Hotel… would she and Jordan have gone on as they were for another year? Two years? A decade?

No matter why light had finally dawned, she couldn't unthink the fact or unsee the reality of her situation. And she couldn't tell him. She owed Jordan her best effort as his fake fiancée and she owed him the chance to say goodbye without guilt.

What would he say if she told him how she

felt? She could imagine his confusion. He'd be flustered, but he'd say something nice. He was always nice. He cared about her, probably more than anyone in his life. She'd been his steady force for years. Dropping a bombshell on him by telling him she was in love with him would be unkind. Unjust even. He couldn't make himself fall in love with her. And he was leaving. His leaving would be bittersweet if she revealed her feelings.

She had to help him leave the island, perhaps even more so now that she understood her feelings and what had been bothering her about the fake engagement. It would be terrible to see him go, but it would be worse to have him stay if she loved one-sided.

"I… It was the key change—I forgot about it. And I'm…thirsty," she said. Jordan handed her his own drink as he had dozens of times before, and she took her time taking long sips, hiding her face behind the rim of the glass. Finally, she handed it back to him and forced a smile.

"All better. But I'm in the mood for a more cheerful song now."

"Are the night spirits getting to you?" her brother asked.

"Hey," she said, trying to lighten her mood and push away her big revelation. No good could or would come of it. "Easy for you to criticize," she said to Ryan. "You just ate your whoopie pie and mine while I was busy entertaining all of you."

Her brother smiled. "But I saved you my key lime pie because I know you like those better."

Ryan was right, and she felt like a heel for concealing her pact with Jordan from her brother. He deserved better.

She deserved better.

CHAPTER SEVEN

Two MORNINGS AFTER the solstice party, Jordan had the day off but he also had a job to do. Maddox texted him early asking him to walk his dog because he'd taken his son, Ethan, to the mainland for a long visit with the boy's mother, Jennifer. Maddox had stayed one night on the mainland since it was late, and his morning flight back to the island was delayed for mechanical problems.

Jordan liked Maddox's golden retriever, Skipper, and he was happy to help. He picked up the dog and went downtown for a walk, intending to grab a coffee and give Skipper a nice long stretch of the legs. He passed the kite shop, the post office, the Holiday Hotel, a souvenir shop and the candy and fudge store.

He paused in front of Violet's boutique. It was early yet. Was she up?

The front door swung open, and Violet stood there with a coffee cup in her hand.

"Two of the best faces on the island," she said. "But one of them needs coffee."

"You're right about that," Jordan said.

She motioned for him to come in. "I made a pot because I was up early dusting and sweeping under the racks and in the fitting rooms. You can bring Skipper in. He won't bother anything."

"I'm supposed to be walking him as a favor to Maddox."

"Is he out on the ferry?"

"Briefly stuck on the mainland because of the plane's mechanical issue. He took Ethan for a visit with his mom."

"It must be strange for Ethan, trying to live in two different worlds," Violet said.

Her tone was wistful, and Jordan wondered if she was thinking about him leaving. Was it really a different world out there?

"I think both his parents try hard to make life seem normal for Ethan," Jordan said.

"They do," Violet agreed. "I'll put your coffee in a mug and then I can walk with you. My shop doesn't open for half an hour, and I'm ready."

She poured and handed him a steaming cup, locked her front door, and then she took the leash and they stepped out onto the front sidewalk with Skipper trotting alongside. The island dogs knew everyone and were practically community property.

"Hey, Skipper," Hadley said as she passed them on her way to work. "You and my dog Betty need a playdate one of these days." She reached down and ran a gentle hand over Skipper's head. "She's guarding a patch of sunlight coming through my living room window right now."

Violet laughed. "I can't decide if dogs or house cats have the better life."

Hadley straightened and tugged her purse higher on her shoulder. "I guess that depends on what you consider a good life. House cats get away with doing nothing, but dogs get to go on car rides and adventures."

She waved and continued toward the Holiday Hotel where she ran the front desk in addition to helping out in the restaurant on occasion.

"I could get a dog when I move to Virginia," Jordan said. "Maybe I'll get a used pickup truck and we could go for rides and hikes on my days off."

Violet smiled. "Sounds perfect."

Did it sound perfect? Dogs were great company, but it was tough to bike with them and skip rocks. They were good listeners, but they weren't going to remind you when a friend had a birthday coming up or invite you over for macaroni and cheese. He swallowed, picturing a new life. So far, he'd imagined himself, polished and respected, managing the Great Island Hotel. He hadn't imagined his days off and long winter evenings.

He tried to shake off the melancholy. Lots of people moved and took new jobs. Made new friends.

"You okay?" Violet asked, noticing his silence.

He nodded. "I was just thinking about how it's so peaceful downtown before the first ferry gets here," Jordan said. He didn't want to tell her what he was really thinking. He didn't want to say it aloud and begin doubting himself.

"I enjoy it every day," Violet said. "The calm before the storm. But you probably don't notice it so much because you're up at the hotel."

"We have waves of people coming around eleven, hoping their rooms will be ready early," he said. "But it's usually pretty steady other than that. The storms don't make it up the hill to the hotel."

They approached the end of downtown where a long green lawn stretched downward toward a marina. Private boats, mostly owned by islanders, bobbed peacefully in the morning sunshine. Jordan knew people who owned boats—Violet had inherited her family's older but still nice motorboat—but his family had never had the means to have their own. Moving to the mountains, he doubted he'd ever own a boat now, but he was happy to make the trade for the opportunity for advancement.

His family's poverty seemed magnified when he reflected that they had lived on an island yet could never afford a boat. It was like living near a highway but not owning a car. He was cut out for more. He just knew it.

A man with a Chihuahua approached, coming along the sidewalk from the other direction. It was the general manager of the Great Island Hotel. Jordan's boss who held a position Jordan could never hope to attain if he stayed on Christmas Island because Jack was respected, anchored in the community and there to stay. He'd been offered a job at the Great Valley, but turned it down twice in the past ten years.

Jordan put an arm around Violet as they paused to say hello and let the dogs touch noses.

"Good morning," Jack Heidelberg said. "I guess the rumors must be true. And you've already got a dog."

Violet laughed. "Skipper isn't our dog. We're walking him for a friend."

Jack nodded. "But you two are engaged?"

"Yes," Jordan said. "Engaged to get married." He mentally kicked himself for saying something so obvious. He sounded too eager.

"And of course it doesn't hurt your chances having a future wife since the Shelleys are all about family." Jack himself had two daughters and a son in the island school and his wife was active in the island community. It had been Jack who'd first told Jordan his chances at a promotion would be better if he was married.

"Love just sort of sneaks up on you," Violet said.

"I was a bit surprised," Jack replied. "When I heard. I knew you were friends, everyone on the island is friendly and I've seen you together, but I just thought the timing was odd, given that you're applying for a promotion to leave the island. Or maybe your timing was just, um, perfect."

Jordan pulled Violet closer and she glanced up at him. Before he could even think, she touched her lips to his in a perfect, sweet kiss. It was a tiny kiss, a mere brush of lips, but Jordan was grateful he had an arm around Violet because he felt as if his world had just tilted.

Jack laughed. "You don't have to prove anything to me. I can see you're both over the moon. I remember feeling like that when Julie and I were first engaged and then married. Still do, sometimes, if you want to know the truth."

He tugged on his Chihuahua's leash and walked past.

"What was that?" Jordan said quietly.

"I think it was a test and we passed."

Jordan meant the kiss, but he didn't want to say it. How could he tell Violet that the three seconds their lips had touched would give him an hour's worth of things to consider? They'd talked about kissing in theory, just in case, but they'd gotten through two weeks of engagement without the need for a single kiss.

He wasn't sure he wanted to risk another one anytime soon.

"I threw in the kiss just in case," Violet said. She looked matter-of-fact and unflustered. "Insurance. I didn't want Mr. Heidelberg thinking you'd fake a relationship just to get a good job."

She gave him a little bump with her hip and started walking as if they'd just avoided a mud puddle or found a penny on the sidewalk. Hadn't she felt anything?

Jordan took a deep, steadying breath. It was far better if she didn't. They couldn't both be tilting. One of them had to be practical and unfazed. Violet was a far better actress than he'd imagined, practically a pro at playing his fiancée. But he highly doubted her acting skills were good enough to pretend that kiss hadn't meant anything. Clearly, she was unmoved—or he would know. Wouldn't he?

While he mused about it, Skipper tugged them toward the marina where he stood looking out at the water as if he was expecting Maddox home anytime.

"He's flying, silly," Violet said. "But I admire your loyalty."

A ferryboat was indeed coming from the mainland. They could see it crossing.

"If I know Maddox, he's on that boat instead of waiting for the plane," Jordan said, glad to have something practical to discuss so he could get his feet under him. That kiss still resonated.

Violet laughed. "Do you think he and Griffin fight over who gets to drive the boat? We seldom drove anywhere when I was a teenager, and my brother Ryan always wanted to do the honors. I was so glad when he went off to college—for the first week, and then I missed him and wished he would come home."

"Are you sad he never did?" Jordan was an only child and had never experienced the frustration and joys of siblings.

"No," Violet said. "He has to live his own life. Just like you do. But if you ever come back to visit, I'll be here in my boutique. Speaking of which, I better get it open before the day visitors get off that ferry."

If he ever came back to visit. How could she think he wouldn't? Of course he would.

All his friends were here. What would Christmas be like anywhere else?

Jordan nodded. "Maybe I'll walk down to the dock with Skipper and meet the ferry."

Violet gave Skipper an affectionate pat, and she turned to walk back toward her shop.

"Dinner tonight?" Jordan asked.

She hesitated. Why did she hesitate? They were friends. It was a simple yes or no, almost always a yes.

"I need your opinion about something," he said quickly. "If you're free."

"What did you want to ask?"

"It's about…my house. I'm thinking about how I could improve it in case I need to sell it."

Violet smiled. "Of course you'll need to sell it. You're going to get that job, and you deserve it. Do you want me to pick up dinner and bring it over around seven and then I'll give you my expert decorating advice?"

He relaxed. Everything was going to be okay. "That would be perfect."

"What would you like for dinner?"

"You know what I like," he said. "Surprise me."

In fact, she'd surprised him already with that kiss. And he didn't know how he felt about it. Maybe he should make a specific request.

"Gotcha," Violet said and she gave him a little wave as she walked away.

SHE WASN'T PROUD of the fact, but Violet hoped for some kind of minor emergency all day that would prevent her from having dinner with Jordan. An electrical outage closing all the downtown restaurants perhaps? A water main break that flooded the street around her shop—not in it, of course—and would require her to remain on premises, just in case. Perhaps a minor turned ankle. A bee sting. A cavity.

Anything that would change her plans and distract her from the string of emotional solar flares stemming from her relationship with Jordan. There had been the summer solstice party that ended in a bright shiny light illuminating her feelings, even though she would have preferred to keep them in the dark. And now, two days later—the kiss.

That wonderful, terrible kiss. Why had she been so impulsive and planted one on Jordan? Hadn't there been any other way to prove to his boss that their engagement was the real thing? Maybe a ring. She should just pick one out of the jewelry display in her boutique that looked sort of engagement-like and start wearing it on her left hand. When Jillian Shelley had asked her where her ring was, Violet had told her it was being resized. Just one more lie they'd racked up.

She pushed back her hair and sighed, and a woman browsing a rack of colorful poplin blouses looked up. "I'm trying not to mess them up," she said. "I used to work retail and I hated it when customers would come in an hour before closing and unfold everything."

Violet smiled. "I'm sorry. That sigh wasn't for you, and I'm happy to straighten the racks. I own the store, so quitting time is whenever I say it is."

Maybe she could beg off on dinner by claiming she had to resize a rack or tag everything with new SKU numbers because of a computer glitch? Would Jordan believe it?

Probably not. Or else he'd offer to come in and help her, darn him.

"You have a beautiful shop and I love the range of sizes."

"I like to fit every body," Violet said. "Every woman is perfect."

"And some men?"

Violet laughed. "Only a few. The rest of them seem to be working on it and driving us crazy in the process."

"Mine is currently fiddling with the motor on our boat. He's not a marine mechanic, so I may get stranded on Christmas Island and have plenty of time to shop."

"I hope so—the shopping, not the stranding, although this is a wonderful island and you could be in a lot worse places," Violet said.

Few people who visited the island were anxious to leave, in Violet's experience. Throughout her lifetime of working for her parents and then taking over the shop, she'd seen countless return visitors, some of them coming back every year like clockwork. She'd watched their kids grow up, getting taller and filling out a little more every summer when they came into the store. Maybe some of the visitors had watched her grow up over the years too, and now here she was running and owning the place where she'd invested her whole life.

Her friends were much the same. Camille, Chloe, and Cara Peterson with the family candy store, and Griffin and Maddox May with their ferry line. Jordan must have felt like an outlier all his life. Having aging grandparents instead of parents at the school function, inheriting only a small house that needed work when his grandparents passed. No wonder he thought opportunity might lie elsewhere.

"Can you recommend a good place for takeout somewhere downtown?" The shopper held a floral blouse in front of her and evaluated her reflection in the mirror. "I think the motor fiddling is going to continue, so I'm taking dinner to my husband instead of waiting around and starving. I've gotten wiser over twenty-five years of marriage."

Violet smiled at the lady who reminded her of her mother who had patiently waited for her dad to finish mowing the lawn so they could go to Sunday brunch on summer days.

"The Holiday Hotel will box up anything on their menu for carryout," Violet said. "But the Mistletoe Melt has dine-in and full-service takeout, and it's a local favorite. I'm probably picking up dinner there tonight."

"Date?"

"Not exactly," Violet said.

"Does this involve a man who is working on perfection but driving you crazy in the process?"

Violet laughed. "I guess you might say that." If Jordan did ever achieve perfection, though, he'd be in another state and she wouldn't be there to see it. She wouldn't be there to do impulsive and dangerous things like kiss him or be tempted to think their relationship was anything beyond friendship. When had that happened?

Since the night of the bonfire at the winery ruins, she'd reviewed two decades' worth of interaction with Jordan, trying to discern and discover when and how her feelings had turned to love. Had it been love when she baked him a birthday cake? Was it love that made her pick him up when he had a flat tire on his bike? Was love behind their joint appearance at the island Christmas party, St. Patrick's Day party, ice-skating get-togethers, canoe races, weddings and funerals, year after year?

If only she could see where her feelings had taken a turn, could she turn them back and save herself the agony of knowing the person she believed she loved didn't return the feelings and was, in fact, using her to escape the island and never come back?

Ouch.

"He has to figure himself out first," she said. "But good take-out food never hurts."

She helped the shopper select two blouses from the rack, try them on and check out. Violet took a moment to straighten her store so it would be ready for her the next morning. Before she walked out the back door and locked it, she gave one last look at the jewelry display. Should she pick out an inexpensive ring, perhaps one that had been around for a while and wasn't likely to sell anyway?

"No," she said aloud in the empty shop. They were already cheating enough, and a false ring would be cheating herself. If she wore an engagement ring someday, it would be placed on her finger by someone who couldn't live without her.

CHAPTER EIGHT

JORDAN PICKED UP the laundry basket he'd left in the living room and stuffed it in his bedroom closet. It didn't improve the appearance of his living room, but it made him look like a better housekeeper. He only ventured into the basement once a week where the ancient washer and dryer he'd inherited were, by some miracle, still running. The basement was crowded with items nobody wanted but hadn't gotten rid of.

Living on an island, it wasn't always easy to discard an old bed frame or a dresser. Having a yard sale at his house off the beaten path was pointless, and he didn't really want strangers or—worse—people he knew picking through his parents' and grandparents' unneeded items. When he did descend the shaky steps into the basement, he tried not to look around.

Other people had happy memories bolstered by family possessions. His childhood had been about surviving the tragic loss of his parents and then getting by with grandparents who were already old when they moved to Christmas Island to raise him. They'd loved him enough to do that, and he'd felt their love, but it was always shadowed by what they'd lost, too. He'd heard them at night on the porch when they thought he was asleep. The smell of cigarettes and night air would steal through his window along with snippets of conversation.

Sometimes, he still smelled the lingering cigarettes on a porch cushion even though both his grandparents had died a few years after he graduated from high school. For almost ten years, he'd lived alone in the house his parents had bought when he was five, and he'd never attempted to make his own mark on it because he didn't plan to stay. And yet, somehow every Christmas he found himself in the same place.

He needed to get out.

If he got the job at the Great Valley Hotel, he would have to clean out and sell this place, and that would mean facing dusty boxes, an artificial tree in a crushed cardboard box, the frame of an old bike, a broken toilet stored in the corner and too many other items that were covered in cobwebs.

Maybe someone would take the house, junk and all.

Jordan pulled aside a graying curtain and saw Violet coming down the road in her white SUV. Clean, of course. Violet had grown up with nice things and she kept them that way. Jordan surrounded himself with nice things at the Great Island Hotel where he picked up his uniforms from the hotel laundry every day, but he'd given up trying to make anything on Scotch Pine Road look good.

Maybe he should have, but it was too late now.

He opened the door and winced as Violet stepped carefully around a splintered board.

"Mistletoe Melt," she said, holding up the bag.

He smiled. "Is there a ham and cheese with mustard in there?"

"Two of them."

"What are you going to eat?" he asked.

Violet laughed. "You can't be that hungry."

"You're right. Just looking around this old place and thinking about how to fix it up so someone wants to buy it takes my appetite away."

Violet didn't try to argue. She knew his place well. She'd cooked in his kitchen, used his bathroom, brought soup to his bedroom once when he was sick. He didn't have anything to hide when it came to her.

Except for the way that kiss had made him feel as if he could fly. He couldn't tell her that. It would be all kinds of unfair to someone who was doing him a favor out of friendship and loyalty. He couldn't complicate things, and he didn't want to. Leaving the island seemed like a greater possibility every day, and it was the only pathway to success for him.

"Let's eat before I start picking your brain on how to refresh this place," Jordan said. He had a picnic table in the yard that he'd purchased himself with one of his first paychecks. Made of a composite material that stood up to wind, sun, snow and time, it still looked good after almost ten years of use. Situated on a small rise, it also had a view of the lake through some pines. Jordan ate outside every chance he could get.

Violet took her usual seat and he sat across

from her. She opened the bag and took out two sandwiches, two bags of chips and two bottles of tea. She held up a white pastry bag. "Cookies. Oatmeal raisin."

"You're the best," Jordan said.

"Although you did tell me to surprise you, I went with the safe choice of the things I know you like. You have plenty of change going on in your life as it is."

Jordan nodded. Trust Violet to understand and be sympathetic.

"But of course it's a lot of good change," Violet continued. "And we're all excited for you. Most people aren't brave enough to take a big risk and completely change their lives."

"You think I'm brave?"

"Most of the time," she said with a smile.

"And other times?"

"Maybe a little foolish for wanting to leave this island paradise and give up fudge and ferryboats and singing under the stars."

Jordan opened his tea and took a swallow. "Am I making a mistake?"

Violet's eyes met his and held just long enough that he knew she was evaluating the cost of what she was about to say. "You have to be the person who decides that. It's your life. And I know you've always felt…"

"What?" he prompted. Did he want to know?

"You've said yourself that you think success isn't possible here—not the kind you want."

"It isn't," he said.

She shrugged. "There are all kinds of success." She took a big bite of her sandwich and took her time chewing it. "For example, I would consider it a success if you got new curtains for every single room of that cute little bungalow behind me."

"Where?" Jordan asked, craning his neck and pretending to look.

"It's all in the presentation," she said. "Sometimes women come into my shop and tell me they never look good in anything. They think they're too tall or too short, too skinny or too curvy to be pretty. I prove them wrong every time."

"And you can work this magic on my house."

"You bet I can. Watch me. As soon as I get dessert, of course."

"Have your cookie, and I'll save you mine for later. You might need it when you take a close look at how big this project is."

"We'll split your cookie later," Violet said.

She finished her sandwich, skipped the chips and ate her cookie while she told Jordan about a shopper who'd special ordered a dress and another shopper whose husband was tinkering with a boat motor and expected to get stranded in the marina. He usually told her stories of his day at work—guests who locked themselves out of their rooms, got caught smoking on their balconies, or who called for room service at all hours of the night and were disappointed.

"I can't help you much with the outside," Violet said as she got up from the picnic table. "I mean, I can suggest a paint color and some complementary shades for trim, but I'm no builder. My brother might have something to say about shoring up the porch or repairing those boards on the edge of the roof."

"I could send him pictures and ask advice."

"You could," Violet said. "But he'll probably tell you to hire a professional, and I'm not sure how much time you have or how much money you want to invest in this place."

"Not much in either case. The new job will start at the end of the summer, and summer is also the best time to try to sell a house on an island where it snows all winter."

"Not much time," Violet said. Her expression was sad.

"Which is why I really need a friend like you," Jordan commented.

Violet reached out and gave his hand a quick squeeze.

"Let's go inside and look for the quick fixes," she said. She wrapped up the remaining cookie and Jordan picked up the rest of their packaging from dinner. They walked up the front steps together, stepping around the splintered board in unison as if they did it every day of their lives.

"You have to fix that," Violet said. "And then paint the porch floor so it won't be obvious there's a new piece of wood."

"I can handle that much," Jordan said. "I think I can get a piece of wood cut to measure at the hardware store."

"And I'll come back and help you paint. Maybe we could do the railing and spindles, too, while we're at it. If we add some plants in pots it would also help make the porch look inviting. It will be a buyer's first impression of their future island getaway."

Jordan laughed. He couldn't imagine anyone viewing this place as a vacation home. "I'll start a list." He led the way to the kitchen where he opened a drawer and took out a pad of Great Island Hotel stationery and a pen. "Floorboard, porch paint, flower pots," he wrote. "Next?"

Violet looked around the kitchen. "Do you have anything in those cabinets?"

He shook his head. "Most of them are empty. I only use the lower shelves over the toaster because you know I eat at least one meal a day at the hotel, sometimes two."

"You eat dinner outside at the picnic table from April through November," Violet said. Of course she knew that because she knew him well and had often eaten with him out there. They had their spots at the table where they always sat, and he usually swiped her seat free of spiderwebs or dew before she sat down.

"I like the view outside," Jordan said. It was much better than sitting at the kitchen table with memories of his grandparents but almost no recollection of his mom and dad. They'd been taken from him too soon.

Violet smiled. "It's a lovely view. Here's

my suggestion for the kitchen. Take off the slightly ugly cabinet doors."

"They're really ugly and dated. You can say it. Remember, I want honesty, and I'd rather hear criticism from you than anyone else."

"Okay, then I would take off the doors and paint the shelves white. It will look open and fresh. Get rid of the curtains that are older than you are. New light bulbs in the fixture over the table and a bright blue rug in front of the sink. And matching towels."

Jordan wrote down everything she suggested. "That doesn't sound too bad."

"We're only in the first room."

"It's a small house," he said.

"Island bungalow and vacation getaway," Violet corrected. "Just wait."

In the living room, Violet pointed to extra end tables and a hand-me-down love seat under the window. "Gone," she said. "Borrow a pickup from Griffin and Maddox and haul them off." She noticed the bag on the couch that was open on one end, revealing the handmade afghan. "Is this new?"

He nodded. "Hadley and Wendy's grandma brought it for me."

Violet smiled. "Penny Pierce. She's a sweetheart and she loves to crochet. I think she's given an afghan to every person on the island. Did you know I have one?"

"You do?"

"It's two shades of violet, of course," she added. "She didn't want me to be cold in my lonely little apartment over my store."

The thought somehow lightened Jordan's mood for a moment. Had the gift been a kind gesture and not the act of charity he'd assumed it was?

"Let's measure the couch and chair you're keeping and we'll order slipcovers online," Violet advised. "And you can stick with blue if you like."

"Won't the room seem empty if we get rid of a lot of furniture?"

Violet shook her head. "It seems crowded and—"

"Say it."

"Dingy," she said with a sheepish look. "Very dingy."

"Why haven't you ever told me that before?" he asked.

"Because it's your house and you didn't ask and… I thought maybe you liked keeping it the way it was when your…family…was still here."

Unexpected pain sliced through Jordan's chest. Was that really the reason he'd never bothered to fix up the place? He'd kept it just as it was when his parents bought it and then his grandparents moved in? They'd never had the cash to make any improvements, but he could have done something. His salary from the hotel had grown over the years as he'd taken on responsibility and he made decent money, especially since he lived on an island and there wasn't a lot to spend it on.

He'd stuck it in the bank instead of fixing up his house, always intending to leave the island if he ever got the chance. Wouldn't his parents have wanted him to, instead of being stuck there with sad memories?

Jordan wrote down Violet's suggestions, carefully numbering them on the hotel notepad. "Paint and rug in this room, too?"

"Yes. Paint isn't too expensive and it makes a ton of difference. I'd paint every wall a fresh white. Get rid of the curtains in this room, too, and maybe paint that little table blue or green for a cottage feel."

"I'm afraid to ask your opinion about the

bathroom," Jordan said. "Although the good news is that there's only one."

"That's the spirit," she said. "Maybe buyers will see the benefit of having only one bathroom to clean in their island paradise."

Paradise. Christmas Island might seem that way to people who had roots and a future here. He'd grown up thinking he'd never grow old and would die here like his grandparents, and he never sat on the corner of the porch where sorrow seemed to linger.

VIOLET WATCHED THE list on Jordan's paper grow and mentally resolved to sit down with him at the end of the evening and prioritize repairs. Trying to do everything, especially doing the work himself to save money, was overwhelming. She knew there was a reason he'd never attempted it before.

"Two bedrooms and a mudroom left, and I have no idea if you're bold enough to look at the basement," Jordan said.

"I've never been in your basement." Jordan had been in hers, a storage space under her boutique. And he'd been in her apartment over the shop plenty of times. Her spaces—even the basement—were bright and orderly, but she wasn't judging her friend. It was a lot easier to keep something nice when you'd inherited it that way and a lot of love and good vibes came with it. Few people knew the sad truth about his parents' car accident, but he'd confided it to her when he heard his grandparents discussing it one night when he was thirteen.

They had run off the road and into the lake and everyone had thought they'd been avoiding one of the deer that lived on that part of the island. It had been dark. But had they been arguing, too, as his grandparents had wondered aloud when they didn't think Jordan was listening? Jordan's mother had never wanted to move to Christmas Island and wanted to leave, but his father had insisted they stay.

It was his father's parents who moved there to raise Jordan, perhaps out of obligation to their son's wishes, but they knew the truth about Jordan's parents' marriage and he'd heard them talking about it those evenings when he listened at the porch window.

Jordan would never know exactly what happened, but he had inherited a broken-down house with heavy baggage. Violet had been amazed he didn't sell it and get a little apartment on the island, and she'd even asked him about it once. He'd mumbled something about it being his family legacy, but she'd seen through that. Jordan hadn't always thought he deserved anything better.

Now he did. Which was all the more reason why she needed to help him get his promotion and start over.

"Spare bedroom," Jordan said, opening a door in a narrow hallway. "Nothing special in here."

"There's nothing at all in here," Violet commented.

"It was my grandparents' room, but I cleaned it out after they passed. Actually, Griffin and Maddox came over and cleaned it out for me, which I appreciated."

"I remember that," Violet said. "That was a bad year for you."

Jordan nodded. "I wonder what they would think of me selling this place and leaving."

Violet put an arm around him as they stood in the doorway of the empty room. "They would be proud of you."

Jordan blew out a breath. "Any suggestions on this room?"

"I'd paint the walls, but there's not much else you need to do."

"Moving on," Jordan said. He opened the next door in the hallway. His room. Violet only remembered being in there once or twice, but it hadn't changed. Dark blue comforter on the bed, dark paneled walls, a simple blind at the window, brown shag carpeting.

"Very masculine," Violet observed. "If your buyer is looking for a hunting or fishing retreat on the island, you may not have to change a thing."

Jordan laughed. "Would my guests at the Great Island Hotel or the Shelleys believe I lived in such an un-glamourous place?"

"I wonder if anyone ever wonders those things?" Violet said. "When I go into a restaurant or a store, I notice what people are wearing because clothes are my thing, but I don't wonder what their shower curtain looks like or if they have a two-car garage."

"Are you saying it doesn't matter where someone is from?" Jordan asked.

"Is that what you need to hear right now?"

Jordan shook his head. "It doesn't change my mind."

"I wasn't trying to," Violet said. "I'm here

because I'm trying to help you get what you believe you want."

Jordan gave her a long look. Maybe she shouldn't have said "believe you want." It sounded like she was saying there was room for error.

There was.

"Speaking of you helping me. I thought about something this morning when we ran into Jack Heidelberg downtown and he seemed as if he'd had a moment of doubt."

Violet wondered if the kiss was what he'd thought about. She sure had.

Jordan strode to his dresser and opened a small top drawer. He took something out and then turned around and opened his hand. "A ring. I should have thought to find one sooner. You can't have an engagement without a ring, and we're lucky no one called us on it."

"Jillian Shelley asked."

"And she believed your excuse about it being resized, but we should make it official. This belonged to either my mother or grandmother, I'm not sure which, but it will work."

He stood there with the ring on the palm of his hand. Was he waiting for her to take it and put it on herself? Worse, was he waiting for her to hold out her left hand so he could slip it on her ring finger? Either scenario was… just…wrong.

Violet debated a moment and the awkward silence grew. Finally, she took the ring and put it in her pocket. "I'll put it on when we might be in a situation where we need it," she said. She cleared her throat. "Now, get your list out. First of all, curtains. Let's measure and we'll order some online. I could sew them for you, but it'll be quicker and easier to just get ready-made ones, and a new buyer will probably change them anyway."

While they stood in his bedroom with his mother's or grandmother's ring in her pocket, she gave him instructions for improving the room so he could rid himself of the house and leave. The tiny ring she'd hardly looked at before she shoved it in there deserved better. It had, at one time, been a gift of love and now it was a token, currency being exchanged for a better life.

Without her.

CHAPTER NINE

JORDAN KNEW SOMETHING was going on the moment he walked into the general manager's office at the Great Island Hotel. Jack Heidelberg had invited him in plenty of times and, in fact, had an open-door policy. Being there wasn't the strange part. The fact that Quentin Shelley's face was on the large computer screen on the corner of Jack's desk was the tip-off that it was going to be an unusual conversation.

His first thought was that he and Violet had been found out and he was kicked out of the pool of candidates for being untruthful. Pretending he cared for Violet and wanted a life with her was, more or less, a lie. He did care for her. He did have a life with her. But romance and marriage? Until he'd proposed a false engagement, he'd never considered the real thing. Was it possible to have everything turned upside down by one kiss?

"Good morning," Jack said. "If you sit there, I think you can see Quentin and he can see both of us." Jack pointed to a chair at an angle from his.

"Is something important happening?" Jordan asked.

"You're about to find out. Quentin asked me to tell you, but I thought it would be better coming from him."

Neither the man at the desk nor the man on the screen looked angry, so the news had to be good, didn't it? What if he was being offered the job right now? Would he take it? An image of Violet's face popped into his brain. She'd be brave but sad as she watched him go. Islanders would be sympathetic, believing the story that their engagement had been very brief and fated and he would be out of Violet's heart and life forever. He'd leave the bad guy, the heartbreaker.

"Long story short," Quentin said. "My general manager is out."

Jordan exchanged a glance with Jack.

"Not him," Quentin said. "The one at the Great Valley. Leaving sooner than expected, which pushes up my time frame for finding a replacement."

Jordan was sure Jack and even Quentin could hear his heart pounding. Were his wildest dreams being handed to him?

"If you're still interested," Quentin began and paused, obviously waiting for some kind of enthusiastic assent from Jordan.

"Absolutely. Yes. Very interested."

Quentin smiled and nodded on the screen. "Good. Our next step is to arrange a visit."

"Of course," Jordan said. "I'd be happy to set aside a suite for you and Mrs. Shelley as soon as it's convenient for you to come to the island."

"Not the island," Quentin said. "The Valley. I want you to come to the hotel where you'd be working if you make the final cut. You need to see the green mountains and valleys of Virginia and then you'll know if you're in love."

In love. Another image of Violet wavered in front of his eyes. Not that he was in love with her or anything…but what would she say about this? He couldn't wait to tell her.

"And you must bring your beautiful fiancée. She needs to be in love, too, or it won't work for either one of you."

"Bring Violet?"

Quentin nodded. "I'll set aside excellent

rooms for each of you, and I know my wife is looking forward to taking her golfing and shopping and sightseeing while you're shadowing and learning more about the Great Valley and the job."

"That's a wonderful offer," Jordan said.

His phone vibrated in his pocket with a message, but he didn't dare take it out and look.

"How soon can you come?" Quentin said.

"Well," Jordan said, his mind whirling, "that depends on what you would like. Of course this is our busy time here on the island."

"Understand perfectly," Quentin said. "And you've got your big July Fourth event coming up in a week and a half. I'm thinking right after that. Watch the fireworks and then fly off that island and see what Virginia has to offer."

Jordan did the calculations. If he left July fifth, that gave him about ten days to persuade Violet to leave her beloved and successful boutique—would she have to close it?—and continue their masquerade hundreds of miles away where she didn't know anyone and didn't plan to get to know anyone.

How could he ask her to do that?

He had to ask her to do that.

"I can see you're worried about all the logistics, and I'm rushing you," Quentin said. "But I don't want you to miss out on a golden opportunity. I see qualities in you I like, and you can go far in this business if you're willing to take a chance. You have to stick your neck out sometimes, but you're luckier than most people because you've got the love and support of a wonderful woman who shares your goals. You can't buy that kind of good fortune."

Jordan swallowed. "So true," he said. His phone buzzed in his pocket with another message. And then another. The insistent messages piling one on top of the other added to his stress. He just needed to breathe. He needed to sit at his picnic table and watch the lake and think. He could find the answers if he just had a moment.

"So can I tell my wife to expect company? The other two candidates from outside the company already said yes to the invitation, and the guy from Georgia is a heck of a golfer, but I noticed Jillian had taken a special liking to your Violet." Quentin laughed. "Maybe it was her golf game."

Great. He'd heard that Quentin had gone boating with the candidate from the East

Coast and now he knew the other one was a great golfer. Violet was his ace in the hole.

Jordan smiled. "It could be anything. Violet is the most wonderful person in the world."

Saying those words had been the easiest part of this conversation. His phone buzzed three more times in his pocket. Did Violet somehow know he was in the middle of a meeting and committing her to a trip to a place far away from her home? What would she say?

He had only one choice.

"I can't wait to see the Great Valley with my own eyes," Jordan said. He looked into the camera mounted on top of the computer screen. "And I know Violet will be thrilled to get an invitation, too. We're in this together."

Quentin smiled. "That's what I wanted to hear. Jack, I know you're going to miss Jordan while he's gone, but I appreciate you letting him go so we can try him out."

Jordan felt odd being discussed right as if he wasn't there, but he was basically a commodity at the moment. An employee who either would or would not serve the company and its owner. As far as he knew, he might be a fish out of water and a terrible fit for the

Great Valley. He could even hate the place and come crawling back to Christmas Island where he'd happily settle back into his rut.

But Violet would be here. Freed from having to pretend anymore, they'd go back to their old harmony and everyone else on the island would forget the brief engagement of two island pals. It wouldn't be so bad...

"And you, Jordan, take Violet out for a nice dinner tonight and tell her she's going on vacation where she's going to love the spa and the shopping. Her little boutique is nice, but wait until she sees the ones in the resort town next to the Great Valley. She'll forget all about Christmas Island when she sees what we have to offer."

Jordan nodded, trying to control his breathing and compose his expression into something that looked like enthusiasm. "I'll tell her. She's going to be blown away."

At least that was the truth. His phone kept up its text notifications in his pocket, and Jordan wanted to bolt from his chair and run outside.

"I won't keep you," Quentin said. "But I will be in touch. You can count on that."

"Thank you. And thank you for this fantastic opportunity," Jordan replied. "I appreciate it."

"You've earned the chance," Quentin said.

Feeling very much as if he hadn't earned it but swindled his way into it instead, Jordan nodded appreciatively and escaped the office before closing the door behind him. He hurried to a little known exit from the office part of the lobby and went outside to a break area only used by hotel employees on nice days. He pulled out his phone and, instead of reading the twelve text messages, he dialed Violet's number.

He had to tell her. And he had to hear her voice.

"Can you believe the good news?" she asked as she picked up. "Of course it's not a surprise and we knew it was coming, but it's still amazing. And I already said we'd be there."

"You did? You know?" Jordan asked. "How?"

Violet laughed. "I think everyone knows now. Cara was at the hotel stable this morning and people were already talking about it there. It's a small island and news like this travels fast."

Could it be this easy? Violet didn't sound upset at all. She sounded elated. Joyful.

"And you don't mind going?" Jordan asked. "I know it's all happening fast and—"

"Are you kidding? I'm over the moon. And I can't wait to help choose a dress. You know I love clothes and shopping."

"Jillian Shelly is excited about that, too," Jordan said.

"Jillian?" Violet asked. And then silence fell on the other end of the line and Jordan realized in that moment that he and Violet were talking about two totally different things.

"Violet," Jordan said after a moment. "I haven't read any of the text messages that came in during the last ten minutes. What is the big news that I clearly don't know?"

He heard her draw a breath. No doubt she wanted to ask him what on earth he'd been talking about.

"An engagement party," Violet said. "Maddox and Camille have finally made it official."

"That's great," Jordan said. Of course it was great. They were close friends and he was happy for them. Finding true love… They were lucky people. Wonderful people. They deserved every happiness.

"It is," Violet said. "But I feel like you might be talking about something else."

Unwilling to spring the news quite yet, Jordan said, "What did you mean when you said we'd be there?"

They were a team, a dynamic duo. They went everywhere together. The whole island had treated them as if they were one person for years, so it wasn't a stretch to plan an outing together. Hadn't he just agreed to that with Quentin?

"The engagement party. This weekend," Violet said. "I accepted for both of us, but—"

"That's great," Jordan said, relieved that the party wasn't after July Fourth. He couldn't ask Violet to miss the party to go on a trip with him.

"Okay, now you have to tell me what news you were talking about and why you didn't read your text messages. It must be pretty big."

"It is."

There was a five-second pause on the other end of the line. "Go ahead."

She said it as if she was blindfolded and waiting for a punch in the nose.

"I was on a video conference with Quentin Shelley. His general manager at the Great Valley is leaving."

"Uh-huh," Violet said. They both already knew that, which was why Jordan was aiming for the job.

"Sooner than expected. Much sooner. Quentin wants me to visit Virginia to see the place and do a little shadowing, see if I'm a good fit."

"That's a wonderful idea," Violet said, her voice gaining some enthusiasm. "You have to get a feel for it and see if you'd like it. Are you the only candidate?"

"No. He's invited two others. And their wives."

In the silence that followed, Jordan knew Violet had put together the entire scenario. There was no point in delaying.

"You're invited," he said.

"That's nice of them, but of course I'm not going."

"But—"

"Virginia is a thousand miles away and I can't leave my boutique in the middle of tourist season."

"It's about eight hundred miles. And they'll fly us."

"No."

"Quentin and Jillian really want you there," Jordan said. "Jillian likes you."

I want you there. You're my rock.

"And Quentin said the golf and shopping and spa are amazing. You might really love it and you get your own room. It's like a free vacation."

"During which I abandon my own business and pretend to be the future Mrs. Jordan Frome," Violet said.

"But—"

"Jordan, you're my best friend and I would do almost anything to help you, but I can't do this. You'll have to go alone and make my excuses. Say I couldn't get away at this time. Tell them I work all year planning for a big summer and I can't just waltz away from it because their timeline has changed."

"Violet, I'm sorry I'm asking you to do this. I had no idea how involved things would get when I asked you for what I thought was a simple, temporary little game of pretending. I had no idea things would end up getting out of control."

Out of control. His feelings when he handed her that family ring, his confusion about possibly leaving her and that kiss that changed everything. He'd chosen this path, but the road seemed to be shifting under his feet, leaving him unsteady.

"I'm sorry, Jordan. But no." Did she sound upset? He'd seen her cry a few times, heard her voice choke with emotion when his own grandparents had died and she'd been there for him. Her voice sounded choked right now. Was she upset with him for even asking? Upset with herself for saying no? Or was there something else?

"It's not until July fifth," Jordan said. "Maybe you could think about it."

If Violet refused to go, what was he going to tell Quentin and Jillian Shelley? Would they suspect things were not as they appeared with him and Violet? Would his chance at the promotion be destroyed?

"There are customers in my shop," Violet said. "I have to go. I'll see you at the engagement party. Seven on Saturday night. Casual attire. I'll arrange a gift from both of us."

She said a quick goodbye and clicked off. He'd been dismissed. For days. She'd see him Saturday night, but this was only Tuesday. Perhaps a few days of separation would make her realize he needed her help more than ever.

He wanted her by his side.

Had he said that on the phone, and would her answer have been any different if he had?

CHAPTER TEN

THE MAY BROTHERS had already poured a year into the project of expanding their ferry dock. Fueled by their ambition and vision and a large cash influx from their honorary Aunt Flora who had chosen to leave them a large portion of her fortune while she was still alive, the dock area was being transformed. Already, workers had reinforced the shoreline and breakwall, and an additional dock waited for a second boat in the fleet.

Most importantly for tonight, the frame of a large building that would be used as part passenger depot and part freight storage, stood against the evening sunset sky. The walls were still open, but the roof was up. Violet had watched the steady progress, but as she walked toward the site of the engagement party for Camille and Maddox, she saw a fairyland. Twinkling white lights were strung from post to post, almost making it seem as if the building had walls.

"Beautiful," she said aloud. She carried a gift box with the engagement present she'd chosen from her and Jordan. She'd signed his name to the card and was planning to meet him there. What would she say to him? He would ask her if she'd rethought her refusal to go with him to the Great Valley Hotel. Anyone would ask that. It was important to him, and he needed her—but how far was she willing to go? This charade had already ballooned beyond what she'd originally imagined. How much deeper in would they both be if they took a trip together?

She'd told Cara and Camille about it one evening after they both closed their shops and they sat on a bench on the front sidewalk. Cara had listened without comment for a long time before finally asking her if the reason she objected to going was leaving her store, lying to the Shelleys or risking falling in love with Jordan.

Stunned into silence, Violet had claimed the mosquitos were eating her alive and had retreated to the apartment over her shop.

But Cara's question had hit the mark with

a painful stab. Did Jordan understand there were layers to her refusal? She was afraid to talk to him about it, a fact that was heartbreaking because the two of them had never held back. Now, pretending to be close was driving them apart. How much worse would that be if he knew the truth about how she felt?

As Violet approached the dock, her mind filled with questions, Jordan pulled up in his car. He wore a new blue Oxford, untucked, with cargo shorts.

"Hotel men's store," he said, pointing to his shirt. "I need some clothes for…"

He trailed off, but Violet knew he was talking about his upcoming trip. Her feelings stung a bit that he hadn't asked her help choosing clothes. She was an expert on clothes. She knew his size. They were best friends.

But she'd also flatly refused to go along on the trip he was buying clothes for.

"Isn't it amazing?" he asked, nodding toward the open-sided building. "It looks like Christmas came early."

Violet laughed. "There's never any shortage of strings of lights on Christmas Island. That's one of the things that makes it special."

"I hope you've…had a good few days," Jordan said.

Violet nodded. "Good. Busy. I'm sure you've been busy, too. Did you get anything done on the list at your house?"

"Several things. I replaced the porch board and painted the porch floor."

"Oh," Violet said. "Wow. That was fast. I was going to help you paint."

"That's okay. I thought I better get moving on it since…"

He didn't have to remind her that the clock had sped up. He was leaving the island in just over a week, and possibly forever not long after that. Of course he'd gotten started on the list of improvements. He was getting ready to leave.

"Not that it was really all that fast," he said. "I should have tackled some of these projects five years ago or even longer."

Violet knew why he never had. He didn't see a future on Christmas Island.

A cork popped, the sound sparkling in the night. Music began pouring through the open walls of the new ferry terminal. The night was warm and calm with hardly a breeze even right by the lake.

"Ready to go inside?" Violet asked. Already, there were people under the roof, some of them swaying to the music.

Jordan took the gift box and tucked it under one arm, and then he reached for Violet's hand. Her left hand. His fingers found the ring she'd decided to wear at the last minute, and he gave her a long look, his mouth open as if there was something he wanted to say.

"It's mostly friends tonight, but I didn't know the entire guest list," Violet said. "I wanted to be safe in case there are people coming to the party that you work with."

"Thank you." His fingers played with the ring, turning it around and around on her finger. "For tonight," he said. "Can we just be like we always were, the best of friends without all the other stuff going on?"

"We still are like we always were," Violet said, even though she knew it wasn't true.

"Let's pretend I never entangled you in this engagement scheme and I'm not leaving the island in a week," Jordan suggested.

"Do you regret that?" Violet asked.

Jordan tried to smile. "Which one?" He let go of her hand and ran his fingers through his hair, messing it up and making him look like the kid she'd known all her life. "I know it seems like it would be easy to chuck all of this and just stay where I am, always one rung below the manager's job, always one step below where I want to be. Believe me, I thought about it as I took down curtains and started the kitchen cabinet battle. But I can't. I owe myself this chance."

Violet nodded. She had to do this for him. She could pretend a little longer. Given the pressing timeline, it might be only weeks or even days and Jordan would be gone. "You do. Tell you what—let's go have fun with our friends and celebrate a real engagement. We'll forget about our fake one for the night."

This time Jordan's smile was real. "That sounds fantastic."

JORDAN RAISED A glass to Maddox when he found him at a table, finally alone, an hour into the party.

"Congratulations."

"Thanks," Maddox said. "It feels good to finally make it official."

"Was there ever any doubt?"

Maddox laughed. "There was plenty for a long time. Camille and I seemed made for each other when we were teenagers, but then I got my priorities mixed up for a bit. Not that I regret marrying Jennifer. Having Ethan is a prize I would never give up."

"He's a great kid," Jordan agreed.

"And proof that sometimes things look like mistakes, but they're blessings. Huge ones."

Jordan didn't believe Maddox was directing any kind of a lecture his way, but he couldn't help wondering if there were things in his own life that seemed like mistakes but were actually gifts.

Asking Violet to be his fake fiancée—was it a mistake or would it turn out to be a good thing in the long run? And how? But then he wondered if he was thinking of the wrong thing. Was pursuing the Virginia job a huge mistake or a blessing that would change his life?

"I heard you're visiting Virginia right after the fourth," Maddox said. "They're giving you a trial run."

Jordan nodded.

"Or maybe you're giving them a trial run," Maddox said. "You have to decide if they're right for you or if you're better off staying where you are."

"Career-wise, I'm definitely better off going," Jordan said.

"Why?"

"Because it will be years before I can move up here. The two people ahead of me aren't going anywhere. They're islanders, born and bred, and they'll be at the Great Island until they retire—or beyond."

"That's what I used to think you'd do, too," Maddox commented. "And what would happen if you did stay exactly where you are? You make decent money, I assume. You have a house and friends."

He had a run-down house and not the kind of money needed to make a substantial improvement—although tearing it down and rebuilding it would be the best improvement he could imagine. The changes Violet had suggested were nice, and they did make the place a little more appealing for him when he got home from work. He liked not having to step around that broken board on the porch. His kitchen was brighter in the mornings. His living room felt larger without some of the handed-down furniture.

"Your business was doing fine, too," Jordan reminded Maddox. "And yet you and your brother decided to expand it, even before you inherited a fortune."

"That's different," Maddox said.

"How?"

"I'd committed to staying here and building something for my son to inherit someday, if he wants it. And Griffin and I agreed to the project, a team effort."

"Well," Jordan said, "I don't have a brother or a family business or anyone to pass my used house and car down to, so going off and finding my fortune somewhere...it's the only thing I can do."

Maddox clapped him on the shoulder. "Maybe you're braver than the rest of us, leaving the island and striking out on your own."

Violet had also called him brave, but sometimes he felt like a coward, turning his back on his past and hoping the grass would be greener somewhere else.

"And you can always come back," Maddox added. "Camille did that, and, needless to say, it's something to celebrate."

Jordan felt a twinge of irritation with his old friend. Didn't Maddox believe he could be successful? Did everyone else think he'd go out and fail and then come crawling back...

to what? A middle-management job at the hotel and a mediocre house on a back road?

Maddox tilted his glass in the air in a little toast and shoved off from the table to visit with other people at the party. Jordan took a moment and stared out at the dark lake. Through the open walls of the new ferry building, the lake was black. Lights on the shore were distant, as if they were far away stars in the sky. Did he really know what was out there? What if it wasn't better than the life he had here?

"As your friend," Violet said as she came up beside him, her arm grazing his. "I came over to rescue you."

"From what?" Did she know about his conversation with Maddox, his doubts…his fears?

"The way you're staring off into the dark water, I was afraid you might be considering running away with a mermaid, and I think they're bad news."

"I believe they're reputed to be good singers."

"But associated with storms and shipwrecks," Violet said. "We don't take chances with either of those things on an island."

Jordan slipped an arm around her. It was

a friendly gesture. Something he might have done anytime in their long friendship. But had he? Everything that had happened in the past weeks seemed to have clouded over the previous years. Was this what it would be like to start over somewhere?

"Thanks for coming over to rescue me from a scary fate."

"Just mermaids," Violet said. "The rest is up to you."

She didn't move away. Instead, she leaned her head back against his shoulder and they watched the lights on the distant shore together. If he asked her right then if she would reconsider going with him to Virginia, would she say yes?

He couldn't do it. Violet would do anything to help a friend, but her initial refusal told him he needed to respect her choice and he was going to have to make this trip alone.

CHAPTER ELEVEN

HIS SUITCASE WAS on his bed, packed with the new clothes he'd chosen at the Great Island Hotel men's shop. He even had new black shoes and a belt. Travel plans, beginning with a flight off the island on the afternoon of July fifth, were set. His shifts at the Great Island would be covered for the five days he was gone. Jordan had everything together, except for the fiancée who wouldn't be going.

He hadn't exactly told Quentin Shelley that Violet would be by his side. But he also hadn't said she wouldn't. There was a plane ticket for Violet from the island airport to a regional airport near the Great Valley waiting in Jordan's email right next to his. There was a room at the Great Valley waiting for her. Right next to his.

She would not be right next to him. Not on this trip, and not if and when he took the new job.

The party atmosphere for the July Fourth holiday at the hotel almost took his mind off his feelings about potentially saying goodbye to Christmas Island. The festive music, balloons and desserts decorated artfully with strawberries and blueberries in flag patterns nearly smoothed over the sting of knowing he might not be there the next summer for the celebration.

"Independence Day, right?" Jack Heidelberg asked as he stopped by the front desk.

Jordan looked up and gave his boss a polite smile.

"In more ways than one," Jack continued. "You'll be free of the island and the year-round Christmas music and cookies."

"I guess you could see it that way," Jordan said. "Not that I ever minded those things."

"And how does Violet feel about it?"

Was his boss just being friendly or was he fishing for something? Had he heard somehow that Violet wasn't going along on the Virginia trip?

"She has mixed feelings like any person would," Jordan said. It was the truth, no matter what happened. He hoped she was happy for him, but he felt sure that she would also be sorry to see him go.

He'd be sad to see her go if she suddenly announced she was leaving Christmas Island. Not that she ever would. Like the May brothers, her family business and legacy were right there, downtown. Violet, Maddox and Griffin all worked hard. He wouldn't take that away from them. He just didn't have those choices himself.

"I'm sure I'll see you both on the porch for fireworks tonight," Jack said.

"Of course." Jordan had invited Violet to watch the fireworks from the Great Island Hotel's porch, just as she had many other times. A barge would anchor in the lake right in front of the hotel, and guests would have a front-row seat. Because the hotel was a good neighbor to the entire island, there was an open invitation to view the fireworks from the massive porch or the wide lawn that swept down to the water.

Most of his friends would be there, practically a going-away party. He'd only be gone five days, but if things went well on the Virginia trip and he edged ahead of the other two invited candidates, it would be the beginning of his goodbye to Christmas Island.

"I've got my eye on the weather forecast," Jack said. "There's a chance of storms, but I'm hoping they will go around us. I don't want to move the fireworks to tomorrow night, but if the storms don't hold off, I'll have to."

Jordan nodded. He'd been part of that decision-making every year, but Jack wasn't asking him for his opinion this year. It appeared his boss assumed, like his friends, that Jordan would get the job in Virginia and be gone. He should be glad people had such confidence in him, but it felt strange to be written off.

"Let me know if you want me to keep an eye on the radar or help make a scheduling change if needed. I'm not planning to go home today until after the fireworks, so I'll be around all day."

It was one of the reasons he'd finished packing early that morning before coming to work. Holidays were long days in the hospitality business, and he wanted to be prepared to get on that flight the next day.

Jack gave him a half smile. "I'll miss you, Jordan."

His boss walked away and Jordan took one

deep breath and then pulled up the weather app the local fishermen swore by. It hadn't failed him yet. He left the app open on half his computer screen where he could keep an eye on it throughout the day, and he tried to focus on treating Independence Day just like any other day at work. He helped guests resolve issues with their rooms, handed out passes to the picnic on the lawn and reviewed the upcoming reservations for the week, just to make sure things were in order for his time away.

Despite being busy, the day seemed to last two days. He texted Violet to ask what time she was coming that night and confirm he'd meet her at the spot on the porch where they always watched the fireworks together. He'd still be in his work clothes, but he'd take off his name tag and just be Jordan, a spectator for the night. With Violet and other friends by his side.

He was almost afraid Violet would decline his invitation. She'd turned down a vacation to Virginia and their friendship felt as if it was on a detour—not traveling the same smooth path, but not knowing exactly where it was going either.

To his relief, she texted back and said she'd

meet him at nine in the usual place. After that, he tried to relax and enjoy the holiday mood in the hotel. He ran several errands, making deliveries to rooms just to have something to do with his restless energy. One room needed towels, another needed a replacement key. One room had a large spider he had to scoop into a paper cup and release outside. It was all in a day's work. What would a day in the Great Valley Hotel be like?

He imagined it would be similar, but he wouldn't know the staff or the hotel guests who came back every year and remembered him. He'd meet new people, new regulars. Wasn't that part of the point in going away?

Finally, Jordan had a late dinner in the employee dining area and the daylight began disappearing. Heavy clouds made the summer darkness come earlier, but the forecast still promised clearing skies in time for the fireworks. After that, they were in for a stormy night, but the hotel had withstood a century of storms. Jordan wasn't worried.

He took off his name tag and locked his office door before he went out to the porch to claim a chair while he waited for Violet. Low clouds hung over the lake and the porch steps were still damp from an earlier passing shower, but it appeared that the fireworks would go on.

"Is the weather cooperating?"

Jordan turned and found Violet with her hand on the back of his porch chair. He got up and pointed to the seat next to him that he'd saved for her.

"You look perfect," he said. She wore a white top with blue embroidered stars and red pants that stopped just above her ankles. Violet had an outfit for every occasion, but she wasn't at all fussy or vain. She fit in everywhere.

"I'm ready for the fireworks if the rain holds off another hour."

"I think it will," Jordan said. "And I'm glad because if we had to reschedule them for tomorrow night, I would miss them."

Violet sat next to him and put her purse on the porch floor between them.

"Can I get you a drink?" Jordan offered. Waiters circulated on the porch throughout the day and evening, and it would only take a lift of his finger to have drinks.

"Just one," Violet said. "I drove because of the weather."

"Then we'll make it something good," Jordan said. "How about champagne?"

Violet nodded and Jordan signaled to a waiter who'd worked there for several years. He ordered two glasses and then sat back.

"Camille and Rebecca are watching from the Winter Palace balcony," Violet said. "They asked me if I wanted to come, but I wanted to do this one more time with you."

"I appreciate it," Jordan said. Every year, Violet turned down their friend group and came up to the hotel so Jordan would have a friend to watch with. In previous years, he'd still been on duty, but tonight he was a spectator. Still, he wanted to see the show one more time before he left.

"Are you packed?" Violet asked.

Jordan nodded. "I bought a suitcase in the hotel shop. Can you believe I didn't own one?"

Violet laughed. "Yes, I can. Who needs to travel when you live on a vacation island?"

"Do you own a suitcase?"

It seemed odd talking about luggage when the heavy subject of his leaving hung in the air that was already tense with humidity and excitement.

"I have an old one. I only use it when I

go visit my parents, but I won't have to this Thanksgiving because they're coming here."

"That's nice," Jordan said. He wouldn't be there to see them. "Will you come visit me in Virginia sometime, if I get the job?"

He hadn't meant to ask her that. Just because he was making the leap and leaving the island, he didn't have the right to ask other people to go out of their way to come see him.

Violet laid a hand on his arm. "Of course I will. If you want me to."

"I do."

Should he tell her how much she meant to him? Was it the right time? He couldn't put into words the way their kiss had made him feel, but he could tell Violet how she had made him feel for a long time. Valued. Trusted. Loved.

Loved. He knew Violet loved him as she loved all their friends. That was all, even though it was plenty.

The waiter put two glasses on the low table between them and Violet picked up hers and held it. "Should we toast to your great success on your trip tomorrow?"

Jordan clinked his glass against hers. "Success," he said.

"And safe travels," Violet added.

They sipped their drinks and a preliminary firework lit the sky, calling people from all over the island.

"Five-minute warning," Jordan announced. "Want to move to the front of the porch?"

She nodded and they stepped to the front railing, claiming a spot before hotel guests filled the porch. Humidity and heat made the crowd feel thick, but the cold champagne was refreshing. He finished his glass and set it on the porch railing next to Violet's empty one. In just a moment, the sky lit up, the low clouds holding in the colors as if they were trying to contain the show just for them.

The explosions and color went on and on until the grand finale shook the floorboards beneath them. Jordan put an arm around Violet as the crowd cheered and began to move. She looked up at him, excitement shining in her eyes. She was beautiful, inside and out, and there was no one else on earth he'd rather be with. Did she feel the same way about him, and would she miss him when he left? Maybe, among the other islanders or the thousands of summer tourists, she'd find someone to take his place as a friend or something more.

The thought made him pull her a little

closer, as if he could hold on to all that they had, even when he was gone.

Violet curled into his side as the applause died. "I love you," she said.

Jordan froze as if he was locked in place by an electric current. Had he heard her correctly? He opened his mouth to ask, but in the next moment, thunder rolled across the darkened sky and rain cut loose. Guests scattered, and Jordan realized his boss, Jack, was right behind him directing guests to the lobby doors held wide-open by hotel staff. Was that why Violet had said those three words? Because they had an audience?

He needed to ask her, but she disappeared into the crowd and he was torn between running after her and assisting guests escaping the rain and wind. He still worked for the Great Island…but would he see Violet again before he left Christmas Island?

He grabbed one of the wide lobby doors and held it open, reminding guests to watch their step even as they ran from the thunder that echoed down the long porch. He couldn't catch Violet, couldn't hold on to that earth-shattering moment when she'd said she loved him. Instead, his sense of duty won out and the old habit of hospitality took over.

IN THE CONFUSION caused by the sudden storm, Violet whispered a quick good-night to Jordan and then dashed down the porch steps and ran for the parking lot. She jumped in her car and sat there, listening to the rain lashing her roof, louder than the beating of her own heart. She put her head on the steering wheel, waiting out the thunder.

Why did she tell him? She could have simply said...nearly anything else. But she tossed three words into the stormy air, right between the end of the grand finale and the beginning of a peal of thunder. Her words had grabbed that moment of silence quite spectacularly, and anyone standing near them could have heard what she said. But Jordan had heard what she said.

There was nothing to do now but retreat. Tomorrow, Jordan would get on a plane and be gone for five life-changing days. He hadn't responded to her words, but there hadn't been time. They'd both been spared by the storm.

She waited for the heavy rain and lightning to pass, but it seemed to be increasing.

Wind whipped her car, and she chose to get home. She could have gone back into the hotel where she would be safe…but Jordan would be there and she couldn't face him. Not after she'd told him she loved him.

Violet found the parking lot exit and made her way along the familiar road through the wind, rain and lightning. Soaking wet, she dashed up her apartment stairs and then took refuge in her cozy bathrobe and snug rooms above her shop, waiting until the storm passed with the bedcovers over her head. She was certain she would never get to sleep between the noise and her brain repeating that moment on the porch over and over. She sang songs under the covers, hoping for a distraction, but one song after another reminded her of Jordan.

They'd sung one at the island Christmas party, another at Cara Peterson's birthday party and another impromptu one in the lobby of the Holiday Hotel one night when Rebecca asked them to accompany her on a guest's special request. Even the national anthem reminded her of Jordan because they'd opened an island baseball game back in high school with that song.

Everything reminded her of Jordan, even the

robe she was wearing because she'd loaned it to him one night when he got caught in the rain and came inside to warm up.

Violet squeezed her eyes tight and thought about her shop's inventory and all the plans she had for late summer and early fall wardrobes. Clothing was her happy place, but she still didn't think she'd ever get to sleep until her phone woke her up, and she opened her eyes to find daylight outside her bedroom window.

"Hey," Camille said when Violet had scrambled out from under the covers and grabbed her phone from its charger next to her bed. "I heard what happened with Jordan last night."

"You did?"

Oh, goodness. Did the whole island know she'd told him she loved him? Anyone who believed the story of their fake engagement would think nothing of it, but her friends… they would wonder why she did it. And, knowing them, they would find some nice way of asking. Was that why Camille was waking her up?

"I'm just glad he wasn't home when it happened," Camille said.

Wasn't home? Of course he wasn't home. They were at the fireworks.

"Wait…what are you talking about?" Violet asked.

"I thought you of all people would know," Camille commented.

"What?" Violet was out of bed, pulling the curtains wide as if she could see the truth somewhere out there on Holly Street.

"A tree fell on his house in the storm," Camille said. "Did major damage."

"But he's okay?"

"Yes. He was still at the hotel. He didn't find it until almost midnight when he got home. He called Maddox and asked for his help with a tarp, but Maddox said the tarp didn't do much good, not with the way the roof was caved in. Of course it was still dark. It might look better or worse this morning. I don't know."

"Jordan is leaving today," Violet said, her head swimming with emotions from her telling Jordan she loved him, to the storm and now this.

"Maddox helped him get his suitcase out of the house, and then Jordan stayed the night at the hotel."

"I have to find him," Violet said.

She thought she heard a soft chuckle from Camille. "Of course you do. Call me later."

Violet tore off her robe, took a fast shower and made up her mind as she rinsed the shampoo out of her long hair. If there was such a thing as signs, this was a big one. She pulled on a pair of pants that wouldn't wrinkle, added a matching blouse and let her hair air-dry while she went to the hall closet and pushed aside hanging coats to find what was stored behind them.

The one suitcase she owned. The only one she'd ever needed.

Five days in Virginia. It was hot there, wasn't it? Humid? She pulled up the weather for Virginia on her phone and added cool tops and dresses and a bathing suit. If the Great Valley was anything like the Great Island, she'd need a nice evening dress. Maybe three. Choosing appropriate clothing for the adventure she'd mentally committed to was the easy part. It was her superpower and it calmed her racing nerves as she carefully folded and packed a huge variety into the large suitcase. With one last addition of a spare handbag, she did a quick job on her hair and makeup, added jewelry and lugged her suitcase down the stairs to her car.

Just outside her back door, a small white dog lay in the grass, nose on paws, and watched her.

"Hello," she said, bending down. She held out a hand and the dog sniffed her, licked her palm and then sat and looked at her as if it expected something. She laughed. "I'm sorry I don't have anything good for you." She balanced her suitcase against her leg and dug through her purse. "Maybe a piece of my breakfast granola bar? It's all natural and there's no chocolate in it."

She broke it in half and let the dog eat it out of her hand.

"Now you have to go home, and I have a plane to catch," she said.

The dog watched her maneuver her suitcase into the back of her car and Violet almost thought it was going to jump in, too, but it returned to the grass where it watched her, head tilted, as if she was fascinating.

"I hope I'm as good a person as you seem to think I am," she said to the dog and then she closed the door and headed for the hotel. In the Great Island Hotel's parking lot, she parked next to Jordan's car. He was still there. Where else would he be? His plane didn't leave for at least an hour, and he now had no home.

No home. It was as if the island was setting him free. He could go to Virginia and give it his best effort, because there was nothing to come home to. Except her. And if she was enough for him, he wouldn't be leaving.

Not that he knew she cared for him as more than just a friend. Even though she had told him…

Violet sighed, left her suitcase in the car, went through the side entrance and made her way to the front desk. She knew every step. How many times had she visited Jordan at work or brought him lunch or had dinner in the formal dining room on special occasions like his birthday or hers? She knew the floral carpeting and the elegant sconces on the walls between paintings. She knew the scent of flowers and the aroma of coffee that would pervade the lobby at this time of day.

Everything was written in her memory, but this time her trip to his office was different.

She paused outside his door. The door was ajar and she heard voices inside. Should she knock? Wait? He'd be leaving soon for the airport. Was he okay? Perhaps he was devastated that his family home had been damaged. Was he thinking of changing his plans and staying? He couldn't do that. Couldn't give up his dream, his chance. She wanted to rush into his office and hold him close and tell him everything was going to be okay.

Instead, she nudged the door open. Jordan stood with his back to the door, looking out the small window. He wore a gray-and-white-pin-striped shirt she didn't recognize. Another new purchase from the hotel men's store? Jack Heidelberg sat in the solitary chair across from Jordan's desk, and he got up when he saw her.

"Violet," he said.

Jordan spun around and Violet gave him a smile that she hoped conveyed everything in her heart. She was there for him. She was on his side, even though his world was upside down. She didn't know what to say in front of Jordan's boss, so she simply said, "My suitcase is in my car, but it's heavy."

Jordan swallowed and then smiled. "I have plenty of experience with luggage."

Violet laughed, the tension rippling from her. The Jordan she knew and loved would joke about his humble beginning as a bellman, and he deserved a chance to reach the top even if it meant climbing over her feelings in the process.

CHAPTER TWELVE

JORDAN PICKED UP his suitcase with one hand and took Violet's arm with the other, and they walked through the hallway to the parking lot without speaking. He wanted to ask her a thousand questions, but he was both afraid of being overheard and afraid of breaking whatever spell had changed her mind.

Violet was coming with him. At his darkest moment, right before what he hoped might be a daylight opportunity in his life, Violet had come through. Given the island grapevine, he knew for certain she'd heard about his house. Had that changed her mind or was it those three words she'd uttered between the firework explosions and the thunder?

He was afraid to ask.

"If I owned two suitcases, I would probably have filled another one," Violet said, her tone light and friendly as she unlocked her car. "You know I like to dress for the occasion."

"I think we're the only people on the plane so we don't have a luggage restriction," Jordan said.

Violet laughed. "Don't tempt me. And, after all, it's only five days and I believe Jillian Shelley mentioned they had a women's boutique and shopping there. I'll be fine."

Jordan put her suitcase in his trunk next to his. "I hope you don't mind leaving your car here in the lot while we're gone," he said. If he focused on courtesy and details, he could keep his nerves under control. The last twelve hours had been one surprise after another, and only the careful, practiced smile of a person who'd worked in hospitality all his life could mask the tension and excitement under his surface. Not that he thought he was fooling Violet.

"It'll be fine," Violet said.

Jordan opened the passenger door for her.

"Are you fine?" she asked.

Jordan leaned against the side of the car. "I'm a mess."

Violet smiled. "I would be, too, if I were you right now. Which is why I'm here. We're going to focus on getting you your dream job and everything's going to be fine."

He liked her use of the pronoun *we*.

They got in the car and Jordan drove toward the small island airport. Should he bring up what she'd said last night? If Violet wanted to talk about it, she would mention it, wouldn't she? Or did she think it didn't mean anything and was just part of their act?

He was the one who'd asked her to pretend in the first place and entangled her deeper and deeper into the charade until they reached their current situation: about to board a plane together for five days in another state. He owed her so much. He definitely owed her the right to steer the conversation.

"Maybe you don't want to talk about it, but I'm sorry to hear about your house," Violet said.

He blew out a breath. "Have you seen it?"

"No. I packed and came straight to the hotel when I heard."

She'd come straight to him.

"Was that what changed your mind about going?" Jordan asked. He wouldn't come out and ask if her words were true and she loved him and that was why she'd changed her mind. He couldn't.

"Yes," she said. She touched his shoulder

as he drove. "It seemed like a sign. You want this job, and you have to get it. Coming back to Christmas Island doesn't seem like an option for you anymore."

"It wouldn't be all bad," he said. "You'd be here."

"And all your friends, and of course we'll miss you, but we're behind you one hundred percent. I'm just the lucky one in the group who gets a free vacation in a glorious show of support."

Jordan took a moment to digest her words. She was telling him it was a practical choice. His house was a wreck. Everyone wanted him to get what he'd always said he wanted, and she was there to help him seal the deal. That was all.

"It might be a working vacation," Jordan said. "So I hope you brought along golf clothes so you can charm Mrs. Shelley on the links."

"Rats," Violet said. "I didn't bring my lucky golf outfit. I thought I'd planned for everything, including swimwear and cocktail dresses and even hiking shoes."

"They have stores," Jordan said. "And I'm buying."

Had he ever bought an item of clothing for

Violet? Jordan remembered buying her an umbrella, dinner, a DVD of her favorite romcom, several books and even a toaster when hers had died right before Christmas one year. Clothing, though, especially to someone like Violet, was personal.

"I'm not letting you pick it out," Violet said, making him laugh as he parked at the airport. They got out of the car and he swung both suitcases from the trunk. They were heavy, but he felt lighter. His friend was by his side, and he was pursuing his dream. What more could he want?

"Ready for this?" the pilot, Canfield, asked. "I don't usually take longer trips like this, so it's an adventure for me. I was asked to give you the red carpet treatment, but I said that would be weird since I've known both of you since you were little kids."

"You could pretend we're millionaires you've never seen before," Jordan said.

Canfield laughed and directed them to get on board the small airplane. "Never thought you'd be getting married and leaving," he said.

Jordan wanted to tell him they weren't getting married and Violet wouldn't be leaving permanently. He couldn't take her away from her home and the island she loved.

"That was awkward," Violet whispered when they'd buckled in and the pilot had taken his seat behind the controls. "When the plane gets loud, we can talk about our strategy while we're there, but for now you can tell me everything you know about the Great Valley so I won't be surprised when I get there."

Jordan pulled up the website on his phone. "I wish I could give you the inside scoop, but I think you're just going to have to experience this place for yourself right along with me." He held his phone so they both could see it and scrolled through pictures.

"It's fantastic," Violet said. "Even larger and fancier than the Great Island."

Jordan nodded. "It draws from a wider clientele. You don't have to be willing to get on a boat or plane to get there, and there's a lot to do in the surrounding area."

At Violet's pensive expression—was it sad?—he added, "That's not a criticism of Christmas Island, though. Where else can you shop at an amazing boutique?"

"And get great homemade candy?" Violet added.

"Snowball fights during the winter."

"And a Santa and Mrs. Claus decked out in real velvet, despite the fact that Santa looks suspiciously like the former postmaster."

Jordan laughed. "No one seems to mind that."

"I'm sure Santa will visit the Great Valley, too," Violet said as she put on her seat belt and settled back in her window seat.

"You sound as if you're reassuring a little kid that Santa will deliver their presents even if they're spending the holiday at their grandparents' house."

"Of course," she responded with a smile.

Jordan couldn't help smiling. "Thank you for everything, especially coming along on this trip."

"I'm glad to be here for you," she said.

A thought suddenly occurred to Jordan. "What about your store, though? Will you have to close it while you're gone?"

Violet shook her head. "Cara has run it for me a few times, although just for a day or two. I called her on my way to the hotel this morning and asked if she could manage her work at the stable and the candy store and also my boutique for five days."

"You'd already decided to come with me before you knew she'd say yes," Jordan said, his heart feeling as if it had swollen in his chest. She'd chosen him over something else she loved and valued.

"I knew she'd say yes," Violet said. "And I would have figured out something else if she hadn't. I decided this was important."

The words *I love you* leaped to his lips. He loved her and appreciated her as a friend, a very good friend, someone who made him laugh and made his day, every day. But he didn't need to say those words. Violet obviously felt the same way about their close friendship.

IT WAS ONLY a few hours via chartered plane to Virginia, and Violet encouraged Jordan to nap. He'd been up all night trying to tarp the hole in his roof, and he needed to store up energy for a week that was basically a very long job interview.

"I brought a book," Violet said cheerfully. She pulled it from her handbag as evidence. "I'll be perfectly happy enjoying this book on the way while you rest."

"I don't want to wrinkle," Jordan protested,

but he yawned and laid his head back against the headrest.

Violet twisted a small section of his sleeve between her fingers and watched it spring back. "You're fine. You had the brains to buy the nonwrinkling fabric even though you didn't ask my advice."

"Sorry," he said with his eyes closed. "This was a last-minute purchase because the suit hanging up in the spare bedroom at my house is currently behind a chunk of ceiling and a tree branch."

"Which is why you need to close your eyes and rest. There's nothing you can do about your house right now, but you can go and impress the Shelleys and everyone else at the Great Valley."

Jordan opened his eyes. "I hope they never find out I've been lying to them about us. They're nice people and it feels wrong deceiving them."

Violet sucked in and then let out a long breath. "You're not deceiving them about being an excellent hotel manager with experience and a passion for the work. The fact that you're a great candidate for this job is the absolute truth."

"I hope they see it that way," Jordan said. He closed his eyes and Violet felt him relax next to her. His breathing became slow and steady, and she watched him sleep for a moment, thinking about how he hated being vulnerable in front of anyone else, and then she turned her attention to her book before her eyes swam with too many tears.

Two hours later, the pilot notified Violet that they were approaching the regional airport in Virginia where they would land. She awakened Jordan and tucked her book back in her purse. As she looked out the window, the green rolling hills of Virginia greeted her. No water in sight, nothing at all familiar, but it was beautiful.

When they landed, Jordan unbuckled and sprang from his seat. Violet laughed. "I thought you were conserving your energy."

"I'm recharged and ready."

"And I have three chapters left," Violet said. "Maybe we should just hang out here so I can finish my book."

Jordan extended a hand. "I promise you'll find time when we get to the resort. And I hope you have fun and you're not miserable pretending you're crazy about me."

"Pretending?" the pilot asked as he came out of the cockpit.

Violet and Jordan froze for a minute and then Jordan flashed the pilot a smile. "I still can't believe it's real—I mean, how lucky can a guy like me get?"

The pilot laughed. "I say the same thing, and I've been married twenty-eight years. Have a great stay, and good luck with the job. I'm already scheduled to pick you up in five days, and I hope Violet hasn't come to her senses by then."

Jordan put their luggage in a waiting green van with The Great Valley Hotel painted on the side, and they got in. Their driver introduced himself and told them about the weather, general traffic information and some local history and news on the ten-minute drive to the hotel.

"Here we are," the driver said as he negotiated a turn onto a two-lane driveway with trees lining both sides. A center barricade with old-fashioned lampposts and colorful flowers separated the two lanes, and Violet could just make out a large white building at the end of the driveway. "It's an impressive approach," the driver said. "Makes you feel like you're getting away from everything—except each other, of course."

The van stopped in a massive circular driveway covered with a green-roofed portico and Violet craned her neck to look up at the front facade of the hotel. "There's no porch," she said.

"It's on the other side," their driver said. "Wait until you see the view from there."

Jordan helped get their suitcases out of the back, but Quentin Shelley and a porter appeared immediately. Quentin gave the porter room numbers, and then opened his arms to Violet for a hug. As she gave him a quick friendly hug, Violet noticed he smelled like pine trees and fresh air. Maybe things weren't so different here than they were on Christmas Island?

"I'm delighted you're here," Quentin said. "My wife wasn't sure you'd leave your boutique and come along, but I won that bet."

"I'm glad to be here," Violet assured him. Other guests, very well-dressed and laughing, passed them and entered the beautiful wide doors of the hotel. Everything around her said *luxury*, and Violet thought for a moment she might really enjoy her five-day acting career.

"And here's our man," Quentin said, extending a hand to Jordan. "Heard about the storm on the island last night, and I'm sorry about your house. If there's anything I can do to help you out, just say the word."

"Thanks," Jordan said. He smiled. "I was doing a little remodeling anyway, and nature decided to help me along."

"Fixing it up to…sell?" Quentin asked.

Jordan nodded. "I certainly am now."

Both men laughed, and Violet walked between them into the hotel while Quentin gave them details about the antique doors and began a hotel history lecture. Jordan reached for Violet's hand and held it as Quentin walked them around the lobby introducing them to Pam at the concierge desk, Robyn at the bell stand and Jay at the front desk. Violet didn't have to remember names—those were printed on their name tags—but it was still pleasant meeting people Jordan would be working with if he took the job.

Nice people. Jordan could be perfectly happy here, even without her friendship and her physical presence only five minutes away, no matter where he was on the island. He could adjust, and so could she. She smiled at the people she met, held tightly to Jordan's hand and gratefully accepted her room key from Quentin when he suggested she might like to relax for the afternoon and he would see her at dinner.

"My wife is looking forward to it," he said, leaning close. "I know she wouldn't admit to a favorite, but we've been together long enough that she doesn't have to say it out loud."

"Will the other candidates and their wives be at dinner, too?" Violet asked.

Quentin waved a hand. "One of them withdrew his application, and we'll have the other one in next week—if this job's still available. This week, it's all about Jordan. And you, of course."

Jordan's grip on her hand tightened and she saw him swallow. If things hadn't seemed real up to that point, they did now.

CHAPTER THIRTEEN

"I DON'T KNOW if you saw this on our website or not, and I'm sort of hoping it's a surprise," Quentin said as he walked Jordan down a long row of shops inside the hotel. He stopped and pointed at a store with a Christmas tree in the front window. Everything was red and green and glittered and "Joy to the World" spilled through the open door. "Does it make you feel more at home?"

Jordan smiled at the crowded window display. The tree rotated and was so weighted down with ornaments, garland and lights, he was amazed it didn't fall over. Under the tree, a red-and-green train hurried around a circular track. One of the ornaments caught his eye—a sailboat in serene shades of blue and ivory. It seemed like an island of peace on the garish tree.

"It's open year-round," Quentin continued. "Guests love it."

"I can understand why," Jordan said. "Guests at the Great Island always admire the lobby tree that's decorated all year long." Although the one in the corner of the lobby at the island hotel was tastefully understated most of the year, only wearing glittering ornaments in December.

"At the end of this hallway, there's an exit to the putting green and the bocce lawn, and it's also where guests can catch the shuttle to the ski lifts in the winter and other outdoor adventures in the summer. I hope you're looking forward to trying those out," Quentin said. "It's good to see everything we have to offer here so you can better assist our guests. We insist that all our employees, from the housekeepers to the concierge desk, try at least two of our hosted activities during their first month of work."

"Only two?" Jordan asked with a smile. "Violet's probably going to want to try them all."

"She's adventurous?"

"She's here with me now, isn't she?" Jordan asked.

"Good thing. You wouldn't want to make a life-changing decision without your partner by your side. That kind of thing never turns out well."

It occurred to Jordan that he hadn't had to ask anyone's opinion or permission in years. He didn't need to call anyone if he was working late. Never had to sit through a movie or a dinner he didn't like just to appease someone. He could trade in his car, repaint his house or get a pet without consulting anyone. It was his life. Just…him.

Of course he usually talked to Violet about everything. She helped him pick out most of his clothes. Had gone with him to the mainland to buy a used car. He smiled, remembering coming back on the ferry with the car and feeling like a million bucks. Violet had been his first passenger.

He never needed Violet's permission, but he liked it. And he trusted her. Would she be impressed with the Great Valley Hotel? If he asked her flat out what he should do and begged her to be truthful, would she tell him to take the job and grab the opportunity?

"I suggest you start on the adventuring tomorrow afternoon," Quentin said. "Tonight, we have dinner and then drinks and dancing.

Of course you could walk in the gardens and watch the sunset, too."

"I'd like that."

"Tomorrow morning, I want you at the front desk working with the current manager starting at eight. If you stay through midafternoon, you get a good feel for checkouts and the early check-ins, and all the things that go along with them."

"Sounds familiar," Jordan said. "Although I'm looking forward to seeing how things are different here."

Quentin laughed. "No one is arriving by ferry, so I think you'll find they bring a lot more luggage. They also want all their tickets while they're checking in, for the white water rafting, the zip line and the horseback rides. People need to schedule their times for golf and archery and hiking tours. It tends to slow things down."

"Have you considered having a separate process for that? Maybe mobile check-in and then a kiosk for tickets?" Jordan asked.

Quentin smiled. "You passed the first test. That's exactly what I want to do, but I hadn't told anyone yet. You and I are already on the same page, and I want your feedback on everything you see that could be improved. Plus ideas on how to do that, of course."

They came to the end of the hallway and stood outside for a moment. Jordan loved the cool hotel air and the smell of polish and flowers that seemed to accompany posh hotels, but the fresh air and the view outside bolstered him and took away the nagging feeling that the Great Valley was a beautiful hotel, but it wasn't *his* hotel.

Maybe not yet.

Jordan continued his tour with Quentin and then they had lunch in the hotel café with windows overlooking the valley. Jordan texted Violet and asked if she wanted to join them for lunch, but she responded and said she was going to grab something light and explore on her own. She didn't say it, but she was leaving him to conduct his interview without worrying about her.

Tiny purple violets in the arrangement on their lunch table caught his eye and reminded him of her. What was she doing? He hoped she found something good to eat and had a nice stroll outside or through the shops. He couldn't wait to compare notes on the wildly exuberant Christmas store.

After lunch, at Quentin's suggestion, Jordan found a seat in the lobby and settled in to observe. His chair was close enough to the check-in desk to get a feel for the wait times and the overall guest satisfaction—judging from their body language and expressions. He'd used the same strategy at the Great Island hotel a few times, taking on the role of casual observer in a lobby easy chair. Of course, there the whole staff knew him, and it was impossible to go undercover.

Here, no one knew him. He just looked like a guest resting his feet or waiting for someone. He glanced around. Where was Violet? He'd been all over the hotel, but he hadn't run into her. She was giving him space. Typical, thoughtful Violet. He'd have to make it up to her by spending the entire evening with her from dinner until dark. They'd be with the Shelleys for part of the time, but he hoped to entertain Violet so that her obligatory trip wasn't total misery.

VIOLET WAS HAVING the time of her life. She got a grilled cheese sandwich and a piece of chocolate cake from the hotel deli, and then she took it outside on the long porch. A deep cushion on a wicker chair sucked her in and made her feel as if she could be on the Great Island porch—if it wasn't for the view. Instead of the lake's blue water, Violet looked out on miles of rolling hills and taller mountains, all covered with trees in various green shades.

Stunning. And so different. The views from Christmas Island, while beautiful, were also limiting. She couldn't see for miles, even from the little hill where Jordan kept a picnic table outside his house. She ate her sandwich, enjoyed an entire slice of chocolate cake all by herself and did some casual eavesdropping on the people seated around her.

They talked about the tennis courts (great surface), the zip line (terrifying but inspiring) and the lawn games (competitive but fun) spread out on the lower lawn. What did people talk about on the Great Island's porch back home? Certainly the lake, the orchestra, the food and drink and the unique atmosphere of Christmas Island.

Here, there was a lot going on. After she polished off her cake, Violet deposited her dishes on the tray, straightened the green floral-patterned pillow on her chair and set off for a walk on the lawn. She descended a short set of steps and was immediately met by a uniformed hotel staffer.

"Are you already on a team?" he asked.

Her first thought was that she was on Team Jordan Frome, but then she realized the hotel employee stood next to a cart loaded with croquet mallets, badminton rackets and sets of colored balls.

"I'm not on a team, but I—"

"I can place you on a team or find you a partner," he said.

Violet glanced at his name tag. David.

"I wasn't planning to, uh…" She broke off and gestured at the people assembled in small groups on the lawn. They were laughing, swinging mallets and rackets, soaking in the sunshine and the scenery.

"I have a bocce team of three waiting for a fourth," David said.

"I don't know how to play bocce," Violet said.

David, who was clearly not taking no for an answer, directed her attention to a tablet on the table behind him that displayed a video screen. "It's a three-minute video on bocce ball, which is a less formal version of the kind played in Italy," he said. "I'll wait while you watch the video."

Violet considered saying a polite no and taking off across the lawn, but David reached down and tapped the play icon on the screen. Having no choice, Violet politely watched the first thirty seconds of the video. Red, green, blue and yellow balls, a little white ball for a target and simple underhanded throwing. She continued watching. She could play that game. It didn't look hard, and the rules weren't complicated. Why not meet a few people and work off her chocolate cake?

"Are you ready?" David asked when she'd finished watching the tutorial.

Violet laughed. "I have no idea, but I'm willing to try."

"Excellent." He gestured with one hand. "Follow me and I'll get you right on a team."

Was this a typical day at the Great Valley? Emphasis on playing and making sure everyone had a good time—even lonely singles with no intention of learning the backyard version of an ancient game?

"Here we go," David said, ushering her into a group of two men and a woman about her age. "This is…" He paused, realizing he didn't know her name.

"Violet," she said. "Like the flower. I don't want to intrude if—"

"Please," the woman said. "I'm Fanny and I could use another female in the group. We can celebrate together when we win."

"Are you sure?" Violet said.

"Are you a beginner?" one of the men asked.

"Don't answer that," Fanny said. "My brother Bart will try to give you tips because he thinks he's an expert."

"This is my first time playing," Violet said. "Today."

Everyone laughed. "You can be on my team," the man his sister had identified as Bart said. "And this is my brother-in-law Wyatt. Would you believe he's a beginner?"

"Should I believe it?" Violet asked, and Fanny chuckled and shook her head.

Violet and Bart chose the red and green balls and took their place. Because she was the newcomer in the group, Violet got to throw out the first white ball that would be the target. She threw it as hard as she could and it landed a decent distance away.

"Experience?" Bart asked.

"Throwing rocks," Violet said. "Skipping them, actually. I live on an island and throwing rocks is a significant local pastime."

Bart raised both eyebrows. "You live on an island?"

"Christmas Island in Northern Michigan. It's beautiful."

They nodded politely, but they clearly had never heard of her beloved home island. It was so odd meeting new people, Violet thought. She saw a lot of strangers coming into her shop, of course. Tourists and shoppers. But she didn't socialize with them, play lawn games or explain where she was from—although she usually opened conversations by asking them where they were from. Joining an impromptu game wasn't how she'd pictured spending her five days in Virginia, pretending to be engaged to Jordan.

This was far better.

Jordan was somewhere in the hotel learning the local ropes and trying to impress people. She'd join him for dinner and already looked forward to hearing about his day. After she put her throwing skills to good use.

Violet gave a smooth underhand throw and landed her ball right next to the target.

"First time?" Bart said skeptically.

"I said it was my first time today," Violet said. "And it is," she added with a grin. She tossed her last ball, placing it neatly beside the target right next to her other one.

"I'm glad you're on my team, but I think I should buy you a drink before you consider switching and defeating me."

Violet shook her head. "I'm no threat."

"A drink after the match then?" Bart asked.

"Sorry, but no. I'm here with someone."

"Oh," Bart said, looking deflated. "I didn't notice your ring."

"It's fine. He's busy inside right now, and I'm enjoying this game."

Bart smiled and then tossed his ball, and Violet took a breath. Maybe she would be okay if her beloved Jordan did move here. He'd be happy, and she wasn't a hermit. She could find plenty of fun and joy back on Christmas Island even if Jordan was hundreds of miles away and she had to learn their duets for a solo singer.

CHAPTER FOURTEEN

JORDAN KNOCKED ON Violet's door an hour before dinner. His brain was swimming with all he'd observed and learned, and he needed a sympathetic ear to spill it all to. There was no way he'd survive a social evening of dinner and dancing unless he decompressed with the best listener he knew.

He knocked again. Was she sleeping? He'd never known Violet to be a napper, but maybe the storm had kept her up the night before, and then her book had kept her awake on the plane. He knocked a third time and was on the verge of texting her when the elevator down the hall pinged and Violet emerged looking flushed and happy with three other people.

Jordan turned, needing to have her to himself, but the other three people were laughing and talking with Violet. He even heard one of the men use her name. They seemed to be talking about a game and who'd won fair and square.

A slice of jealousy cut through Jordan's heart, but then Violet saw him a moment later and smiled, and he felt as if the sun had come out after the rain.

She said goodbye to her friends who went to rooms down the hall and then came to Jordan, who was still standing at her door.

"You look as if you need to put your feet up and have chocolate," she said. She rubbed his arm and then keyed into her room. "I know this because I'm in the same boat," she added.

Relief rushed through him. He and Violet were always rowing together. He never wanted that to end, even if he was moving three states away. They could call and have video chats. It could be almost the same. "Do you have chocolate and footstools?" Jordan asked.

She smiled. "Is my name Violet Brookstone?" She pulled two thick chocolate bars from a bag on the counter and pointed to two easy chairs by the balcony doors. "I can't take credit for the chairs. Your hotel has conveniently provided them. But I did stock up at the gift shop on my way to this room earlier. I knew we'd need chocolate at some point."

"Let's split one and save the other for an emergency," Jordan suggested.

Violet laughed. "What could happen? We're here at a fabulous resort and all we have to do is convince people we like each other." She snapped a chocolate bar in the middle and offered him half.

"You're too good to me. I'm sorry you were stuck entertaining yourself all afternoon." Although she hadn't looked unhappy when she got off that elevator. He wanted to ask what she'd been doing, but he didn't want to sound like a prying ogre. She could do anything she wanted. She wasn't there as his employee.

She waved a hand. "It's easy to entertain yourself here. I had lunch on the porch, wandered down to the lawn where I ended up on a winning bocce ball team, and then I had lemonade while we walked through the gardens. It was nice."

The use of the pronoun *we* stuck out. She'd walked through the gardens with someone else…and without him. He'd been looking forward to seeing the gardens with her.

"As nice as Christmas Island?" Jordan asked. He felt a sense of loyalty to his home island and his home hotel, even though there was no doubt The Great Valley had a lot to offer with its massive size and wide choice of amenities. Of course most people would trade the smaller island hotel for the larger vibrant one nestled among scenic mountains, wouldn't they?

Violet bit off a chunk of chocolate and put her feet up on the footstool where she rubbed her heels together and said, "There's no place like home."

They both laughed, and Jordan's tension slipped away. He kicked off his dress shoes and put up his feet, too, so they could enjoy the view together. His feet tingled with relief as soon as he elevated them.

"It's not my hotel," Jordan said after a moment.

"What?"

"You said a minute ago that my hotel had provided these chairs."

Violet smiled. "That's because I assumed you were wowing everyone and they were going to snap you up so fast you wouldn't even have a chance to go home and pack. They'll just keep you."

Not go home. Jordan thought about what was left in his house on Christmas Island. In his luggage, he had his good clothes, his laptop and the electric shaver Violet had gotten him for Christmas. What, of value, was left in his damaged house? Photographs of his parents and grandparents. His grandfather's snow shovel, its handle smooth with age and use. An old lawn mower. Assorted dishes from meals cooked in that little kitchen he'd just painted. A comfortable chair on the porch. His bike in the shed. His favorite picnic table in the yard.

It wouldn't be much to most people, but it was all he had. So far. With this job and the pay that was nearly double his current position, he could replace his bike and lawn mower and snow shovel.

"Where would you live?" Violet asked, seeming to read his thoughts.

"I'm going to ask that question at dinner," Jordan said. "I looked a little online, but I didn't get a good sense of where employees live. I could ask around, but I'm sure the Shelleys will have some ideas."

"Do you think you should visit apartments or meet with a Realtor this week while you're here?"

He turned to Violet. "Do you want to come along so you can make sure I don't choose an ugly place?"

"Not at all. If you want to torture yourself with wood paneling and shag carpet and tiny windows that face north, that's your business. I won't have to see it."

She wouldn't see it. Would possibly never heat up leftovers in his kitchen or watch a movie on a snowy day in his living room—even though he would almost certainly find a place with a nicer kitchen and living room than the one he was leaving. Jordan blew out a breath. "One thing at a time. Who knows if they'll even want to hire me? They still have the other candidate."

"But you're here first, increasing your chances to even better than they already were," Violet said. She finished her chocolate bar and got them both a small bottle of water from the mini fridge in the room. She set them on paper coasters on the wood table between their chairs, and then opened the door that led to the balcony.

"I like smelling the pine," she said, "but the inside chairs are cushier than the ones on the balcony. And the fabric is wonderful."

"Familiar?"

"Very," Violet said. "I knew, in theory, that the two hotels had the same interior designer, but until I got here and saw the similarities I didn't really process it. Same carpet in the lobby, some of the same patterns on the curtains, and I've seen quite a few chairs in the lobby and hallways with the same floral brocade as the Great Island." She sipped her water. "It's a nice touch of home so you won't miss us too much."

"I'll miss you," Jordan said. It was the honest, simple truth. He'd miss everyone on the island, but no one more than Violet. It would be so nice if… But that thought was impossible. She wasn't coming, too. She wouldn't be moving to Virginia. It was ludicrous to even consider asking her.

Violet patted his hand as if she was a kindergarten teacher encouraging a kid to get on the big yellow bus at the end of the day.

"Our flight this morning was only a few hours, not a twelve-day voyage away. It'll be fine."

Had it only been that morning? He'd awakened on Christmas Island and now he was breathing the air of a different state through the balcony doors—or was the fresh outdoor scent coming from Violet who had enjoyed an afternoon on the lawn with her new friends?

A lot had happened since they took off from the island that morning.

"Do you think you could be happy here?" Violet asked. The question took him aback, and he blurted out the first thing that came to mind.

"Do you?" His intention was to ask if she could be happy there, but it would be safer if she chose to read it differently—as if he was asking her opinion about his own happiness. Why did he feel off-balance in Violet's company these days and then snap back to their easy friendship? What if the off-balance feeling stayed and he could never put things back to the way they were?

Violet's mouth opened and she shifted her glance from him to the hills beyond the open balcony door.

"It doesn't matter what I think," she said, not turning her blue eyes back to him. "This change is totally up to you."

Everything was up to him, including doing his best to impress his future boss. Jordan swung his feet down and put his shoes on. "Can you be ready for dinner in an hour? I asked for an early seating so we could have more time to enjoy a walk afterward and some dancing this evening."

Violet smiled. "Absolutely. I'm wearing a blue dress if you want to coordinate your tie."

"How did I know you'd suggest that?" he asked.

"We're a team," she said.

AN HOUR LATER, Violet walked into the formal dining room with her hand curled around Jordan's arm. He still wore the gray suit, but thanks to her, he had a variety of ties, and the blue one he'd chosen was a good match for her dress. Same hue, a shade darker, as if they'd planned it but weren't too cutesy.

Meeting Quentin and Jillian Shelley reminded her of the night a few weeks earlier when they'd had dinner together at the Great Island. Their game of pretending to be a couple had been fresh then. In the ensuing days and weeks, it had taken on some deeper flavors at times and had, at other times, felt a bit stale. Like a fantastic birthday cake that had sat on the counter a few days beyond the big day.

What had caused the flavor to turn a bit? She hardly admitted it to herself, but she knew. Every moment she spent with Jordan was a risk. She kept trying to put up barriers so she wouldn't fall any further toward heartbreak, but it was hard. She loved him, and there was nothing she could do about it except help him say goodbye.

"This dining room is huge," Jordan said.

The aroma of wonderful food filled the air, but Violet had no appetite.

"Don't be nervous," she told Jordan.

"Strangely, I'm not," he said.

He wasn't nervous? Who was this guy? The Jordan she knew had been trying to prove himself since he was old enough to know what it meant to seek approval. The guy who hadn't wanted any of the kids in their school to know where he lived was now striding into an elegant dining room with confidence?

She couldn't take credit for it, not with the swarm of butterflies in her own stomach. There was only one explanation—he was confident about getting the job and starting a new life here.

Jillian Shelley waved from a table and then stood to hug Violet. "You really left your boutique and came," she said. She shook hands with Jordan. "That's a good sign for you, isn't it? If Violet's happy, you're happy."

"Violet is my rock," Jordan said. He pulled

out her chair for her and she was glad because her knees felt wobbly. Maybe she was hungry after all.

Several people passed their table and she heard her name and looked up to find Fanny, Bart and Wyatt.

"So you're the lucky guy," Fanny said. "Better watch out, though. Violet has an excellent throw."

Jordan laughed. "I know. She's currently the rock-skipping champion on Christmas Island, but I hope to get another chance to take the crown this summer." He shook hands with them and they introduced each other, and then Fanny's group moved on to another table.

"Making friends already," Quentin commented. "You'll find this is a friendly place."

Violet heard her phone ping in her purse and she grabbed a quick glance at the screen as everyone settled into their chairs. Cara.

"I'm sorry," she said. "I need to check this message from the person running my shop."

"Of course," Jillian agreed.

Violet swiped the message. There was no text. Just a picture of an adorable white dog. Dirty, but adorable.

"You're frowning," Jordan said. "Is everything okay?"

Violet held up the phone and showed him the picture of the dog. "Cara sent this."

"She adopted a very dirty white dog?"

Another message came in. I found her sleeping on your back steps this morning and she stayed all day.

Animals love you, Violet texted back. Thanks again for taking care of my store.

Easy peasy, Cara texted.

Violet put the phone back in her purse. "One of my friends is an animal magnet and a stray dog that showed up just as I was leaving is still hanging around."

"You have strays on that small island?" Jillian asked. "I'd think everyone would know whose dog is whose."

"Mostly, we do. But there are litters born in parts of the island that are more secluded and woodsy, and sometimes the dogs and cats wander downtown where the action and the food are."

"Speaking of animals," Jillian said. "Someone reported seeing a bear on one of the hiking trails, but I'm not sure I buy the story. I think it might have been inflated for a post on social media. At least I hope so, because I'm taking you down one of those trails tomorrow. You're going to love it."

"I'm sure I will," Violet said.

"And I'll set up fun activities for the three days after that, too," Jillian said. "I know Quentin will be keeping Jordan far too busy—almost like he works here already."

"I'm ready," Jordan said eagerly, and everyone laughed. Violet's heart was in two large pieces. One of them was excited for her best friend that his dream was coming true. The other one was going to feel sad as she watched Jordan get further and further away from her. Every instinct told her to be nice and help Jordan get what he wanted. There wasn't room for her to assert herself and take what she wanted because their goals were polar opposites.

While they waited for their food, Violet sneaked another peek at the dog picture on her phone. A stray who'd found its way to her shop at just the moment she'd vacated it. She was a stray, too, enjoying the temporary hospitality and food in a place where she knew she would never live.

CHAPTER FIFTEEN

THE NEXT MORNING, Violet glanced at her phone and found a text from Jordan before she got out of bed—a very luxurious bed with a pillow top mattress and plenty of pillows. The moment she opened her eyes, she'd seen mountains out her window. So different from her view of downtown Christmas Island with the shimmering blue lake beyond.

I'm talking to the manager of the boutique right now and she's asking if you'd like to meet for coffee.

Violet looked at the time. It was only eight, and she'd noticed the boutique didn't open until ten when she'd popped in the day before.

I'd love it. Thirty minutes?

She says yes.

Thank you.

Actually, thank you. It would look pretty weird if you didn't want to.

He was right, of course. If he was genuinely considering the job, and she turned down a chance to get the inside scoop on the boutique, people might think she wasn't serious about coming along as Jordan's bride. If he got the job.

Violet popped out of bed and showered quickly before selecting one of the chic but classic outfits she'd brought along. She was downstairs in just under thirty minutes, and Jordan waved at her from behind the front desk. There was only one other person behind the desk and she was at the other end, so Violet walked over to Jordan.

"Good morning, Miss Brookstone. I trust you slept well," he said in a posh formal voice.

Violet laughed. "Like a very well-cushioned rock."

"Me, too."

"Liar," she said with a smile. "You lay awake half the night worrying about today."

"You think you know me so well," he said.

"Am I wrong?"

He grinned. "The important thing is that you have a nice breakfast with Lisa at the boutique. I sent over a breakfast tray with croissants, doughnuts and coffee a minute ago."

"You thought of everything. Thank you."

"I'm in hospitality. It's what I do," he said.

Violet tilted her head. "Do you arrange private breakfasts with boutique managers for everyone?"

"Every day," Jordan said.

Violet laughed and gave him a little wave as she turned toward the long hallway where the shops were located. She peeked in the front windows of the still-closed shop and saw a woman in the back who quickly waved to her and opened the door.

"I'm Lisa, and you must be Violet, and you're just as beautiful as your fiancé said you were."

Jordan had said she was beautiful?

Violet held out her hand. "I'm Violet Brookstone. Thank you for having breakfast with me."

She glanced around the shop that was not physically larger than her own back home, even though it seemed larger. Everything was painted white: the walls, ceiling, shelving, and frame around the wide front windows. Without any exterior windows, the paint color kept the store from appearing dark and the colorful clothing popped in contrast with the walls. Violet's Island Boutique had a different feel with its dark wood floor and walls and the copper ceiling. It never seemed dark though, because of the wide front windows overlooking Holly Street. Sure, she turned all the lights on during gray winter days to chase away the gloom, but she loved the character.

The Great Valley's boutique had style and class, but it didn't have character or history—at least not for her.

"My pleasure," Lisa said as she ushered Violet to two white chairs near the fitting rooms and floor-to-ceiling mirrors. "Jordan already won my heart by sending a coffee and goodie tray, and I love having someone to talk about clothes with."

"He's very thoughtful," Violet said. "Seeing this beautiful place does make me homesick for my little boutique, though."

"Coffee and pastries will help, and then we'll talk about our favorite suppliers and what we've ordered for fall—although you might just be here this fall and you'll see for yourself."

The warm feeling in Violet's chest cooled a little. This nice lady thought there was a solid chance Violet would be moving to Virginia. But she wouldn't be. She'd be shifting her merchandise with the season back on Christmas Island.

JORDAN KNEW HE shouldn't pick at the loose button on his cuff. If he just left it alone, it wouldn't come off. Unless it caught on something. And then it could come loose at exactly the wrong moment. What if he was trying to impress someone with his smooth hotel skills and his button flew off and rolled across the plush carpet?

Are you available? he texted Violet. It was almost lunchtime and he hadn't seen or heard from her.

In my room dreaming about lunch.

I could eat.

Where?

I'll come get you.

He wanted to meet her at the same hotel café where she'd eaten the day before, but he couldn't have her sewing on his button at the table. In five minutes, he knocked on her door.

"Can I come in?"

"Sure."

He held out his cuff and Violet's sharp eyes found the loose button immediately. She grabbed his wrist and pulled him to the easy chair he'd used the day before.

"The light is good right there," she said. She opened a bag on the counter and came back with a sewing kit. "Did you catch it on something?"

He shook his head. "I noticed it was loose this morning after I saw you."

"Some shirt manufacturers don't do a very nice job with details," Violet said. "This is not one of the shirts I ordered for you, and I like reminding you of that fact."

"Lesson learned."

Violet threaded a needle with light blue thread that matched his shirt perfectly. She propped his wrist on the arm of the chair as if he was a doll she was dressing. "Hold still."

She unbuttoned his cuff and began passing

the needle back and forth through the four tiny holes.

"Are you willing to do something wild tomorrow afternoon?" he asked.

She paused with the needle in the air. "Is it fun?"

"I assume so, but I've never done it before so we'll have to find out together."

"What is it?"

"A zip line tour through the trees and across a huge valley," Jordan said. "Quentin insisted I take an afternoon off and do something fun with you."

"Is that why you're doing this?"

Jordan laughed. "Heck, no. I've always wanted to try something like that, and it will be a lot more fun with you than anyone else. Will you?"

"Absolutely. I brought cargo shorts and sneakers just in case."

"It's a date," Jordan said. He thought he noticed Violet's hand pause when he said the word *date*. Was she nervous about zip-lining with him? "I'll let you know the time, but if you change your mind I'll understand."

"I won't change my mind," Violet said.

"When else am I going to have the chance to do something like that?"

Violet's fingers were on his wrist and he wondered if she could feel his pulse racing at the thought of zip-lining. He didn't think that he was afraid of heights, but he'd had very little opportunity to find out on an island where the tallest building was three stories. Challenging himself seemed to be the theme of his summer.

"How was your breakfast with Lisa?" he asked, searching for a safe topic.

"Wonderful. She's my kindred spirit when it comes to picking out and ordering a line of clothes. She also told me about a supplier in New Jersey she likes and gave me the website and a phone number. They have great wholesale prices, even with smaller volumes like I have on the island."

"That's great," Jordan said. He watched her needle and thread moving methodically through his cuff, even though he had no worries about her stabbing him.

"Of course I didn't tell her I'd be back on Christmas Island this fall. She was really nice about discussing a role I could have if I were going to be here."

"Maybe you'll fall in love with the Great Valley and move here," Jordan said.

The needle paused in the air, and Jordan glanced up at Violet's face. "The pillows are delightful and the food is good here," she replied. "But I don't think I'd enjoy biking on all these hills."

"Or giving up rock skipping for bocce balls," Jordan said, playing along with her light tone. Of course there was no question of her moving there. He couldn't and wouldn't ask that of any of his friends from back home. If he was doing this, he was accepting the solitary state of his decision.

"Definitely not," Violet said. "My beginner's luck with that game could run out fast."

She tied off her thread and snipped it with a small pair of scissors, and then she rebuttoned his cuff.

"Lunch?" Jordan asked. "Same place as yesterday?"

"Did I tell you where I ate?"

"I heard from one of the hotel staffers. It's a tight-knit group here, and they already like you. They're probably hoping I get the job so they'll see you again."

While he was glad Violet's general sweetness and kindness to people had already won their approval, it was going to make it more awkward for him if he took the job and showed up without her. That, though, was a future problem he'd worry about after he secured the promotion.

CHAPTER SIXTEEN

THEIR GROUP IN the sightseeing van included two other couples and a family with two kids. One couple was in their midfifties, and the other was about Violet and Jordan's age.

"We're on our honeymoon," the woman Christina said. "Just got married a week ago."

"If that wasn't scary enough," her new husband added, "I'm discovering my bride is a daredevil."

"You didn't already know that?" Jordan asked.

The man Justin shook his head.

Jordan swung his gaze to Violet. "I don't think there's anything about you I don't know."

Everyone laughed except Jordan, and Violet could tell he was dead serious. And he was right. Except for the one major secret she had about being in love with him. She couldn't tell him that one.

"We live on an island," she explained. "And we all know each other a little too well."

The older couple exchanged a grin. "There are still surprises even after raising three kids," the husband said.

One of the little boys from the family in the back of the van yawned loudly. "Can we watch something on your phone?" he asked his mom.

"Look out the window," she said. "The mountains are better than any videos."

The boy sighed, but his mom was right, Violet thought. The mountains rose on all sides of the road that seemed to have been cut through them. The heavy midsummer growth of leaves came in green of all colors, and there were rocks and streams among the trees. Although Violet was accustomed to nature and beautiful scenery on the island, this was different.

"How long have you been married?" the new bride asked.

Violet shook her head. "We're not. Just engaged. Jordan's here for a job interview, and that will decide our wedding date if we're moving here."

She amazed herself by chatting about her relationship with Jordan as if everything was completely normal. For a moment, she imagined what would happen if she really did marry him and move to Virginia. If she wanted to start an entirely new life, it would be a beautiful place. Her parents had moved off the island and her brother, too. Was it such a stretch to imagine?

Of course, one major stumbling block was that she might be in love but Jordan wasn't. Nothing about his behavior suggested to her that his feelings had changed. He didn't tend to be vulnerable and open about his emotions with other people. She was one of the few on the island who knew the whole story about his family and its impact on him. If he felt anything for her beyond a deep and lasting friendship with some gratitude thrown in for her current performance, she would be surprised.

"We should move here," the new groom said to his wife. "Especially if we could live at that hotel."

"For enough money, you could," Jordan said, and the adults in the van laughed. Rooms at the Great Valley weren't priced completely out of range of a working-class family, but the hotel was definitely a luxury people would experience for a limited time.

"We could come back for our big anniversaries," the bride said. "It could be our tradition."

"Lots of people do that," Jordan said.

"Here?" the bride asked.

"Sort of," Jordan said. "I work at the sister property of this hotel, the Great Island Hotel on Christmas Island in Northern Michigan. It's just as beautiful, although smaller—small enough that I recognize our yearly visitors. I've been there long enough to see people come back for their tenth anniversaries."

"Why would you want to leave?" the older man asked.

Jordan shrugged and paused, and Violet wondered how he'd manage that question.

"A big promotion," he said.

The older man nodded. "Makes sense."

"And," Jordan continued, "there's ziplining and white water rafting and other things we don't have on our little island."

He hadn't needed to elaborate. The older man had accepted his reason without a flicker of doubt. Was Jordan trying to talk himself into moving? He didn't need to justify the move to anyone, especially her.

Violet reached over and put a hand on his,

and he stopped talking and nodded at her as if he understood her message. He had a right to improve his life, even if it meant starting over.

The groom turned to his new wife. "You don't want to go white water rafting, do you?"

She gave him a crooked smile and he groaned. "I should have asked more questions before we planned this honeymoon."

Everyone laughed, except the kids who had taken their mother's advice and had their faces glued to the van windows.

The van pulled into the lot at the Mountain Adventure Company, and everyone got out and lined up for their instructions. The zip line offered single and tandem rides, and everyone in the group chose tandem. Jordan stood close to Violet in line, his arm around her shoulders, as they listened to the guide's safety lecture, and then they helped each other put on their harnesses.

Jordan held out a red and a blue helmet. "Your choice."

"Blue," she said.

"I knew it," he said, and the honeymooners next to them laughed.

"At least I know what my bride's favorite

color is," the groom said. "You want the red one, right?"

She shook her head and grinned teasingly, and then she reached for the red one. "You're right," she answered.

Violet felt Jordan's tension as they waited for the other adventurers to take their turns. Was it trepidation at zip-lining for the first time, or was it a combination of everything? Probably everything, she thought. She'd be thrumming with nerves if she was planning on moving away and taking a new job.

When it was their turn, they climbed the steps to the platform, handed their harness carabiners to the guide to hook up and then settled into the tandem chair. Jordan took Violet's hand as they waited to be released over a massive mountain gorge, and she was glad to feel his fingers around hers. The engagement ring pressed into her palm, but she wouldn't have let go of Jordan's hand for anything— except the one thing she couldn't have.

HE HAD PLENTY of experience flying on small planes, and he knew that sensation of leaving the ground and soaring, but watching Violet's face as they began zipping along the narrow cable through the trees was an entirely new feeling. Her blue eyes were wide with excitement when she glanced over at him, and the breath left his body.

The trees thinned out and he realized they were soaring like birds high above a deep valley with a narrow river running through it far below. But he hardly saw any of that. Instead, he saw Violet as a little girl and then the teenager he'd walked to school with, and then the woman at his side.

He loved her. That wasn't new. But this feeling of flying as he looked at her face was something more. It was love. He was in love with his best friend. He swallowed and tried to suck in a deep breath. In love. For the first time in his life he felt the wild abandon of knowing his heart was beating alongside someone else's.

"Do we know a song about flying?" Violet asked.

Jordan couldn't think of a single song title. *He was in love with Violet.*

"Although this takes my breath away, so I doubt I could sing anyway," she continued.

He wanted to sing. He wanted to shout. But his mind focused on one single thing. He was in love with Violet Brookstone and there was nothing he could do about it.

"Are you okay?" she asked. "You look as if you're going to be sick."

"I'm fine," he croaked.

"Don't you like this?"

"I love it." *I love you.*

"Me, too."

She squeezed his hand and leaned forward to look down into the valley. Soon, they were at the first landing station where they transitioned to the next zip line. They took a moment to get their land legs while other group members hooked on to the line. Violet stood at a railing and gazed out over the mountains and valleys, and Jordan took his place right by her side.

He wanted to tell her. He told Violet everything. She knew him better than anyone, could read his thoughts most of the time.

Did she already know?

"Picture?" the woman from the older couple asked. "I'll take one of you if you'll take one of us."

"Of course," Jordan said, snapping into hospitality role. "You first."

He took their phone, waited until they were

ready and snapped three pictures in a row, just to make sure they'd have one they liked. He gave them back their phone, and then Violet pulled out hers and handed it to them. She slipped an arm around Jordan's waist and pressed herself against his side. Jordan tried to compose an appropriate smile, but he was afraid the picture would reveal a profoundly goofy and bedazzled expression.

That was how he felt.

"We're up," Violet said. She snapped her phone into a cargo pocket on her shorts and tightened her helmet. "Are you sure you're ready for this?"

"Do I have any choice?"

She chuckled. "No. We're in this together and there's no going back."

There was no going back. Once he realized he was in love, how could he possibly go back to just friendship with Violet? Worse, how could he leave her?

This time when they zoomed out over the tree canopy, Jordan remembered to take a deep breath first. He held tight to Violet's hand and enjoyed the ride even though he had no idea what he was going to do about the newfound realization that he loved her.

Lately, he'd been bolder about chasing after his dreams, but there were two hearts involved in this situation and he couldn't hurt Violet by persuading her to pretend she loved him and then telling her it was real. For him.

No, he thought as they soared through the sky, weightless and fearless, loving Violet was all the more reason to take the job in Virginia and leave her feelings out of it. She deserved someone better than him, and she deserved someone who was going to stay right there on the island she loved.

On the next platform, they took more pictures and talked with the other adventurers while they transferred to the next and last zip line. The two little boys had long forgotten their desire to watch a video, and they were clamoring to be first to take off in a tandem swing with one of their parents. The honeymooners went next, holding hands and kissing as they took off. The middle-aged couple chugged from their water bottles before their launch.

"We're the last ones," Violet said as they stood on the platform waiting for a staff member to give them the go-ahead and hook them up. "Of all the things we've done together, this is the most exhilarating."

"You feel it, too?" he asked.

She nodded. "We don't have height and distance like this anywhere on Christmas Island, and it makes you see things differently."

He wanted to kiss her and thought perhaps if he did at that moment, she would know what was in his heart. But the adventure staff member hooked their line and gave them the thumbs-up, and they were off, soaring through beautiful but unknown territory.

CHAPTER SEVENTEEN

THE NEXT TWO days at the Great Valley passed quickly for Jordan. Before eight in the morning each day, he arrived at the small office behind the large check-in desk. The previous manager had already left, and Jordan's on-site interview felt more like a dress rehearsal. The job still wasn't guaranteed to be his, but there were no internal candidates and the other staffers treated him as if he was already their boss. It was exciting and frightening to think the job was his to lose.

Each morning, from across the lobby, he watched the sun through the windows transition from pink rays to bright streaks. By late afternoon, a tall mountain caught the sunlight before it got to the lobby and the tables and chairs took on a cozy glow from the interior lighting.

He could get used to it. The view would be great in the fall and winter. Would he be there to see it? During the evenings, which he spent with Violet after quiet dinners in the main dining salon, he tried to convey to her the subtle shifts in light, the guest requests that differed from the Great Island and how he was doing meeting people and fitting in.

In exchange, Violet told him about her day, which usually involved some outdoor activity. She'd gone hiking and then shopping with Jillian Shelley who had told Jordan, again, what a treasure Violet was.

He already knew. She'd sent him the picture from her phone, and the look on his face gave away his feelings entirely—at least she thought so. She'd said he looked gobsmacked by the adventure, and it was easy to play along with that assessment.

Each of the previous nights, he'd left Violet at her door late in the evening, and even though they said good-night, the words hung in the air as if there was more to be said. Maybe it was being far away from home and surrounded by strangers all day, but Jordan found himself straining for a glimpse of Violet in the lobby or outside the windows. He looked for her at lunch. He looked forward to dinner all afternoon long.

He wanted to be with her every moment of the day. How was he going to move permanently to the Great Valley in a few weeks or months if he missed Violet when she was on the same property? Knowing she could walk past his desk at any moment distracted him until he reminded himself he was there to serve the hundreds of other guests. They deserved the best service, and hospitality was the thing that had saved him as a lonely teen yearning for a nicer life and was now giving him the opportunity of a lifetime.

After dinner on the final night, Violet took his hand and pulled him toward comfortable porch chairs where they could watch the moon over the mountains. They'd sat in the same chairs the previous night after a few dances in the ballroom, and Jordan knew he would never hear the night insects and see the moon rise over those mountains again without thinking of Violet and this precious time during which he could pretend she was his.

"I want to show you something," she said. She sat in a chair and pulled out her phone. "Look."

"As long as it's not that goofy picture of me on the zip line platform," Jordan said.

In the picture, a white dog sat on a blue cushion with its head tilted up as if it heard something magical in the air.

"She's back?" he asked.

"She never really left," Violet said. "Cara took her to the horse barn every night and found her a place to sleep, but then she found her on my back step every morning."

"So she's definitely a stray?"

Violet nodded. "She looks cleaner and happier in each picture, and you know Cara is probably indulging her."

"It's odd," Jordan said.

"I know. It seems like she's waiting for me to get home even though I only met her once, the morning we left. I stopped and petted her for a minute, but I was too focused on getting my luggage to my car and getting to you that I didn't pay much attention."

"It might have been enough to make her fall in love with you," Jordan said.

Just saying those words aloud made his heart race. It would be so easy to fall deeper in love with Violet if he let himself. How had he never considered that a possibility? Was it the change of location, the situation...his situation? Being in charge of his own life and future made everything seem different, sharper somehow. Scary. As if the risk was greater but so could be the reward.

"Maybe I'll adopt her when I get back," Violet said. "I'd always thought of getting a shop dog to greet customers and wag her tail from her perch by the front window. It'll keep me from being lonely when you're gone." She smiled. "Maybe I'll name her Jordan."

Jordan laughed. "You'd replace me with a stray dog?"

"I could never replace you."

Her tone was serious and regretful. Did she feel the shift in the air between them, too?

"I could never replace you either," he said.

Their eyes met for a full ten seconds. Hers shimmered. Were those tears?

"Am I making a mistake leaving Christmas Island?"

"No," she said quickly. Too quickly. As if she didn't even want to consider the question.

Jordan sat back and looked at the moon that had grown full each night they'd been there. His heart was full, too, but he felt trapped by the weight of his own dreams. "This is our last night."

Violet nodded. "I've tried not to ask you how

you think you're doing with your working interview."

"Afraid to stress me out about it?"

She looked down at her hands twisted in her lap. "Afraid to learn the truth maybe." She looked up and met his eyes. "I know you've done an amazing job. You know what you're doing, you're smart and personable and… well, they'd be fools not to hire you."

"Thank you," he said. "You've always had more confidence in me than I deserve."

"No, I haven't."

He opened his mouth but didn't know what to say. She hadn't been confident in him?

"I mean it wasn't anything you didn't deserve. You deserve everything good that has ever happened to you, but you're the only one who never seems to see it," Violet said.

"That's not true."

"Yes, it is. You can't keep thinking you're the poor kid from a little house."

"A little run-down house that currently has a tree on the roof."

"See what I mean?" Violet asked. "You took my words and somehow twisted them to reflect badly on you. Don't you see that you're respected and valued by your friends for who you are, even though your parents never got a chance to make the best of their lives?"

"Short lives," he said.

"But yours won't be. You've got a golden future just waiting for you."

A golden future. He thought of the gold dawn light coming across the lake in the mornings as he drove from his house to the Great Island Hotel for another shift at the front desk. There was no future in that job. If he wanted to move up the chain, he had to take a chance and move on from Christmas Island. Wasn't that why he was here?

He swallowed down the frustration that had seemed to hang over him his entire adult life. Did he always have to prove himself? Why? Who was he proving himself to now? His family was gone and his friends would eventually forget him when he left.

Only Violet. He looked into her beautiful eyes and realized she might be right about a lot of things, but she was wrong about one. She'd said he deserved everything good that ever happened to him, but he didn't deserve her or her love. Not the way he was using her to get ahead.

"We should get back to our rooms and

pack," he said abruptly. "The hotel van will pick us up at eight for our flight."

EVERYTHING WAS DIFFERENT. When she'd told him she loved him after the fireworks, she hadn't waited for a response. But now she'd said she could never replace him and his words were swift and—she had to believe—true. *He could never replace her either.*

They stood side by side in the elevator. His fingers brushed hers and then curled around her little finger. She held her breath.

The doors opened at their floor and they walked together to her door as if they were coming home from a date. How many times in their lives had they walked home together, dropped each other off, waited while the other one fumbled for a key in a pocket?

This time was different.

Jordan still had hold of her hand. He turned to face her at her door and took her other hand, the one with the fake engagement ring. The hotel hallway was silent as they stood, hands linked, outside her door.

This might be her only chance.

Violet swayed toward him and tilted her face up to his, closing the distance and keeping her eyes on his the entire time. She wanted him to know what she was about to do was intentional.

Before she could touch her lips to his, he suddenly let go of both her hands. She'd made a mistake, misunderstood the tension between them, destroyed their—

Jordan put both hands on her shoulders and kissed her cheek, right next to her mouth as if he was testing the waters. They hadn't spoken a word since they left the porch, but they didn't need words. Jordan's lips lingered near her mouth, and Violet turned her head just enough for her lips to contact his for a long, sweet kiss that contained more feeling and longing and history than they could ever have said.

There was no one around to see them. It wasn't for show to prove their relationship. This kiss was because she loved him and she was willing to take the risk of showing it to him. Even though it could ruin everything between them and complicate Jordan's life, for the first time since their false engagement, Violet decided to put her feelings and needs first.

Jordan pulled back.

"I'm sorry," he said.

"What?"

"I shouldn't have done that."

"I did it," Violet said.

"But I started it."

Violet nodded, searching his expression for clues to his feelings. Was he really sorry or did he think she'd be upset?

"For two people who've known each other forever, we're making a mess of this," Violet said.

"Which is totally my fault. We had the perfect friendship before I ruined it with this whole thing."

"Did you?" Violet asked, irritation starting to replace the emotion she'd felt while kissing him.

"Of course I did. I can't kiss you and make you think I—"

The words hung in the air for a moment until Violet decided she wasn't playing any more games.

"Make me think what?" she asked.

"That...our relationship is real."

"Our relationship is real," she said. "It's been real all our lives when we were there for each other and cared about each other. It was real when we rode bikes and had winter dinners together. It was real when I agreed to this fake engagement, and it was very real when I got on the plane to come here so I could help someone I loved achieve his dream even though it meant saying goodbye to him. It doesn't get any more real than that."

Jordan took a full step back, creating space between them. His mouth opened and she watched his chest rise and fall quickly.

"You love me?"

"Of course I do," Violet said. "I've shown you that a thousand times over the years."

Jordan nodded. "Over the years." He said the three words slowly as if they possessed the key to understanding her meaning.

She knew what he was doing. He was processing her statement that she loved him as an extension of friendship. Like the way she loved all their friends on Christmas Island. She opened her mouth to tell him there was a big difference between loving someone and being in love with him, but then she closed it again.

He was floundering, searching for a way to make everything make sense. If she told him she was in love with him, he might turn down the job at the Great Valley and return to Christmas Island where he would settle into his old life and come to regret their relationship. If there was one thing she could never do, it was to stand in the way of his happiness.

"You've shown me that, too," Violet said. "When you handed me the best rocks for skipping and let me pick out almost all your clothes. You know I love that."

He nodded and his shoulders lowered as if he was relieved. Violet wanted to cry, but instead, she applied herself to searching through her purse for her room key. "And I better get packing because it's going to be a tough job fitting it all in one bag after the shopping I did here."

She'd acquired a new dress, a sweater, a swimsuit and a pair of shoes. But she'd gained a lot more on this trip. Understanding and resolve. She'd chosen to help Jordan get what he believed he wanted, and she had to go through with it, even though the sweetness of their friendship had acquired an unfamiliar edge. In chasing a big promotion, was Jordan losing a little bit of himself?

As his friend, was it her job to tell him that and offer an alternate suggestion—her love?

"Good night," she said brightly. If she didn't dash through that door and close it in five seconds, she was either going to cry or tell Jordan that she was in love with him. That would ruin everything. If thoughts about their relationship being more than just friendship were going through his head, it would add to his stress and confusion. She wouldn't be responsible for him making a mistake, not when he was so close to his goal.

"Wait," Jordan said. "You can't just say good-night like that."

"Sure I can. We tried a kiss and it went about as well as that first one we did in front of your boss back on the island. Sadly, no one saw this one because I think we were more convincing this time. But believe me, this kiss didn't change anything."

"You didn't feel something?"

Violet hesitated just a moment. "I felt… well, it was very nice. You're a decent kisser, which will really come in handy for you someday."

She hated herself at that moment. Reassuring a guy that maybe he'd find a great gal to kiss one day and he should go into it with confidence. Did that make her the best or the worst friend Jordan had ever had?

"Someday, but not with you again," Jordan said in a tone that was a statement, not a question.

"We're leaving tomorrow and then I'm sure it won't be long before you're back here in an office with your name on the door in gold letters."

There would be a for sale sign in his yard and a huge hole in her life. Maybe she could adopt that little white dog and have someone to take on long walks, even picnics. She could call her Daisy with her pretty white fur. Violet tried to concentrate on how nice it would be to pick out a pretty pink collar and train Daisy to greet customers. It was better than thinking about saying a final goodbye to Jordan.

"Is that what you think I want?" Jordan asked. "My name on a door?"

"Everyone knows what you want, Jordan," she said. "You've been very clear, and the last thing any of your friends—me included—want to do is get in your way. Forget the kiss."

And then she keyed into her room and closed the door.

CHAPTER EIGHTEEN

JORDAN FELT A lot of emotions early the next morning as he zipped his suitcase and did a final sweep of his room to make certain he hadn't forgotten anything. At the Great Island, he'd seen everything from computers to phone chargers to toys left behind. One person had left a giant wad of cash in the safe, and Jordan and another manager for a witness had carefully retrieved, counted and stored it in the hotel's main safe.

People's minds were elsewhere when they were on vacation, and for the first time Jordan understood that phenomenon. Of all the emotions he felt as he rolled his luggage from his room, the strongest one was fear.

So much had happened professionally, he was afraid he would lose momentum if he left now. So much had happened personally with Violet that he was afraid it would fade into the past, some kind of unreality, if they left Virginia without truly addressing it. They couldn't just leave their unresolved issues behind them in another state. He'd tried bringing up their relationship and his job prospects the previous night and Violet had stopped him.

Maybe she was the wise one. If she suspected he was about to tell her he was in love with her, it was a good thing she hadn't let him. What was the point of opening up his heart only to be rejected? He was leaving anyway. He had to. How many more chances like this were going to come along?

Violet opened her door at the same time he did and pulled her large suitcase into the hall where it teetered and flipped over. Jordan reached down and grabbed the handle.

"I've got it," he said.

She hiked her purse onto her shoulder and let her door close. "Thank you, but it's heavy."

"Experience," Jordan said.

She laughed. "Did that experience tell you my suitcase would be heavier going home than it was coming here?"

"You did warn me."

This was going well. They were having a friendly conversation, no talk of the kiss, no discussion about their relationship. It was as if things were…settled.

"Do we have a minute to grab coffee and rolls from the bakery in the lobby?" Violet asked. "I'll admit I'm going to miss those."

"Of course," Jordan said, using his hospitality tone. "I'll order on the app while we're on the way down. Can I guess your order?"

"Of course," Violet said, mimicking his tone with a smile.

In the elevator, Jordan was happy to pull out his phone and use the hotel WiFi to place their breakfast order—two coffees with cream, no sugar, a bagel with cream cheese for him and a cinnamon roll with maple icing for her. It gave him something to think about instead of remembering his fingers curled around hers the previous night in that same elevator.

The doors opened and he maneuvered their luggage out while Violet strode ahead of him toward the bakery at the far end of the lobby. All day long, the aroma of coffee, cinnamon and sugar teased the senses of anyone in the lobby and added to the bakery's daily sales. Maybe the Great Island Hotel should add a bakery like that in the lobby? Jordan planned to suggest it when he returned to work the next day. He could ask Destiny about it. He even thought of exactly where it would go and suggestions for breakfast items guests would be sure to ask for.

And then he remembered it might be none of his business what happened in the lobby of the Great Island. Quentin Shelley had texted him a goodbye late the night before and an assurance he would hear soon about the job.

Don't bother unpacking much, was the actual wording of the text. Jordan's first inclination had been to show the message to Violet so she could give him her interpretation of it and celebrate with him, but he hadn't contacted her after she slipped into her room.

They could talk about it on the plane today. It was going to be a long trip home with a lot to think about.

On the plane, Violet pulled out several catalogs and buried her nose in them, sending him a strong signal that she didn't intend to talk. Jordan leaned his head back and closed his eyes. The working interview had been fun most of the time, informative all of the time, and—he realized now—completely exhausting. On Christmas Island, he didn't need to put on a strong front at all times. Everyone knew him. But at the Great Valley Hotel, he'd had a lot to prove and show.

As he drifted toward sleep, it occurred to him that he'd always been trying to prove himself on his home territory, but going somewhere else had shown him that he didn't need to do that at home. The thought was like a flash of light, but then he let sleep take him and only awakened when they touched down on Christmas Island.

"It's pouring rain," Violet said. "Do you have a raincoat in your suitcase I could dig out for you?"

Groggy, he shook his head.

"I wish I had a spare coat, but I do have an umbrella," she said.

Jordan struggled up from his seat and from his dreams. He'd dreamed of his childhood on the island, his dad teaching him to ride a bike down the road by their house and his mom bringing his lunch to school one day when he'd forgotten it. It had to be right before she died. He remembered a birthday party for his grandfather with a homemade cake made by his grandmother that had a lopsided 60 on it. He'd always thought sixty must be very old because it was his grandfather's last birthday.

In his dream, his childhood home—his home now—was bright and cheerful. Had the rooms darkened over the years or was it an illusion?

"I...don't mind getting wet," Jordan said. It might feel good and wake him up.

"It's not much of a welcome home," Violet said as she looked out the small window while they waited for the pilot to give them the all clear to leave the plane.

Maybe it was just the welcome home he needed. A big wet, windy dose of reality contrasting with the sunshine they'd left behind in Virginia. The plane's door opened, and Jordan muscled their baggage to his car, getting soaked in the process. Violet hopped in the passenger seat, her purple coat glistening with rainwater.

"I'll take your suitcase up to your place and then we'll go get your car from the hotel parking lot," he said. "That way you won't have to haul it."

"I can manage."

"No," Jordan said. "Let me do this for you after all you've done for me."

He pulled out of the island airport and took the road toward town that led right past his house on the way. He almost didn't want to look. The fallen tree and the tarp covering the roof had almost faded from his mind while he was gone, but now that he was back, he was going to have to face it.

He heard Violet gasp before he saw it for himself. What on earth?

Rain blurred his windshield, but there was no doubt something was different. Jordan pulled in his driveway and put the car in Park. The wipers flicked back and forth across his windshield, giving him brief clear glimpses of his home.

The fallen tree was gone. The hole in the roof repaired. The entire exterior which had peeling white paint when he left had been repainted. The porch railings and shutters were a contrasting color—he couldn't tell in the rain if it was gray or green. Even in the rain, the white siding gleamed and made the house appear new.

He hardly recognized his own home.

"I can't believe it," Violet said.

"Who did this?" he asked. Surprise and shock was turning quickly into frustration in his mind. He didn't ask anyone to repair his home. Didn't get quotes and sign contracts.

"I don't know," Violet said. "Honestly."

He turned off the car and stalked to the

front door. When he unlocked it and entered, he found that nothing inside had changed. Not one thing in the entryway and kitchen was moved from when he'd left. He went into the spare bedroom where the hole had been in the roof. There was still plaster and wood on the bed that had fallen from the ceiling.

No one had been inside.

He felt a hand on his shoulder.

"Are you okay?" Violet asked. "I know this is a surprise, but it's a good surprise, isn't it?"

"It's still my house, and it's my responsibility to take care of it. Not some Santa figures who swoop in and drop off new roofs."

Violet laughed.

"It's not funny," Jordan said. "It's obvious Maddox got some of our other island friends and did this. I'm sure they were just being nice, helping out the poor kid from the crappy house that was even worse after the storm. A pity job."

"Stop it," Violet said. "You sound like a jerk. People did something nice for you because that's what people on this island do. And you should be grateful because it'll make it this much easier for you to sell the place and turn your back on all of us."

She headed to the car, leaving Jordan feeling as if there was a hole in his chest, not unlike the one that had been in his roof. Did they think he was turning his back on all of them and their friendship? Didn't anyone understand? He'd thought Violet had.

He closed the door of his house and didn't bother locking it. Violet sat, arms crossed, looking out the window instead of at him. "Just take me straight home," she said. "I'll get my car from the hotel lot later."

VIOLET HELD HER umbrella over Jordan's head as he carried her bag to her back door. Tension rolled off him like the rain and she was torn between lecturing him and hugging him. They were on Christmas Island, their home turf where everything made sense in its cocoon of familiarity. The kiss, the feelings, the confusion and sea changes they'd experienced in Virginia were behind them, left somewhere in the air over the states they'd flown over.

"Thank you," she said as Jordan put the suitcase inside her apartment door. He breathed heavily from carrying it up the stairs. "Do you need a glass of water?" she asked.

He shook his head and a raindrop fell off

and landed on Violet's cheek. He reached up and wiped it off.

"Sorry," he said. His finger lingered on her cheek. "I need to go." His voice was low and gruff. "I have…a lot to think about, and you've put up with enough already."

He turned and left, and Violet moved to the window over her kitchen sink that overlooked the back of the building. She hadn't tried to stop him because it was true that he had to have time to process all that had happened in the past few days. A million emotions had to be going through his heart.

She had a similar problem.

She watched Jordan emerge below her and trudge toward his car. Before he opened the driver's door, though, he stopped and turned. He moved back toward the building and she saw him crouch and hold out his hands. Even through the rain, Violet saw a flash of white launch itself into Jordan's arms.

The stray dog.

Jordan held the dog, shielding it from the rain, and sat down on the back stoop, hunching his shoulders over his companion.

Violet had always loved Jordan and had recently admitted to herself she was in love with him, but now her heart utterly melted. He wasn't perfect. Didn't always say the right thing. Was probably leaving the island because of a complex and a goal she couldn't understand.

But she loved him.

She ran down her stairs and flung open the back door. "Come inside."

Jordan stood and opened his arms just wide enough for her to see what he was shielding.

"Bring Daisy, too," she said.

Jordan's brow wrinkled in surprise, but he came inside and stood, dripping and clutching the small white dog.

"Come upstairs and I'll get some towels," she said, pushing back the wet white fur so she could see the dog better. "Welcome home," she said to the dog, but she could have been talking about herself and Jordan. Violet reached out and pulled Jordan close, heedless of his wet shirt and the dog's wet fur. They held each other with the shivering dog between them.

It was unwise to give her heart to Jordan and to a dog she hardly knew, but she couldn't help it. Finally, she released her hold on both Jordan and Daisy and led the way up the stairs just as she had minutes earlier, but Jordan carried the dog, which was much lighter than the suitcase.

"Let's use the bathtub," Violet said. "I hope Daisy likes water."

"Do you have any supplies for washing a dog?"

"Believe it or not, Cara left me a doggie care package because she said I was going to come home to a new friend. She seems to know what animals are thinking."

Jordan carried the dog into Violet's bathroom and she grabbed the dog shampoo from the care package and pulled towels from a long cabinet next to the enclosed tub. The green walls and purple accents soothed Violet every morning, and it was nice to be home. Although she had enjoyed her luxurious bathroom at the Great Valley Hotel, she'd missed her own cozy space.

Violet got out a dark green towel and put it on the floor for her and Jordan to kneel on, and then she set a matching towel next to the tub. She knelt and ran the water until it was warm but not hot and then Jordan knelt beside her and lowered the dog slowly into the tub.

"Have we ever bathed a dog together?" Violet asked as they watched Daisy get her footing in the tub and then sit down in the shallow water, trusting them.

Jordan shook his head. "I thought we were done having new experiences together after the last five days."

Violet laughed. "Apparently not."

Jordan reached into the tub and touched the dog's head. "Do you remember when we were maybe ten or eleven and we found that stray kitten on the bike trail behind the school?"

"We heard it mewing from the bushes," Violet said, nodding. Its little cry had seemed so helpless and then it had emerged from the tall grass, gray ears barely visible among the blades. They had returned to the school to get a box or a basket to put it in so it wouldn't fall through Violet's bike basket, but it was gone when they went back to the spot where they'd first seen it.

"We looked for it for hours," Jordan said.

"And we finally found it and our teacher adopted it."

"You hate giving up," Jordan said.

The dog put out a paw and slapped it on the water, testing the unfamiliar environment, and both Jordan and Violet laughed.

"It's like she was waiting for you to come home," Jordan said. "And how did you know her name was Daisy?"

"I didn't. But when I saw the pictures Cara sent, I thought it would be appropriate because of her white fur. Plus, I have a fondness for flower names."

Jordan rubbed a slow circle on Violet's back as she worked her fingers through Daisy's fur. Next to her, Violet felt Jordan shiver.

"Your clothes are wet and you must be freezing," Violet said. The bathroom felt warm and sticky to her, but her clothes had remained dry under the raincoat she'd shed and she had her hands in the warm water.

Jordan sat back on his heels. "I'm okay."

"Are you?" Violet asked softly, giving him a quick glance.

"I'll be okay. I just…"

"You need a little time," Violet said after a moment. "A lot has happened this summer and this week and just in the last ten minutes."

"For you, too."

Violet acknowledged that statement with a nod, but she didn't state the obvious—that she wouldn't be changing her job, her address, her life.

"What will you do with Daisy?" he asked.

"I'd like to keep her. Cara has checked around and no one on the island is missing a dog. She's shown up here for five days straight." Violet smoothed back Daisy's fur. "So I believe I have a new friend."

She rinsed off the soap, drained the water and Jordan helped her wrap the towel around Daisy and lift her out of the tub. Violet dried her fur and her paws and carried her to the living room where she made a little bed from dry towels Jordan had grabbed as he left the bathroom.

"You've still got your old friend," he said as they sat on the floor and petted Daisy.

"I know," Violet said softly.

"I mean it. Nothing has to change, even if I leave. We'll still be friends."

"If?" Violet asked.

"Nothing is final. Yet."

That little addition of *yet* extinguished a nascent flame of hope. Jordan got up, touched her shoulder and left. This time, Violet did not go to the kitchen window to watch him leave. Instead, she sang to Daisy until the dog went to sleep on her new bed, oblivious to the rainy afternoon outside.

CHAPTER NINETEEN

AN HOUR LATER, Violet entered the back door of her boutique and gave Cara Peterson a warm smile.

Cara waved at her from the front of the store where she was folding sweaters on a table. "You've been back an hour and you're finally checking in. Does that mean you're really confident in me?"

"Totally confident. And I appreciate your running my store for days. They must have missed you a lot at the candy store and the horse barn."

Cara shrugged. "I caught up by working in the evenings."

"Then you need a vacation. I can recommend a great resort in Virginia if you really want to get away."

Cara laughed. "Too far for me, but I'm looking forward to hearing all about it. The pictures you texted were beautiful." She came to Violet and hugged her. "I noticed Jordan was here."

Violet nodded. "He dropped me off and then we gave the stray dog a bath. I named her Daisy."

"So you're keeping her?"

"I hope so."

"Good. Not that you had much choice. Even when I took her to the barn, I'd find her here the next day."

"She's a beautiful dog, especially now that she's clean. I just want to hug her and make her a sweater. Or a raincoat," Violet added.

"Daisy could be your mascot and you could sell a line of pet accessories," Cara suggested.

Violet clapped her hands together. "Little sweaters and collars, pet beds with custom embroidery. I love that idea. Thank you!"

As she spoke, Violet browsed through her shop, reacquainting herself with each rack and display. She'd missed it. The coordinating jewelry and curated outfits waited for just the right person to try them on, but they were also Violet's balm. She controlled the effect each ensemble created. The right clothing made people beautiful and confident and helped them enjoy special occasions and face difficult ones.

There was no wardrobe for watching Jordan sail out of her life. Not the lovely blue shirtdress in the front window, not the yellow swimsuit, not the red capri pants with the cute sailor buttons.

"I don't want to pry, but as the youngest of three daughters, I do have experience listening to love story problems," Cara said as she stood opposite Violet over a rack of linen blouses.

Violet forced a smile. "Can we talk about my new dog instead?"

"Animals are easier than humans," Cara said. "But humans have their advantages." They walked to the sweater table at the front of the store and continued refolding the stacks of summery cardigans. "Has Jordan seen his house yet?" Cara asked.

Violet blew out a breath. "On the way here."

"Was he surprised?"

"Yep."

"And not in a good way, I'm guessing," Cara said. She stacked three cardigans and moved to the next pile. "I tried to tell Maddox and Griffin that, but they were in hero-friend mode and I didn't want to be the Grinch."

"They meant well, and what they did is honestly amazing. Jordan sees that, of course, but he just… Well, I understand his feelings, but I also don't," Violet responded. "It's his house and it has always bothered him that the place he inherited came with…some flaws."

"But he didn't change it," Cara said.

"No, he didn't. I thought it was because he didn't know where to start, or it was just overwhelming, or he was busy, or just didn't have the money. Or all of those things."

"It probably was," Cara agreed. "He's not alone in that."

"Insurance would have patched the roof and repaired the storm damage, but the exterior paint, shutters and railings and all—that was a very nice extra that wouldn't have been covered."

"And it bothered him?" Cara asked.

Violet nodded. "He seemed upset."

"Interesting. Animals are territorial, too. They wouldn't want anyone messing with their dens and lairs and nests. But, then again, he's leaving, right?"

"I believe so."

"And now his house is too nice to leave?" Cara asked. "Could that be the problem? He sees it differently now and it complicates his decision? Or…"

She stopped and Violet felt heat in her cheeks. She didn't want to look up and meet her friend's gaze.

"Or is there something else that is too nice to leave?" Cara finished. "His feelings are a twisted-up mess like that tree that fell on his roof."

Violet sighed. Was Jordan upset about leaving her? As a friend or something more? Her feelings were also tangled like the roots of that tree. "Animals are easier. Maybe I should take Daisy for a nice long walk."

"It's raining. You have to face your feelings about Jordan and be honest with him. He's always depended on you, and now he needs your honesty more than ever."

"What am I supposed to tell him? That I finally realized I'm in love with him just as he's about to leave? That's like fixing up your house and then selling it."

"Not exactly," Cara said. "Most people fix up their houses so they can sell them—which has always seemed weird to me, but what do I know?"

Violet smiled. "You know enough not to

pretend to be engaged to someone and make a royal mess of your life."

"You got a free vacation," Cara said.

"Not quite. I need to repay you for your time running my store."

"Or you could wait. One of these days, I'm going to run off with a handsome man for a week, and I'll need someone to feed my horses and shovel out the barn while I'm gone."

"I'm writing you a check right now," Violet said.

JORDAN SHOULD HAVE stayed home. It was a Friday night in July, so the voices in the bar were gaining volume with every minute. His head would be pounding worse than it already was by the time he had one drink with Maddox—who wouldn't take no for an answer—and played a round of darts.

He didn't need the drink, the darts or the company. He wasn't worthy of any of them at the moment, and the only way he was getting through the night was quickly and with his mouth shut.

"You could take a swing at me," Maddox said, "but we'd have to go out in the parking lot. We're either too old or too young to fight in a bar."

Jordan lined up a shot and tossed a dart. "Is there an optimal age for bar brawling?"

"Somewhere between twenty-one and stupid," Maddox said.

"I'm right there."

He'd been foolish in multiple ways, but none of them bigger than drawing Violet into his promotion scheme. What if he'd just tried for the job on his own merits instead of trying to pretend he was something he wasn't? Wouldn't he have had a chance?

Now he'd never know, and that was one of the things burning his biscuits as he'd wandered his lonely little house seeing every flaw as if for the first time. Why hadn't he ever done anything about the missing switch plate in the hallway? He could have changed the light bulb in the hall closet, could have fixed the broken shelf in the basement stairway so stuff didn't spill onto the one below it and cause an avalanche of junk. He'd never bothered, and now he was kicking himself.

"Okay," Maddox said. "So no sucker punch in the parking lot. Can't say I'm disappointed." He propped a hip onto a table near the dartboard. "I guess I'll settle for letting you beat me at darts."

"Letting me?" Jordan said. "Don't you think I can do it on my own?"

He knew his tone was grouchy and he didn't care. He didn't see a whole lot to like about himself at the moment. Who knew why Maddox had even called and insisted he come out for the night?

With every step he'd taken recently to prove he wasn't a poor kid from a sad family, he'd proven even more that he was still taking a handout from concerned people, still taking advantage of his friends—especially Violet.

It didn't sit well. Didn't fit, just as his hand-me-down clothes from the island rummage sale every spring didn't fit. It was a small island. He recognized his winter coat as one Griffin May had worn several years earlier. He knew the book bag he used throughout middle school had been carried by Violet's older brother Ryan for at least a year. He'd even found the initials RB inside.

No one on the island had ever said a word when he'd shown up wearing their old clothes. But he knew it.

"I'm glad I'm not a dartboard," Maddox

commented. "At least not the part in the middle. You're definitely going to beat me fair and square if you keep up the bull's-eyes."

Jordan still had a dart in his hand, but he tucked it in his shirt pocket and turned to face Maddox. "Thank you." He drew a long breath. "I didn't know what to say when I saw my house this morning through the pouring rain."

"I was afraid you'd either kiss me on the lips or be mad," Maddox said.

"I was mad," Jordan said. "For an hour."

"And then you got over it?"

Jordan picked up his glass and took a long drink. "I hate being a charity case."

"You're not. No one sees you that way."

Jordan didn't answer. He pulled the dart from his pocket, aimed and missed the target by a foot.

"You see yourself that way," Maddox said.

His tone was kind but pitying, and Jordan was trying to formulate a response when Maddox punched him on the shoulder.

"Get over yourself, Frome. So your porch needed painting and a tree had the audacity to fall on your roof out of all the roofs on the island. Guess what? Everybody I know needs help, sometimes a little, sometimes a lot. If you'd stop trying to prove you don't, you'd look around and be a whole lot happier."

"I'll be happy when I get off this island and get somewhere," Jordan growled. He spoke in anger, but did he really mean it?

"Do you think so?" Maddox asked.

And that was the meat and potatoes of the question. Was he really going to be happy just because he got a promotion, met all new people who didn't know his grandparents and parents and made twice the money?

Jordan sat down and Maddox sat across from him.

"My insurance company would have repaired the roof and removed the tree," Jordan said. "They were going to come out next week and do an estimate."

"It rained today."

"I know. I thought about that. And they wouldn't have painted the place, especially the porch railings and shutters."

"Not unless they were damaged in the storm," Maddox said.

Jordan nudged his glass toward Maddox's and clinked them together. He swallowed. "Only true friends would do that."

"You're darn right. True friends who wish you the best, no matter what you want to do."

"Thanks. For everything."

"You're welcome. However, I am authorized to say on behalf of a certain lady and her friend that if you hurt Violet in all this business, your true friends will kill you as a courtesy."

Jordan nodded. "I appreciate that. And I'm buying tonight."

"Good. Now I believe I'll finish off our dart game, and I won't feel sorry for you at all when you lose."

Jordan laughed and sat back. He looked around the downtown bar frequented mostly by locals, even during the tourist season. Christmas decorations were left up all year and nothing had changed in ages. He used to meet his grandfather there after school and walk home with him, and he'd never thought that was strange until he was old enough to think about it.

His parents and grandparents weren't perfect. Their house reflected it. But Jordan began to think his friend Maddox's words were as true as they were tough—that it didn't reflect on him unless he let it.

CHAPTER TWENTY

JORDAN SIFTED THROUGH guest reviews of the Great Island Hotel as the morning sunshine warmed his back through his office window. The five-star reviews were gratifying and almost universally mentioned the historic feel of the place, the beautiful porch, the lake views, the food, the decor and the service. He couldn't agree more. The hotel was a slice of luxurious paradise on an island not lacking in history, charm and scenery. He loved those complimentary reviews and tried to respond with a note of thanks to all of them.

However, it was the negative reviews that offered room for improvement. He couldn't take credit for the positive ones, but he felt the critical ones in his bones. A guest had requested additional towels on Monday and didn't get them until Tuesday morning. Room 250 reported noisy guests in room 251 and no one had addressed it or followed up. The check-in for a large family reunion party had not gone smoothly and they were not offered any apology or compensation for something that was clearly the fault of the front desk.

Had Jordan been there, he would have addressed all of those things. There wouldn't be three online reviews that reflected badly on his hotel. He would have knocked on the door of 251 and smoothly made suggestions where they could be more comfortable to enjoy their loud music and conversations, and then he would have followed up with a call to 250 and offered them complimentary guest passes to the lunch buffet the next day.

He should have been there to help check in that large family reunion group. They'd had very specific requests for adjoining rooms and rooms that needed to be separated by at least a floor. An aging member of the group had asked for proximity to an elevator, but got a room way down the hall, adding too many steps to her day. Jordan shook his head when he read the report.

He should have been there for that family.

He wrote personal emails to the parties involved and offered them discounts on their stay plus further amenities if they chose to return. He wanted to add a note telling them to ask for him by name when they returned… but would he be there?

"Good morning," his boss, Jack, said as Jordan took a place behind the front desk. It was much too early for anyone to be checking in or out, and it was one of the times Jordan liked best. The sun slanted in the lobby windows and the whole building with two hundred rooms was slowly waking up to a beautiful day on Christmas Island. Coffee and scrambled eggs scented the air.

"Morning," Jordan said. He nodded and smiled at his boss.

"Well?"

"It went well," Jordan said. "The Great Valley is a wonderful hotel with a terrific location and a staff I would be proud to work with."

Jack's shoulders slumped. "I was hoping you'd hate it."

"I didn't hate it. I even went zip-lining." Jordan grinned. "We don't have zip-lining or white water rafting here."

"Do we want it?"

"No. But we could add bocce ball sets to the lawn games. I saw people enjoying that."

He'd heard about Violet's game, but he

hadn't taken the time to play himself. He should have asked her if she wanted to play a round of tennis or some other game on the lawn. He'd gone on the zip line with her, but he could have spent more time with her.

Should have.

"I'll suggest bocce to our recreation department, but I don't think there's any chance of building a zip line on the island," Jack said.

"Can't have everything," Jordan said. He took a micro cloth and dusted the monitor screens at the front desk and then the counter. He straightened the pens in the desk organizer so guests wouldn't see a haphazard display.

"Did Violet like the Great Valley?" Jack asked.

Jordan's first reaction was to ask him why that mattered, but then he remembered his boss didn't know about the false relationship.

"I think she liked it very much," Jordan said.

"Which is good news for you. It would be tough for you to take that job if she wasn't serious about moving, too, although I can't picture her leaving the island."

"Her brother left the island," Jordan offered. Ryan had gone off to college, found work on the mainland and never returned to live on Christmas Island full-time. In a way, Jordan had always admired him for it. What was it like to have easy access to all the things on the mainland instead of relying on the ferry or plane schedule?

"You look happy," Jack commented. "The last week was a trial run for me to find someone to replace you. I moved someone up to your position, but I got constant phone calls and guest service slipped." He leaned on the counter and glanced around as if there was something more he wanted to say but without an audience. A seasonal worker came up and started sorting through papers on the desk nearby. Jack shoved off from the counter.

"You have a right to go where the wind blows you, though," he said.

Jack walked away and Jordan was left wondering what unspoken things his boss had kept close to his vest. Did he know something about the Great Valley job or Jordan's chances of getting it?

Jordan almost turned and headed into his office, but he noticed a familiar person striding toward him. Ryan Brookstone walked as if he had a definite purpose. Had he found out about the fake engagement and he was here to tell Jordan to get out of his sister's life?

"I never thought I'd say this," Ryan said. "But I could use a room if you have one."

"A room?" Jordan stammered.

"You do rent those, right? I know it's July, the busy season, but I just need something for a few days and I don't care if it has a view of the dumpsters."

"Dumpster view," Jordan said. "Let me just check." He studied the screen in front of him, scrolling through the limited room options available. "Three nights?"

"I think so. It should be enough."

"Don't you…usually stay with Violet when you're on the island?" Jordan was familiar with the spare bedroom at Violet's place with its subtle gray-and-white tones, perfect for any visitor who needed a quiet, welcoming place. Her parents stayed on occasion, and her brother. Jordan had even stayed over once when there was a winter storm that closed all the roads.

"I texted her from the ferry and decided I'd be better off somewhere else. Maybe you haven't heard, but Violet has a new complication in her life."

"A complication?"

"A dog." The way he said it, it was as if Violet had contracted a disease.

Jordan smiled. "Daisy. She was waiting for us when we got home."

Ryan gave him a confused look. "Home from what?"

Violet hadn't told her brother she'd gone on a five-day trip with Jordan to another state? And now he had to make up a story fast. Ryan was a perceptive, protective older brother. He'd trusted Jordan to walk his sister home after school or island events. Jordan got invited along to birthday parties in the Brookstone family. Ryan trusted him and treated him like family, and he had no idea how far Jordan had crossed the line. If Ryan knew he'd kissed Violet...

"I had a business trip to the Great Island's sister hotel in Virginia, and I could take along a friend. Violet had her own luxury room and kept me company while Cara ran her boutique."

It was true, and he laid it out in a matter-of-fact way. Really a simple thing, right. Just two friends. Ryan was going to be furious with him when he found out how he'd used his sister.

"Wait a minute," Ryan said. "Your story doesn't pass the smell test."

"It doesn't?" *Here it comes.*

"I don't really believe that Cara ran Violet's boutique. Does she even care about clothes?"

"I guess she cares enough. Violet seemed fine with the management, and the dog was waiting in the rain for Violet when I dropped her off."

Dropping her off sounded unserious—like a friend simply dropping off another friend. Jordan had wondered if Ryan, a builder, had been involved in the repair on his house, but he clearly had not. Why was he here now?

"I have a room with a queen bed overlooking the rear of the hotel for three nights," Jordan said. "Don't you like dogs?"

"I like them, but I'm allergic. Violet was clearly not thinking of her only brother when she decided to take in a stray."

Jordan cleared his throat. "You know Violet. Always looking out for others with her big heart."

"Too big," Ryan said. "She thinks with her heart sometimes and I'm afraid someday she's going to get her heart broken."

Jordan felt a stab of guilt. Was Violet thinking with her heart when she'd agreed to help him? Of course she was. But he never wanted to cause her any heartbreak.

He cleared his throat. "The dog did look pretty desperate for a good home."

"And she really left her store for a trip to Virginia?" Ryan asked.

"Maybe she needed a vacation," Jordan said, trying to sound casual. "Anyway, she had lots of fun shopping while I worked."

"Now that doesn't surprise me," Ryan said.

"Are you here for just a friendly visit or is there something else?"

"Checking out some property for a client," Ryan said. "Nothing concrete," he added quickly. "I always like a good excuse to come stay on the island, although now I'm going to have to think ahead about a reservation instead of taking a chance I can find a room in the height of the tourist season."

"I'd be happy to help you with that."

"But you'll be gone," Ryan commented. "I heard you were looking… Oh, wait. That's why you went to Virginia for a business trip. Was it like a job interview?"

"It was," Jordan said, having no reason not to be truthful about it. He didn't mind Ryan knowing about his plans, and now he wished he'd told Violet's brother about her involvement from the start. If Ryan found out now, he wouldn't be happy. He'd think there'd been something to hide.

There hadn't been. Not at first. But weeks into the fake engagement, Jordan had plenty to hide. He was in love with Ryan's sister and there was nothing he could do about it.

The thought that Ryan had left the island and thrived gave Jordan a little stab of hope. He'd never seriously considered that Violet might go with him, even if he got up the nerve to tell her how he felt about her. But her brother had...so maybe she could, too? Couldn't she start a boutique anywhere, maybe somewhere where there were tourists all year round without the long quiet months of winter dragging down the yearly balance sheet?

It was too much of a long shot, and he had a hotel guest standing in front of him waiting for him to do his job. Jordan forced his hospitality smile.

"You're in luck," Jordan said. "That room was empty last night, so I can give you the keys right now and save you from Violet's new houseguest."

"You're a good friend," Ryan said. He handed over his credit card. "Let's get together for a drink later and catch up. You know where to find me."

Jordan completed the check-in process while scanning his brain for any good excuse not to have a one-on-one conversation with Violet's brother.

RYAN'S EARLY MORNING text telling her he was catching the eight o'clock ferry had awakened her at six-thirty, and Violet had gone back to sleep. She was dreaming about a childhood trip to Ohio where they'd visited a theme park and ridden roller coasters all day long. In her dream, her parents were in the front seat of the car on a tall blue coaster and she sat behind them with Ryan.

After she texted Ryan a picture of the dog sleeping next to her bed, he'd sent her a frowning emoji and said he was staying at a hotel on the island. She'd have to make it up to him later by buying him dinner downtown.

She closed her eyes, hoping to return to that magical amusement park when she and Ryan were little and roller coasters were fun instead of being an analogy for her current life.

When she woke up the second time, Daisy was sitting next to her bed, thumping her tail on the hardwood floor. Violet opened an eye. "The store doesn't open for two hours."

More thumping and wagging ensued and then Daisy put her front paws on the side of the bed and licked Violet's face. The poodle had to stretch to reach her, and Violet laughed.

"Fine. I'm up before you decide to jump up here and shove me out of bed."

She put on her robe and slippers and went downstairs with Daisy at her heels. She wasn't worried about putting her on a leash so she could wander the patch of grass behind the boutique building. Daisy had shown up of her own free will and apparently intended to stay. There was very little car traffic on the island, and none early in the morning that would threaten a wandering dog.

Daisy could live a life of peace and freedom with Violet. Just the two of them happily cozying up in her apartment and going for long walks. Maybe Daisy would enjoy running alongside her bike or riding in the basket.

"We're going to be fine," Violet said aloud as Daisy finished her business and trotted back to Violet's perch on the back stoop. She didn't add *without Jordan* because there was no sense burdening an innocent animal with her problems.

Violet threw herself into her work in the boutique. She decided to have a sale on select items, rearrange the display in the front window and expand her collection of socks—especially the fun socks with clever pictures and witty sayings. It was partway through July, but it wasn't too early to start thinking about wool socks and parkas and big comfy sweaters. She texted her brother and asked him to pick a restaurant.

Violet let Daisy out at noon and then again when her store closed, and then she grabbed her purse and walked to the Holiday Hotel, which Ryan had selected. It should be a safe choice. The May brothers knew about the fake engagement, and they knew that her brother didn't. Rebecca was a trusted friend and wouldn't blow her cover. Hadley wasn't likely to be in the dining room because she'd mostly transitioned to the front desk.

Hopefully, no one would say anything about Jordan, and she and her brother would have a nice dinner.

However, the moment she walked into the restaurant, her plans exploded. Jordan and Ryan sat at a table by the front window. They both stood when they saw her, and she tried to smile despite the turmoil in her chest. The two men she loved most in the world were waiting for her at a dinner table, and it was a total disaster.

"I hope you don't mind," Ryan said. "I asked Jordan along and I wouldn't take no for an answer."

Jordan sent her an apologetic smile.

"This is great," she said. Violet scanned the room and saw Hadley coming their way. Rotten luck that Hadley would be working there and hadn't been let in on the secret. She couldn't be expected to *not* say anything. The cat was going to be let out of the bag and there was only one way to head it off. Get there first.

"I'm glad you're both here because Jordan and I have some big news," she said. Her heart was physically painful at what she was about to do. Lie to her only sibling, right to his face. It had to be done. If Ryan found out the engagement was fake, he wouldn't like it. He'd always been protective of her and thought she put other people's needs in front of her own.

Even though she hated admitting her sibling was right, there was no time to ruminate on it. Hadley was about to expose their secret, and there was only one solution.

She slipped her hand in her pocket and wiggled the ring onto her finger and then held it up. "We're engaged."

Jordan's face froze in shock and horror, but Violet knew he'd understand in five seconds.

"Here's my favorite lovebirds," Hadley said. "Did you come to celebrate, Ryan?"

"I…guess so," Ryan said, looking just as shocked as Jordan, but not in a bad way.

"You need a moment before ordering," Hadley said. She held up a finger. "I'll be back in a few."

"When were you going to tell me this?" Ryan asked.

"At dinner," Violet said, shocked at how smoothly she was lying. She hated herself. "But you must have been using your sibling radar and accidentally invited my partner in the big news." She grabbed Jordan's hand and was relieved when he had the sense to lean down and press a kiss to her cheek. She breathed in his scent and enjoyed the warmth of his kiss. If only they weren't acting. If only they were truly in love and getting married and Jordan wasn't leaving and they weren't living an absolute disastrous farce.

If only.

"Well," Ryan stammered. "Finally." He threw up his hands and then hugged them both at the same time. "You two have finally figured out what everyone else knew." He laughed. "I was afraid to say anything for years and Mom made me swear I wouldn't, but you two were destined for each other since we were kids."

She couldn't stop the tears, and she didn't bother to try. Ryan thought everything was finally right and wonderful, and it was as wrong and terrible as it could be. Her tears should be happy tears, pure joy at finally acknowledging the love of her life—who happened to be standing there like a stone statue with an expression that suggested he'd just broken a tooth biting into something.

There was nothing she could do except stick with the plan. They were engaged and when Jordan left and she didn't follow, she had license to tell everyone he'd broken her heart and was a villain.

Not that anyone on the island would believe

Jordan Frome was a villain. Violet hadn't even made up a story yet for why they broke off the engagement. Why on earth would two people who were perfect for each other break off an engagement—oh, wait, how about if the engagement was never real?

Her love was real.

"Don't cry," Ryan said. "This is great news. Do Mom and Dad know? When did this happen? Why didn't you tell me? When are you getting married?"

"Whoa," Violet said. "Let's sit down and order some food before you kill me with questions."

Did their parents know? Of course not. It was a miracle that they hadn't heard it from someone on the island, and the only explanation was the fact that they were on a month-long camping trip out West. There had been pictures of mountains and redwoods and national parks coming through occasionally, so Violet knew they were alive and well, but the reception wasn't great and they promised a visit in person later in the summer where they'd catch up. Her mom had sent a selfie from the Grand Canyon the previous evening with a short message saying they were turning in their rental RV in Phoenix and flying back to Florida in a few days.

It wouldn't be long before they found out. Violet had known the day was coming, but she'd hoped the fake engagement would be over quickly and she could tell her parents it was a brief silly thing they got out of their systems before Jordan moved to Virginia.

"How's this going to work?" Ryan asked. "You're moving," he said, nodding to Jordan, "and you're the last Brookstone on the island. What about your store?"

"We haven't worked out the details," Jordan said. Violet recognized his customer service voice. It was the one he used on hotel guests when he needed to assure them everything was under control and it was his pleasure to be of assistance. She wanted to throw her napkin at him. How could he be so calm?

Maybe because he wasn't lying to his family. He had no family, no one to answer to. A free agent who could do whatever he wanted without a care for anyone—except her, perhaps, but clearly that wasn't going very well. Jordan might recognize what a tough spot Violet was in, but he couldn't empathize. His family was gone.

"Are you selling your house?" Ryan asked.

"Yes."

"I've always liked that place," her brother said.

Violet could hardly take any more surprises. Her brother was all delighted that she was engaged to the person she was "destined" to be with, and now he liked Jordan's run-down house.

"You like that place?" Jordan asked.

Ryan nodded and picked up a menu. "Great location on that little hill, no neighbors close by. I liked eating at that picnic table in your yard a few summers ago when Violet and I brought takeout. View of the lake is super."

"But you build houses for rich people. My house isn't a whole lot more than a shack."

Ryan shrugged. "Could be nice, though. With a good location and some planning, the right person could turn it into an island get-away."

The right person. Violet knew what her brother meant, but she could also guess how Jordan would take those words. He wasn't the right person. He should just sell the place and leave the island. Start over.

"Maybe the right buyer will come along," Jordan muttered.

"So let's hear about this hotel in Virginia where you interviewed," Ryan said, diving back into the conversation and ploughing ahead, unaware of the obstacles in the road. Violet admired her gregarious brother who was all arms and legs and appetite as a teenager, but was now coordinated, polished and successful doing what he loved. He'd built birdhouses by the dozen as a kid, moved on to other projects like fences, a shed, a back porch on their family's home. No one was surprised when he became a contractor and then expanded into investing in subdivisions and large projects. He was just over thirty, but he'd already carved a place for himself in the building world in Michigan and the surrounding states.

"It's a great hotel," Jordan said. "A sister hotel to the Great Island, but much larger with a lot more amenities and surrounded by mountains, not water."

"What did you think of it?" Ryan asked.

"I—" How did Ryan know she'd gone along? What did he think about that?

"I heard you went along, and now that I

know you're engaged, I get it. Hey, wait, did you get engaged on your trip?"

"No," Jordan and Violet said together.

"It was a few weeks ago," Violet explained.

Ryan frowned. "Can't believe you didn't tell me."

"I was waiting," Violet said.

"Until your whole family could be together to hear the big news," Jordan added to Violet's astonishment. It was a plausible explanation, but her stomach twisted when she thought of her parents and brother walking into a lie facefirst. They deserved better.

She deserved better.

They placed their drink orders and then Ryan gave Violet a crooked smile. "Mom and Dad are coming for Christmas in July, and I thought I'd come along. I was considering asking you if you'd partner with me in the Holiday Hustle this year for once, but I'm sure you're going to want to be with your fiancé."

The Holiday Hustle was an island-wide race during the Christmas in July weekend each summer. Teams needed some athleticism because the challenges usually involved biking, often included kayaking and sometimes there was a flat-out run to the finish line. Along the way, participants had to complete challenges such as figuring the length of the island's runway without a tape measure, stepping along a line of canoes tied together without falling in, and ringing the church's bell to a recognizable tune. The challenges were different every year and kept under lock and key until the day of the race.

Violet and Jordan had competed together every year since they were old enough. They'd come in second place, third place and even dead last one year when they had the misfortune of Violet's flat bike tire, Jordan's turned ankle and a decision to flop down on the grassy hill at the marina and laugh instead of trying to salvage their race.

Would Jordan still be there in two weeks for the July 25 event? And how was she going to manage her parents and brother in addition to everything else? It all depended on whether Jordan had a job offer by then. All she could do was smile cheerfully, prepare to compete in the race and find some way to steel herself for Jordan's departure.

It was a good thing she had Daisy to lick her tears, make her laugh and give her someone to love.

CHAPTER TWENTY-ONE

HE'D BEEN BACK on the island a week. A long seven days of waiting to hear from Quentin Shelley. That message Quentin had sent him right before leaving Virginia, *don't bother unpacking much*, now seemed strange. Who didn't unpack for a week? Maybe the other candidate Quentin had coming in for a five-day interview had blown Jordan out of the water. What if he was more experienced and better suited for the job? Maybe the other guy, in addition to being a good golfer, had grown up with mountains and zip lines and not on a tiny island.

The person whose job Quentin was replacing had already left the Great Valley. Shouldn't there be some urgency? At least a rejection that would put him out of this constant state of uncertainty.

A rejection. On one hand, it would destroy his hopes of being a general manager with the prestige and paycheck it afforded. He'd be stuck here on Christmas Island where his parents had died too young and his grandparents had tried to take their place. Worse, a rejection would keep him on Christmas Island where he would have to break off an engagement with Violet...or do something about their relationship. How could he see her every day and never confess to her that he was in love with her?

Yes, a rejection would inflict serious pain and complications in his life.

On the other hand, it would mean he could continue fixing up his house—a job that, once he started, he was sort of taking pleasure in.

"Anybody home?"

From the hallway of his house, where he was working on a project, Jordan recognized the voice of Mike Martin, who owned the bike rental downtown and was soon to be married to Hadley Pierce. They were also expecting a baby in the fall. No one had seen that relationship coming, but they seemed happy. They'd been friends until they were much more.

Could it be like that for him and Violet?

"In here," Jordan called. "Just a second."

He lowered the light fixture from the hallway leading to the bathroom and second bedroom onto the carpeting and went to the front door, which stood open. Through the screen door, he saw Mike holding a gallon of paint in each hand.

Jordan opened the door and gestured for Mike to come in.

"How did you know I needed paint?" Jordan asked.

"Violet. I saw her downtown when I was going into the hardware and she asked me if I'd bring yours to you. She said you'd be busy and wouldn't want to stop and go downtown."

"She knows me," Jordan said, smiling. Violet had offered to pick it up for him, but he hadn't wanted to pull her away from her store again. She'd already done enough for him.

"Are you sure you wanted plain white?" Mike asked. "The guy at the hardware said you could come back and have it tinted if you change your mind."

"Thanks for picking it up. Violet suggested white, especially for the ceilings and the hallway so it doesn't look dark and dingy. I need to think about first impressions from buyers."

"She's good at stuff like that. Maybe I

should have asked her what she thought about my bike rental and if I should repaint it in shades of green, but I went with Hadley's opinion about that."

"Good idea," Jordan said. "Hadley's practical. She'd give you good advice."

Mike leaned against the counter in the kitchen. "So you're really selling this place."

"If I get the job."

Mike nodded. "And, if, on the wild chance you don't get the job, you'll have a bright, cheerful house to live in."

His words echoed Jordan's thoughts as he'd changed light bulbs, removed unneeded items and painted walls and shelves. The old house seemed to be coming alive as if it was waking up to a sunny morning. Without the drapes in the living room, he could sit in his chair and see the lake through the window. Of course, he'd gone through half a roll of paper towels scrubbing the glass now that the windows weren't covered and he could see how filthy they were.

How had he lived with the house in its shabby condition? Why had he never taken an interest in it other than just a place to store his clothes and lay his head at night?

"I was thinking that," Jordan said. "Although I'm really hoping that job will come through." He shrugged. "You never know what people are looking for or what other candidates are out there."

"True," Mike said. He shoved off from the counter. "A few months ago I considered changing jobs because I thought I needed something more stable than my seasonal bike rentals, but I talked myself out of it with a little help from Hadley. You have to put your happiness and the happiness of people you love in front of any big ideas about becoming a millionaire."

"I don't want to be a millionaire," Jordan said.

"But you do have some big ideas about changing your life and starting over."

Jordan nodded. It was hardly a secret.

"And you don't think that just maybe…" Mike began and then he trailed off. An uncomfortable silence filled the entryway of the house.

Jordan liked Mike and wasn't going to press him into saying something he didn't want to. Mike had driven up the road just to bring him paint, but he'd done more than that.

"Thanks for being on the fix-up crew when the tree fell," Jordan said. He didn't have to ask if Mike was there. Griffin and Maddox may have led the efforts, but other islanders had clearly joined in.

"Happy to help."

"I know people think I'm making a mistake by wanting to leave," Jordan said.

Mike shrugged. "People make all kinds of mistakes. I almost made one by not recognizing what Hadley and I had together, but I got lucky and ended up with exactly what I needed, even though I'm still not sure I deserve her. Maybe you'll get lucky, too, and get exactly what you want."

Mike and Hadley had a lifetime of friendship together—everyone knew that. A surprise pregnancy only made that relationship stronger. Everyone was happy for them, just as Jordan hoped everyone would be happy for him if he got the job at the Great Valley Hotel.

Mike started for the door. "Good luck with the house project."

"Thanks again for going out of your way to bring my paint," Jordan said.

Mike laughed. "Violet was looking out for you, like always."

Jordan watched Mike turn around in the driveway and head back toward town in his old pickup. Violet had been looking out for him as always—but in his quest to get what he wanted, had he been looking out for her? Mike's words about almost making a big mistake with Hadley stuck in his mind as he rolled fresh white paint over the dingy walls of his childhood home.

REBECCA, CAMILLE AND Violet met up in the back of Violet's shop after closing time. The official reason was to admire Rebecca in her gown and check the hem with the shoes she'd recently ordered. Violet wasn't worried about the fitting. She knew Rebecca well enough to know she'd choose a two-inch heel that was dressy but not a trip hazard, and the hem she'd basted in was going to be fine.

There was another reason she was anxious to talk to her friends.

"We're getting dinner after the fitting, right?" Rebecca asked. "My treat, and I feel like Mistletoe Melt. It's a bit cool out this evening for July, and some of their comfort food sandwiches are calling my name."

"Sure," Violet agreed. She didn't have plans.

On another night, she might have called Jordan to see if he wanted to sit outside and eat, but she was glad to have her friends.

"Where's Daisy?" Camille asked.

"Upstairs," Violet said. "She's very good, but I can't take a chance on her jumping on Rebecca in this dress. She gets a little excited and forgets her manners sometimes."

"Don't we all?" Camille said.

Rebecca put on the gown, and Violet zipped her into it, being careful not to snag the white satin and lace. The toes of her new shoes were barely visible.

"Perfect length," Rebecca said.

"Still not talking you into a train?" Violet asked. "When else are you going to get away with wearing a dress with a train?"

"I can live without it," Rebecca said.

"Do I sense some waffling there? You know I can add one if you just say the word. I have superhero sewing skills."

"This dress is perfect just as it is," Rebecca said.

"In that case, I wonder if we could use my sewing skills in another way." Violet drew a deep breath. "You know how we just haven't seen perfect bridesmaids' dresses for you, me and Cara," she said to Camille. "And time's getting short for ordering them especially if we're going to need alterations and hemming."

"We're not wearing old prom dresses our mothers saved in the hall closet?" Camille said. "I was really looking forward to a powder-blue dress with way too many ruffles."

"Does it have a train?" Rebecca said. "It might be perfect."

"So," Violet said, forging ahead and ignoring the ridiculous conversation. "I was thinking I would have time to make three dresses."

"You'd make my bridesmaids' dresses?" Rebecca asked.

"If you want me to," Violet said. Although nearly all the stock in her store was ordered ready-made, her true love was fabric, thread, trim and possibilities. She'd made her own prom dresses in high school and they weren't powder blue with too many ruffles. She'd made custom gowns for special occasions for other islanders. Two summers earlier, she'd hand sewn a simple but beautiful wedding dress for an islander a few years older than she was and she'd had the pleasure of attending the wedding where she couldn't take her eyes off the dress.

Fit, movement and a hint of shimmer were everything.

"Desperately," Rebecca said. "I'd love it."

"Oh, thank goodness," Camille responded. "I couldn't picture myself in anything I've seen online, and I know whatever you make will be perfect."

"Do you think Cara would be fine with this?"

"I'm sure she would," Camille said. "She claims not to be caught up in frills and lace, but she likes it. And she wants to look good. This is a fantastic idea we should have thought of from the start."

Violet smiled and her heart felt light and happy. She'd thought about offering to make the three bridesmaids' dresses months ago, but she'd still held out hope Rebecca would find something perfect online. The weeks had flown past and it was time to make a decision and get moving on it.

She had another reason for the offer. With Jordan's upcoming departure, she had time on her hands. Evenings when they might have gone biking or sat on his picnic table watching the sunset would now be time spent alone. If she had a project she was passionate about, it would give her brain, her fingers and her heart something to do other than wonder how she'd ever let Jordan go.

"I have some ideas about style and length, and you have the color already chosen," Violet said.

"Which I'm flexible about, by the way. I don't want to get so caught up in having every detail fussed over that I forget what the day is about."

"Stop being so nice," Camille said. "It's your wedding, and we're going to wear burgundy dresses to go with your fall color scheme. It's not exactly a sacrifice since that color works on all three of us. Now, orange I might have argued against."

"I do have some orange fabric leftover from the matching pumpkin costumes I made for me and Jordan last Halloween," Violet said. "I could do sashes or trains."

They'd had a marvelous time bumping around the island in their huge pumpkin costumes with green stems on their heads. She had a picture on her phone she was really glad someone had taken for them. They'd never wear those costumes again.

"You look sad," Camille said in a low, sympathetic voice. "Jordan used to bring a smile to your face every time you mentioned him, but not anymore. What are you going to do about the fact that you're in love with him?"

Violet sank into one of the pink velvet chairs in the back of her shop. Her face felt hot and her eyes burned. Maybe it was time she gave up and talked it through with her friends. "I didn't say I was in love with him."

"You didn't have to," Rebecca said. She went to the chair next to Violet and almost sat down.

"Don't," Violet said, holding up a hand. "You'll wrinkle."

"Let me take this off." Rebecca turned so Camille could unzip her. She went into the dressing room, but they could still hear her. "I think you and Jordan are both playing a game of chicken."

Violet and Camille exchanged a glance and Violet sniffed.

"You know what I mean." Rebecca's voice drifted out from under the dressing room door. "You both have finally realized you love each other, but neither one of you is brave enough to go first and say it out loud."

"I can't," Violet said. She swallowed, trying to push down her feelings. "He needs to keep his head clear and make a good decision. I don't want to be the reason he stays here."

"You're the one who has to stop being so nice. That's a much bigger deal than the color of bridesmaids' dresses," Rebecca said.

"Do you have any reason to believe he loves you?" Camille asked.

Violet got up and took the wedding gown from Rebecca as she emerged from the dressing room. She placed it on its padded hanger and covered it with a large piece of white muslin. Did Jordan love her? There had been several moments in Virginia when she had wondered. The porch, the zip-lining, the kiss in the hallway outside her door. Every word he said or thoughtful thing he did demonstrated he cared for her. But was he in love with her? If so, it was a new thing, hatched as a result of their fake engagement. When the engagement dissolved, would his feelings, too?

"Maybe," Violet said. "But what does it matter if he's leaving? I can't go with him. I don't want to leave Christmas Island or my friends. My life is here. And even if there was something between us, it would be far less painful to just let it go instead of dragging it out when we'd be miles apart."

"He'd leave anyway if you told him you loved him?" Rebecca asked.

"He has to. He believes he'll only find happiness and success if he gets to start over somewhere with a big promotion."

"He's wrong," Camille said. "Speaking as someone who left the island and chose to come back, I could tell him a thing or two about the grass being greener somewhere else. There's no green like Christmas green. He'll find that out if he really does leave and he'll be back someday."

"Which is all the more reason not to say anything. He needs to figure out his own life and make choices without being clouded by my feelings, or his."

Rebecca laughed. "What's life without being confused by feelings? I'm absolutely certain of my feelings for Griffin, but I still have moments when I search my face in the mirror just to see if I really know myself."

Violet glanced toward the floor-to-ceiling

mirror where she and her friends were reflected. Despite its faithful representation of their appearances, the mirror couldn't help Violet understand what to do with her feelings beneath the surface. Her friends were right and she knew it, but what could she do? If she fought for Jordan's love as her heart was telling her to, she believed she'd win and he'd stay. But would forcing him into that choice be the best thing for their long-term happiness?

She sighed. "The only thing I know for sure is that I'm ready for dinner, and you both need to demonstrate your friendship by reminding me to bring leftovers home for Daisy."

"She can have some of mine," Camille said. "I stress ate five cookies this afternoon because my mother was firing questions at me about my wedding."

"Have you set a date?" Violet asked. She picked up her purse and got out the key for the back door.

"Christmas, I think. I wasn't going to do Christmas because that's what Chloe did, but then I decided it didn't matter if people wanted to compare my wedding to hers. She did what she wanted, and I can do that, too."

Camille did what she wanted. Violet wanted to do the same, but selecting a wedding date seemed easier than telling her best friend he had to make a life-changing choice.

"Oh, my goodness," Violet said. "Please tell me you're in the mood to talk about your Christmas wedding dress over dinner. I need a distraction, and dresses are my favorite kind of distraction."

Camille grinned. "Get ready for it, then." She leaned in and whispered in a stage voice, "I want a long train."

"Yes!" Violet said. She felt better already after just thirty minutes with her friends. Everything was going to be okay.

Rebecca hip-bumped Camille. "I think you should have red-and-white-striped bridesmaids' dresses so we all look like candy canes. People will have expectations from one of the island's candy girls, and it will definitely be different from Chloe's wedding."

Camille laughed as Violet locked the back door and they started toward the downtown restaurant. "I may dress you all as gumdrops, which will require custom work from the best fashionista we know."

Violet smiled. "I can picture us now."

She did picture Camille in a shimmering white gown with a long train and the wedding party and venue accented with Christmas colors. Nothing suited a Christmas Island romance better than a Christmas wedding. She could imagine the dresses, but she couldn't imagine who she would dance with at the reception with Jordan far away.

CHAPTER TWENTY-TWO

JORDAN WALKED WITH Violet to the dock early on Friday morning of the big Christmas in July weekend. He'd insisted on going with her to meet her parents. Ryan had sworn he wouldn't spill the beans on the engagement, but Jordan found it hard to believe that Violet's parents, who were back from their vacation and were still well connected on the island, wouldn't have heard.

He had to be there to support Violet and also to reinforce the belief in their engagement. Quentin Shelley had texted him to say he would have a definite answer within days, and this was no time to let down the curtain on their performance. Jordan also knew the Shelleys were coming to the Great Island Hotel for the Christmas in July weekend. They'd been there for the event in previous years, so their presence didn't necessarily mean good news for Jordan's job prospects.

But they'd be on the island, and they had sharp eyes and minds. If they caught a hint of a fake relationship, his chance at the job could be ruined. Worse, he would have put himself and Violet through a very difficult month for nothing.

"Only a few more days," he said aloud as they watched the ferry dock.

Violet turned her head to look at him. "A few more days until what?"

He put an arm around her shoulders. "Until you don't have to pretend anymore."

She put a hand on her shoulder, covering his hand. "This is going to be the biggest test yet. My dad takes things at face value. If I tell him I'm blissfully happy at the thought of being your bride, he'll believe it. My mother, however, has a way of running X-ray vision over my face and knowing my feelings."

"She won't believe we're engaged?" Jordan asked.

"She might believe it, but she'll suspect there's something complicated about it."

There would be something complicated about it, even if it was true. Weren't there always complications involved in every romance and wedding and marriage? Not that he would know, since he'd hadn't been emotionally involved with anyone. Except Violet. And that was as complicated as it could get. He loved her, but he couldn't tell her. He was using her, but he was also sincere. He wanted to be with her, but he needed to leave the island. It was beyond complicated.

But did it have to be? There was a dramatic way to uncomplicate their situation, even if it meant giving up his dream. No one was forcing him to leave Christmas Island.

He pulled Violet a little closer. The dockworkers were tying up the ferry and he could already see Violet's parents waving enthusiastically from the deck. They'd be among the first people off the boat. There were only seconds left. Should he just tell Violet how he felt?

He cleared his throat. "It is complicated," he said, his voice a shaky whisper. Was this the time? Would it make it better or worse, easier or harder if he confessed his feelings for Violet right now before her parents reached them?

She nodded. "You're right. Mom will see that I must make a terrible choice between loving you and staying on the island I love. She'll see that dilemma right away and believe it accounts for anything that seems… amiss. That can be used to our advantage because who wouldn't see how difficult that is?"

Difficult? It was impossible. A thought hit Jordan like a wave and soaked him as Violet's parents approached. He felt as if he'd been knocked down, even though the weather was clear and dry and sunny.

He could turn down that job.

He could take control of his life in a way he never really had. He'd lived in a run-down house and done a job he thought was holding him back—but what if he was the person holding him back? What if the only thing stopping him…was him.

What if he believed he was capable of and deserving of a wonderful life and a bright future, despite the shadows of his past. Was that what other people saw when they looked at him?

"Violet, I—" he began.

"There's the happy couple," Rob Brookstone said as he came up and offered a hand to Jordan while Elaine Brookstone pulled her daughter into a big hug. Jordan shook hands with Violet's dad who then tugged him in for a hug. Not unusual. Jordan had practically been an honorary member of the Brookstone family for years. Which made his situation even worse. They trusted him and cared for him, and he'd drawn their only daughter into a fake engagement and then realized he was hopelessly in love with her.

Rob Brookstone should be punching him in the nose.

"What do you mean by *happy couple*?" Violet asked.

Her parents exchanged a glance.

"Ryan blabbed, didn't he?" Violet asked.

"He was so happy for you, he couldn't help himself," her mother said. "And it is happy news. Jordan, I can't imagine anyone more perfect for Violet than you. I've always thought so, and I'm so glad for you both."

Elaine Brookstone hugged him, and Jordan wished a rogue wave would knock him into the lake. He was deceiving them all, even Violet who he had almost told the truth to but didn't. Was now the time?

Violet's dad pulled up the handle on his suitcase and her mom hooked her shoulder bag to the handle. While her parents were distracted, Jordan turned to Violet and took her hand. Every ounce of hospitality in him wanted to unburden Violet's parents of their luggage, but he couldn't miss his chance. He was determined to finish what he started because he didn't know when he'd feel bold enough to say it if he didn't grab the chance. "I love you, Violet," he said.

Her parents turned their attention back to them, and her mother sighed.

Violet's expression told him immediately that she assumed this was part of the game. It was her *of course you can wear that color* or *let me find you a slightly different size* smile that she used in her store.

"I love you, too," she said brightly, and then she took her parents by the arms. "I hope you're not mad that I didn't tell you weeks ago. I wanted you to enjoy your trip instead of thinking you should rush home and congratulate us."

Her mother smiled. "We might have done just that."

"See?" Violet said. "And now you're here, we can all celebrate together."

"Perfect," her dad said.

Her mother nodded, but Jordan noticed the subtle question in her smile. Did she suspect something was amiss and that was why Violet hadn't been quick to share the news of their engagement?

"I can't wait for you to meet Daisy, and she'll be delighted to have guests," Violet said, plunging forward with the conversation. "Poor Ryan couldn't stay with me when he visited because of his allergy, but I have my guest room all ready for you."

"I hope Daisy is a good traveler," her dad said, "since she'll have to make the trip to Virginia if what we hear about your prospects pans out."

"Details," Violet said. "This is a weekend to celebrate instead of fussing over details. I want everyone to swear we'll just be happy and enjoy the festivities."

"That's easy enough," her mother said pleasantly, although she gave Violet a long glance. "If that's what you want."

"And you two are doing the Holiday Hustle together, right?" Violet's dad asked.

Jordan cleared his throat. "Of course. We never miss it."

He and Violet had agreed to it, partly because they were a great team and also because people would expect it. It could be their last time. Next year, would Jordan be in Virginia?

He put on a brave face for Violet and her parents, declined their invitation for dinner because he was working late at a special reception for the festival weekend and promised to see them all the next day at the start line.

He leaned down and kissed Violet on the lips, just a quick touch of their lips. Chaste. Appropriate in front of her parents. Enough to play the role, but not nearly enough to demonstrate the love in his heart that he just couldn't seem to express in the right way or at the right time.

The brief kiss wasn't enough, and Jordan knew, as he walked away, that the choices he'd hoped would open up the world to him had actually closed him into a cage of his own making.

VIOLET HANDED JORDAN a stretchy headband meant to absorb perspiration and identify them as a team. She already had her red-and-green sweatband in place and her hair in a ponytail. The Holiday Hustle T-shirt was also red with an image of a green Christmas tree wearing running shoes.

"I liked last year's headband that was red and white like a candy cane," Jordan commented as he adjusted his. The other teams milling about downtown were waiting for the envelope that would give them their first clue in the race that was part athletic, part scavenger hunt, part adventure and all kinds of silly.

"Is this our year to come in first?" Violet asked. "We've played by the rules every year, and we deserve a win. Especially since this is our—"

She didn't have to say it. Jordan knew. Everyone knew. Some of the other racers and spectators thought Violet and Jordan were likely to leave the island as a couple, and some of the nearby teams knew the truth. Violet would need a new partner next year.

She looked around. Of course she had many friends on the island. There were other choices. If her brother was available, he'd come home and do the Holiday Hustle with her—especially if she asked him to. He'd believe he was helping her out since her fiancé had broken her heart and decamped a year earlier. Deceiving her family made her breakfast bagel weigh heavily in her stomach. If she told them the truth right now, they wouldn't betray her secret on purpose, but it would make it very hard for them.

Letting them believe, for just a few more days, was easier for them. She could bear her own misery.

"What if it's not our last year?" Jordan said, completing her sentence. "I may not get that job and you may be stuck with me forever on this little island."

Violet forced a laugh. "If you become sulky, I may have to push you into the lake, so you'd better get that job for your own good."

Jordan gave her a wistful smile. "There are times I wonder what really would be for my own good."

"Winning this race is a start," Violet said. "The prize would give you a nice pot of money for moving expenses. I hear that can be pricey, and you'll have to set up an apartment in Virginia and you'll need all sorts of things like a shower curtain and rug and dishes." She smiled. "We better focus on winning."

Jordan took her hand. "I don't really care about winning. In fact, Violet, there's something I need to say."

Shirley from the chamber of commerce blew a whistle loud enough to awaken lost shipwrecked souls from the lake. "Are you ready to get out there and show your stuff?"

she asked over a loudspeaker. Her enthusiasm alone could propel a runner across a finish line, and she had a reputation for being almost dangerously passionate about all things Christmas Island.

Whatever Jordan was about to say, Violet sensed it was important. Heaven help her, she didn't have the emotional strength to hear it and she was glad Shirley had assaulted all their eardrums. Jordan could table whatever conversation he intended.

"Line up," Shirley said. She held a stack of red envelopes in her hand, fanned out like a deck of playing cards.

"I love you," Jordan said, low enough that only Violet could hear.

But she did hear.

There were teams all around them moving toward the start line, stretching, bouncing, getting ready for the starter's pistol to set them off on a race around the island. Her parents were among the onlookers, and her brother was farther down the line of competitors with his last-minute teammate, Cara Peterson.

But Violet felt the force of Jordan's low words as if they were standing alone on a craggy cliff above the sea.

"I'm in love with you," he said. "I've never felt this way before, and it took me a while to know what it was."

"A while?" Violet asked.

"Years," he admitted, "although the process has sped up a lot in the past few weeks."

Weeks? He'd been in love with her for weeks? But not before the fake engagement. Since then. Was that the catalyst…and if so, was his love built on a lie?

Shirley moved down the row of racers and shoved an envelope into Violet's hand, and Violet gripped it as if it contained an explanation for Jordan's proclamation. Why was he telling her this now? Why here? Had he just figured this out?

Those were the practical questions in her mind as she stared at Jordan, mouth open, completely without words. The rush of emotions his statement aroused made her feel as if she could run across water. Perhaps running was the best idea.

"Ready, set, open the envelopes!" Shirley called over the bullhorn and a pistol shot rang out.

Around them, teams were ripping open envelopes and slivers of red paper drifted past on the breeze. There was a pause while racers read the location and nature of their first challenge, and then teams scattered.

Jordan and Violet remained, locked in each other's gaze, the unopened envelope in Violet's hand.

"Go!" someone from the crowd yelled.

"I mean it," Jordan said. "I finally understand my feelings for you, and I don't want to let you go."

"We have to go," Violet said, casting a glance at the racers who were way ahead of them, jumping on bikes and taking off on an island road.

"We don't," Jordan said. "We have to have an honest conversation about our feelings and what we're going to do, and we haven't had a minute alone since yesterday."

We don't. Just the way he'd said it raised Violet's hackles. As if he was in control. As if he was the one who decided that honesty was the best policy.

In defiance—or self-defense if she was being honest with herself—Violet tore open the envelope as if she was throwing down a glove before a duel. She hadn't asked to be a fake fiancée. She hadn't asked to fall in love with her best friend. And she certainly hadn't asked to be in this ridiculous situation.

"Here's an honest conversation for you," she said. "People are going to wonder why we're just standing here. Not as much as they're going to wonder about the fake story I eventually am forced to circulate about our breakup, of course." She kept her voice so low that it took on a villainous quality. "In fact, not one thing about this stinking summer has made any sense except for this. We're going to kick butt in this race and collect our prize. That's the one thing I feel competent about controlling right now."

She hadn't said *I love you, too*, even though the words wanted to claw their way out of her. He'd finally given in, weeks after she had. He'd won the game of chicken Rebecca had accused them of playing. But it wasn't going to do either of them any good. It was up to her to keep her head.

Jordan reached out and snatched the clue from the open envelope. "We're not going until we talk about this."

Violet reached for the clue, but he held it over his head, just as he had when they were kids goofing around, playing keep-away, laughing, not having a care in the world. Violet stood on her tiptoes to try to grab the paper. The effort created heat in her body matching the heat in her brain. How dare he do this when they were in the middle of the most important conversation of their lives and were already falling behind in a race? Not to mention the dozens of people watching from the sidelines.

"You're resorting to childish games," she said. That was it. He was retreating to a safe place. Was he afraid to embark on a new life, and he was only telling her he loved her as a life raft, an excuse not to leave Christmas Island? Could she believe him—and did he even trust himself? Jordan had never been in love, as far as she knew. Then again, neither had she.

"You have to go," Violet's dad yelled. "You're getting behind."

What did it really matter? Maybe Jordan was right and they needed a serious conversation. Not that this was the place for it.

"Are you going to let your brother beat you?" her mother called.

Jordan's serious expression shifted and his

lips twisted just enough for Violet to know her mother's taunt had gotten through to him.

"I don't have a brother, but I'd be willing to beat yours if that's what you want," he said.

"He's practically your brother," Violet said.

"Only if you actually marry me," Jordan said.

"I won't."

"Even if I ask?" Jordan said.

They stood and stared at each other. The crowd had fallen silent again, waiting. Violet knew they couldn't hear her conversation with Jordan because of the street noise and the shouts of the other racers.

Violet took a deep breath and let it out. "We stop this conversation and this whole charade right now. Like the time we resolved to never again bring up my embarrassing performance in the school talent show when I thought I'd practiced the flute enough. We pretended it never happened for so long that I started to believe it never had."

"I don't know what you're talking about," Jordan said with a hint of a conspiratorial grin.

"Exactly. We stop talking right now, and we start racing."

"On one condition," Jordan said. "We talk later. After the race."

"I said we weren't going to bring up what you just said."

"That I'm in love with you or asking you to marry me?"

"You're not in love with me. I know you well enough to know you're confused. You're in love with…something else."

She couldn't believe he was in love with her, wouldn't let herself believe it. Because if it turned out not to be real, she wasn't going to make it worse by indulging in false hope and letting Jordan do the same. He was leaving the island, had to leave. It was his dream.

"That's what you really think?" Jordan asked.

Violet squared her shoulders and nodded.

"Then let's start racing," Jordan said. "I'm not giving up."

Violet didn't ask if he meant the race or their relationship. Instead, she switched into all-business mode. If she kept her mind on completing the Holiday Hustle and beating her brother's team, she could keep her emotions together and not fall apart.

CHAPTER TWENTY-THREE

DESPITE THEIR HEROIC efforts at biking uphill, counting the courses of brick in the front wall of the fire station and finding a tiny jingle bell hidden among a dozen docked kayaks, Jordan and Violet were still, to the best of his guessing, in third or fourth place.

The penultimate challenge was laid out near the hardware store on a downtown backstreet, and Jordan sighed when he saw it.

"I bet you wish you were racing with your brother," he said. Ryan Brookstone and Cara Peterson were nowhere in sight, which told Jordan that they'd completed the task quickly and moved on. Of course Ryan completed it quickly. The task was to assemble a birdhouse resembling a gingerbread cottage. Why hadn't he developed any woodworking skills himself? He didn't have the luxury of a dad who could have taught him, but what had been stopping him from learning on his own?

"I'm sure we can handle this," Violet said. "Ryan didn't get all the building talent in the family. I can follow directions and put things together."

Jordan surveyed the table assigned to him and Violet. There were pieces of precut wood, decorating accents, nails and a hammer. A sample birdhouse sat on a table nearby. But there were no directions.

"I can also look at the sample," Violet added.

Jordan admired her tenacity and perseverance, but he also knew it was a defense mechanism. If she gave the challenge all her attention, she could avoid looking him in the eye. She hadn't wanted to hear he loved her. He had to admit it was poor timing right at the start of the race. He'd blurted it out, but she hadn't said the same back to him despite her blurting out the same words before.

There'd been an audience at the fireworks, and he'd dismissed her proclamation as part of the ruse. There'd been a large audience at the start of the race. Had she similarly dismissed his words?

No. He'd spoken quietly, for her ears only. It wasn't for show and he knew she knew it, but she still all but clapped her hands over her ears. Did she find him so foolish or incapable of love? Did she really think he was just confusing his feelings and seeking something to hold on to?

Was he?

No.

"And you're not helpless at this either," Violet said. "You helped me assemble new display racks at my store and put up a new mailbox. You've got skills."

Her confidence bolstered him, but she'd always seen the best in him whether he deserved it or not.

Violet took up the hammer and started tapping in nails at the base of the birdhouse. "Hold this wall up," she said, her face all concentration. Jordan stood so close to her he could smell her shampoo and feel her hair brush his cheek. It took him back to their zip-lining adventure. He should have told her then that he loved her. Would she have believed him?

Two more teams arrived, hot on their heels in the placings. "We have to hurry," Violet said. She ran over and looked more closely at the example birdhouse, running her hands over it as if she was trying to memorize it so she could re-create it.

"Ryan would be better at this," Jordan said.

"Stop it. You're good at lots of things. We can do this if we put our heads together."

"I haven't been a good friend this summer."

Her hammer slipped and she whacked her finger. Jordan took her hand and kissed the finger. Violet stilled and didn't pull back her hand.

"We're still in this race," she whispered, but her pulse beat in her neck.

He held her hand a moment longer and then released it. He began picking up the sidewalls of the birdhouse and holding them in place, trusting Violet to hammer close to his vulnerable fingers. To his amazement, they finished the structure and tacked on the Christmas decorations well ahead of the other two teams, and the moderator handed them their next clue.

They read the location together and then exchanged a glance.

It was their special place. The rock-skipping beach.

"Could we be so lucky?" Jordan asked.

"We'll see when we get there."

They grabbed their bikes and pedaled toward the beach they knew so well. Every turn in the road was familiar, and having Violet by his side, speeding along, wind in their hair, took Jordan back to all the good times they'd shared. He would miss this most of all, the joy and freedom of the island roads and especially the joy and freedom he felt when he was with Violet.

Joy and freedom. Wasn't that what he'd been seeking all his life?

They jumped off their bikes and got their instructions. Already, there were three other teams lined up at the water's edge with race judges standing nearby. The challenge was for the team to skip rocks, and the first team to have a combined total of sixty was the victor.

"Thirty each," Jordan said.

"We've done it before," Violet said.

Hope was a living thing in Jordan's chest. This was their race to lose at this point. Was it a sign that the final, deciding challenge was the one best suited for them? The race challenges were dreamed up by a committee during the winter, and the members were sworn to secrecy. Everyone on the island took the competition seriously and there had never been a leak.

This was fate.

Jordan glanced down the line of competitors who'd made it this far only to be thwarted by rocks, surface tension and luck. The other two teams ahead of them were Ryan and Cara and Andy, one of the maintenance guys at the Great Island Hotel, with a woman Jordan didn't know. Andy had both hands on his head and his companion was crouched down, apparently searching for a good rock. Ryan threw a rock without even attempting to skip it and Cara laughed. How long had they been there without successfully completing the task?

Jordan and Violet's chances were very good.

Violet nodded to the judge to get his attention, and then she skipped a wide flat stone across the lake's surface. Ten skips.

"Warming up," she said. She tried another and got fifteen skips, way below her usual skill level.

"Don't overthink it," Jordan said.

Violet turned toward him. "That's probably my problem. I'm trying so hard not to think about anything that I can't concentrate on anything."

"Watch this," Jordan said. He glanced at the judge to make sure the judge was ready to count, and then he tossed a rock out and counted as it skipped over the surface of the water. "I counted twenty-nine," he said. "And you could end this quickly by grabbing a thirty-one, which I know you're more than capable of."

"Usually," Violet said.

"Always," Jordan said. "You're the confident one out of the two of us. You've always known what you're about and what you want. I'm the one who's floundered around and thought I wanted something I didn't have."

"What do you want?" Violet asked. She held a perfect skipping stone in her hand. She could toss it and secure their place at the finish line. But she waited for his answer instead.

Joy and freedom. Why didn't he just say the words? Joy and happiness came from the island he'd finally realized he loved and from the people there. Freedom was a tougher one. He'd wanted freedom from memories, reputation, poverty, lack of opportunities. But what good would it be if he didn't use that freedom to do what he wanted, be where he wanted, be with people he loved?

He couldn't say all those things. Not with

Violet's exasperated expression boring a hole through him, a rock clutched in her hand. Not with the fate of the race teetering on their performance. If they won, he could use his half of the prize money to further improve his house—not to sell it, but to stay in it with a fresh perspective.

"Jordan," Violet said. "What do you want?"

He knew she wanted a bold answer, and she deserved one. But he needed time to rethink everything. "Working on it," he said. He glanced at the water and then back at Violet. "Right now, I want to win this race and we're perfect for this task. We've been training for years and didn't even know it."

Violet gave him a long look. "Fine," she said. She rubbed the rock, did three test throws and rolled her shoulders, and then sailed the skipping stone over the water, garnering an amazing thirty-three skips. The judge counted the last one aloud, and the other teams stopped and turned to watch.

"Of all the rotten luck," Ryan yelled. "My sister would get a rock-skipping challenge."

"You did it," Jordan said.

"You helped," Violet said. "But now we better hustle to the finish line before another team manages to complete the skipping task. Time's flying."

Just hours before, Jordan had thought time wasn't on his side, but now he realized he was in control of his own timeline. The choice was his.

CHAPTER TWENTY-FOUR

VIOLET THOUGHT HER day couldn't have any more wild twists and turns. There'd been the scene at the starting line in which Jordan had claimed to be in love with her and even brought up marriage, possibly for real. Then they'd raced, enduring ups and downs until their final victory. And now the dinner at the Holiday Hotel that was supposed to be a victory dinner courtesy of her parents was obviously something else.

Congratulations, the big banner hanging over their table said. There were fresh flowers on the table and a large box gift wrapped with paper that had wedding rings and bells on it. White paper wedding bells also adorned the table.

"Here are the big winners," her father said as Violet approached the table with Jordan, who had met her at her house and walked down the street with her.

"We have two things to celebrate," her mother said. "Your big win today and your engagement."

Ryan stood up and shook Jordan's hand. "Congrats on winning the race. Sorry I ran my mouth about the engagement, but they would have found out the minute they got here anyway, and no way could I stop them from throwing a party."

"There's a party?" Violet asked. She glanced around and saw her friends pop out from behind the bar, their faces a mixture of frozen smiles and trepidation.

"Just a few of your best friends," her mother said. "Your friends, too, Jordan. I know everyone on the island is just so happy you two have finally found true love. While we're here, we want to talk about the wedding, and of course we want to pay for it."

Why wouldn't her mother stop gushing and looking so happy? Violet wanted to pop this balloon and put everyone out of their misery by blurting out the truth, but at that moment, Quentin and Jillian Shelley entered the dining room and waved to her and Jordan. She saw them glance up at the Congratulations banner and the wrapped gift on the table.

The wedding bells on the table would convey that the congratulations weren't just for the Holiday Hustle win.

She couldn't blow Jordan's story in front of the Shelleys. He wouldn't do that to her. There was nothing she could do except smile.

"You're my only daughter, and I've always wanted you to have a big beautiful wedding," her mother said, embracing her. "You'll be the prettiest bride and I'm sure you've already started thinking about your dress."

Violet had not thought a single moment about her wedding dress because she was not getting married. That had never been part of the plan. And now her parents were practically hiring a band and booking flights for a honeymoon.

Everything had gone too far, and Violet couldn't speak the truth without ruining all the efforts Jordan had made. She would destroy his job prospects, but her other choice was lying to her parents and brother.

"I can't wait for you to open your engagement gift," her mother said. "It's breakable, so you'll have to handle it carefully."

Handle it carefully. And that was her life in a nutshell right now, Violet thought as she opened a beautiful set of four matching champagne glasses. They would be perfect for toasting at a wedding if she ever received a proposal that wasn't a sham. She considered Jordan's words at the starting line earlier: *even if I ask?* But she put that thought aside. He hadn't asked, not for real.

And he could have. She'd practically begged him on the rock-skipping beach to just go ahead and say the words. She'd asked what he wanted, and all he needed to say was that he wanted her.

How much longer was she going to kill her own feelings to save someone else's?

JORDAN FROZE A smile on his face and wondered how he was ever going to regain the trust of Violet's family. Her parents and brother had readily believed he and Violet had a sincere engagement. Would they ever trust him again? He sat and watched Violet open the gift of champagne glasses while trying not to let his attention drift over to Quentin Shelley and his wife who sat across the restaurant. Quentin had a room for the next three nights at the Great Island Hotel, but

Jordan hadn't yet talked to him because he'd been occupied with the Holiday Hustle.

Quentin could be on vacation, and he could have come with big news for Jordan. Losing the trust of the Brookstone family was going to be emotionally painful, but losing the trust of his employer if everything came to light would have devastating consequences of a different kind.

There was only one way through it all. Marry Violet. Then, he could turn down the job in Virginia and say there was a family conflict. He could stay on the island and not have to make up any more stories or acknowledge that the engagement had been a lie. Their closest friends would keep the secret. It would be the easiest way.

And the worst. Violet was not going to marry him. Especially not because it was an easy solution to his problems. If she truly was in love with him…that would be different, but then it would be wrong to continue the relationship without being completely truthful. Starting a lifetime together based on a lie wouldn't work.

"That's the owner of the Great Island and the Great Valley Hotels," Violet said while they waited for their drinks. She nodded toward the table where Quentin and Jillian Shelley sat sipping drinks. "Mr. Shelley and his wife are lovely people and they think highly of Jordan," she continued.

How was Violet making polite conversation and continuing the ruse while Jordan felt as if the walls were closing in and about to squeeze the truth out of him? Was Violet not as emotionally wrapped up as he was?

"This is going to be so hard," Violet's mother said. "I never thought you'd leave the island, but I can understand that you may need to if Jordan's work is in Virginia."

Violet tilted her head. "Do you think his work is more important than mine?"

What was she doing? Making an argument for no reason?

"Of course not," her mother said. "Although you could start a boutique somewhere else."

"Jordan could be a hotel manager somewhere else," Violet said. "Like here."

An uncomfortable silence fell around the table, and Jordan held his breath. Was Violet trying to ruin the party, or was she sowing seeds of dissension to better explain away their upcoming breakup? It would be a brilliant move, and her intelligence and perception were two of the many things he admired and loved about her.

If he had to make a choice between marrying Violet—if she truly loved him—and a dream job, what would he do?

Jordan took Violet's hand and kissed it. "I want us both to be happy," he said. He hoped that would gracefully end the conversation, although kudos to Violet for starting it.

"Then this could get very difficult for you," Violet said.

So much for a graceful exit. Violet was doing a convincing job of laying the groundwork for the end of their engagement, but the thought of ending it and taking back the ring made Jordan feel as sad and empty as he had when his parents didn't come home that night when he was a kid. He remembered the pajamas he wore when his grandparents had come into his room to give him the worst news.

Violet's family had become his, and the May brothers, and the Petersons and numerous other island families. When his grandparents passed not long after he graduated from high school, his friends had tried to ensure he wasn't lonely. Why was he inviting the inherent loneliness of a new life in a different state?

Violet's father cleared his throat as if he was about to say something, but they were all spared any more awkward talk by the arrival of their food.

While they ate, Jordan noticed the Shelleys only had drinks and appetizers. They were probably having a late dinner at the Great Island. Sure enough, they got up from their table before Jordan and Violet's family finished their meal.

"We don't want to intrude," Quentin Shelley said as he paused near Jordan and stuck out a hand. "I can see you're celebrating the happy couple and their big win today."

Jordan stood and introduced the Shelleys to the Brookstones, and then Quentin and Jillian left after a moment of polite conversation.

To Jordan's great relief, the Shelleys hadn't brought up anything about him taking a job off the island, and Violet also didn't renew the line of conversation. No one else steered anywhere near it, but it was still the calm before the storm. And the storm was coming.

At the end of the night, he gave Violet what he believed was a convincing good-night kiss in front of the Holiday Hotel, and she walked home with her parents.

Ryan Brookstone hung out for a moment longer with Jordan. "My sister always puts everyone else first. When I was a kid, she let me win arguments and gave me first choice on everything from cookies to which bedroom I wanted when our parents got a new house when I was in middle school."

"She lets me pick first, too, unless we're talking about clothes," Jordan said.

"I was a little surprised at dinner tonight when she implied she didn't want to move away for your job," Ryan said.

He wasn't the only one. Had it been tactical brilliance or was there more going on in Violet's mind and heart?

"We'll work it out somehow," Jordan said.

Ryan gave him a friendly pat on the shoulder and turned to walk up the hill toward the Great Island Hotel. Jordan got in his car and headed home. He hadn't left a light on, and he usually dreaded approaching the house in the dark with its aura of sorrow. A faint gleam left from the sunset provided just enough light, though, to give the house a golden glow. He imagined Violet sitting on the front porch, waiting for him to come home from work, her dog by her side.

He'd never pictured her in his home before, and the image stayed with him as he laid his head on his pillow. He was looking forward to seeing Quentin Shelley the next day, but wondering with all his heart what he was going to do.

CHAPTER TWENTY-FIVE

"AM I TOO EARLY?" Jillian Shelley nudged Violet's front door open a crack even though Violet hadn't yet turned the sign to Open.

Violet looked up from the computer at the register desk and smiled. "You're welcome anytime," she said. "I'm sorry we didn't get a chance to chat much at the Holiday Hotel last night."

Jillian waved a hand. "You were having a party with your family. We didn't want to intrude. You look so much like your beautiful mother, and your brother is a younger copy of your dad."

"I'm very lucky to have them in my life," Violet said.

"And I'm sure they're excited about the wedding, which is what I wanted to talk with you about this morning."

Violet felt her heart jump in her chest. She hadn't spent any time or emotion thinking about or planning a wedding, and that oddity was something her parents had brought up the previous night at her apartment before they went to bed. Violet glanced up at the ceiling as if she could see them upstairs or they could hear her.

"I haven't really thought much about the wedding," Violet stammered. "It's the busy season here on the island, and with Jordan being up in the air…considering the potential job change, I mean… I guess we haven't gotten to that step yet."

Jillian swept the room as if she was checking to be sure they were alone, and Violet sank back onto the stool behind the counter. She really should offer her guest a seat, but her knees felt weak. Lying to and fooling lovely people like the Shelleys was almost the worst part of playing a fake fiancée. Almost. Lying to herself had dug a crater in the side of her own heart.

"I'd like to make a suggestion about your wedding, but I don't want to step on toes or cause offense anywhere, especially after seeing your family last night," Jillian said. She leaned on the counter and toyed with a pair of dangling earrings in the jewelry display.

"What is your suggestion?" Violet asked.

"I don't know exactly when you were planning the ceremony."

"We don't have a date," Violet said, glad she could at least be truthful about that.

"Every season in Virginia is beautiful," Jillian said. "Fall and winter are my favorites."

Violet began to realize where Jillian was going with this. Was she hoping Violet and Jordan would have their wedding in Virginia?

"Which is why I'd like to offer to host the wedding at the Great Valley," Jillian continued. "Quentin and I have enjoyed getting to know you and Jordan, and we don't have any children of our own, so it would be such a pleasure to be part of your special day."

Violet felt her eyes sting with tears. These sweet people had no children of their own and wanted the chance to be part of her wedding with Jordan. What kind of monster would she be to let this sham go on any longer?

"I don't know what to say," Violet said, her voice thick.

"I'm sorry," Jillian said, putting a hand on Violet's. "I'm afraid I'm intruding. Your parents probably want an island wedding, and of course you'd want to get married here where all your friends are. Even though you'll be living in Virginia soon—or at least Jordan will while you tie up loose ends here—it would be possible to hold the wedding at the Great Island." Jillian smiled. "I should have thought of that first instead of suggesting Virginia."

Violet took in a deep breath, but she still felt dizzy. Jillian had as much as told her Jordan had the new job. He'd be living in Virginia soon. Of course that was why she and Quentin were there. Quentin could be offering Jordan the job at that very moment.

"Oh, my poor girl," Jillian said. "I'm sorry. I can see I upset you with all this wedding talk and moving talk. It's the most exciting time of your life, but also frightening and emotional. I remember marrying Quentin and starting a new life, even though it's been a long time. I shouldn't barge in."

"It's not that," Violet said. "It's so nice of you to offer to help with our wedding."

"I'm offering more than help," Jillian said. "You can use either hotel as your venue free of charge, catering included. It's the least we can do for upending your life and stealing you both away from Christmas Island."

A free and beautiful wedding. Violet let tears spill down her cheeks. If only she and

Jordan were getting married for real, the prospect of having their ceremony and reception at the Great Island Hotel where they'd danced so many times before and made memories and where all their friends could attend—it was beyond generous and perfect and…utterly impossible.

"We'll talk later when this has had a chance to sink in," Jillian said. "I only bring it up because your parents are here, and I thought it might give us a chance to coordinate and work together. These types of plans are so much easier to make face-to-face, I always think."

"Thank you," Violet choked out.

"I believe I'll see you at dinner tonight," Jillian said. "There will be another reason to celebrate, if you know what I mean."

With another friendly smile, Jillian left Violet's Island Boutique, and Violet dried her tears with her sleeve and picked up her phone with steely resolve. Enough was enough. All her life she'd believed that being kind to people in her orbit was also being kind to herself. And it usually was. Her friends returned her love and loyalty. Her family did the same. But now it was time to tell Jordan that her feelings and her desires meant just as much as his.

We need to talk. Now.

She texted Jordan instead of calling him out of respect for the morning routine at the hotel front desk. If he didn't call her back within—she checked her watch—five minutes, she was going to either call him or climb the hill to the Great Island Hotel and find him. The game had gone on too long.

QUENTIN SHELLEY SMELLED of aftershave and coffee as he looped an arm around Jordan's shoulders and walked him to a quiet place at the end of the Great Island Hotel porch.

"It's a heavy topic for this early in the day," Quentin said, "but I'm about to change your life."

Change his life. Jordan had dreamed of that for so long he could hardly believe it was about to happen. There was no question what was coming. The only question was what he was going to do.

"Can I get you some coffee or a breakfast tray first?" Jordan asked. Why was he stalling and putting off what should be the news he'd wanted for a long time?

Quentin laughed. "Ever the epitome of hospitality. That's what I love about you, Jordan. You seem to know exactly what people want."

"Shall I get that breakfast ordered, then?" Returning to the familiar role of host helped Jordan get his feet under him.

Quentin shook his head and put both hands on Jordan's shoulders. He steered him to a chair and deposited him in it. "I already had coffee and breakfast with my wife. She wanted to eat early and get downtown because she wanted to see Violet before her shop got busy."

"She wanted to talk to Violet?" Jordan asked.

"It's a secret between the ladies right now, but it does involve your wedding so you'll hear about it sooner or later."

Jordan's phone buzzed in his pocket, but he couldn't get it out and look at it. His boss was holding an earnest and life-changing conversation with him. The text would have to wait.

"I won't beat around the bush any longer," Quentin said. "I'm here for a visit, yes, but my main purpose is to offer you the job at the Great Valley. You won out fair and square over the other candidate, even though we did give him an honest chance. But we had our eye on you from the start."

"You did?"

"Yes. I'm always looking for talent in all levels of management. This is a people business, and I need to make sure I have the right people. I never thought a native of Christmas Island who'd worked a decade at the Great Island would move, but when I heard you were open to it and then we met your wonderful Violet and she seemed open to the move, too, well, Jillian and I knew we'd found our next general manager for the Great Valley."

At any other time in his life, Jordan would have jumped to his feet and shouted his acceptance to the rafters of the historic porch.

His phone buzzed again, but it was the least of his problems. He was about to do something life-changing and permanent, probably damaging, certainly dramatic.

"I have to tell you the truth," Jordan said. "I respect you and your wife immensely, not just as the owners of the hotel where I work, but also as people. After getting to know you over the past month or so, I've learned something important."

"I hope this is leading up to a yes," Quentin said.

Jordan sat back in the wicker chair that should have been comfortable and comforting, but he only felt the weight of what he'd done.

"When I heard about the job opening and I considered the fact that you were known to favor married managers, I made a choice."

"Is that when you asked Violet to marry you?" Quentin asked.

"Yes and no." Jordan swallowed. What he was about to say could never be undone. "I asked her to pretend to be my fiancée so I'd have a better shot at a promotion."

Quentin's face was like a cloud passing in front of a bright sun for a moment and then it cleared. "I don't believe that."

"It's stupid and wrong. I know, and I'm sorry."

"No, what I don't believe is that you and Violet aren't actually together. I've never seen two people who have such chemistry, not counting me and my wife, of course."

"We've been friends all our lives," Jordan said. "The stories we told you were true."

"But she's not really engaged to you and you're not getting married."

Jordan shook his head. "I'm sorry."

"I'm sorry for you, then. You're the one missing out."

"I know." Jordan assumed he meant missing out on the job, and there was no arguing the fact. He didn't deserve a promotion, and, truthfully, he didn't want it anymore. Pretending to be engaged to Violet had made things strangely real to him. He wasn't leaving Christmas Island, even though he knew he was likely to be fired from the Great Island Hotel for lying to the owner. And he had no one to blame but himself.

"I don't mean the job," Quentin said. "You're missing out on something with Violet. Any woman who cares about you enough to put herself through that much misery is worth making any sacrifice for. You're missing out if you can't see that."

"I see it," Jordan said. "But there's nothing I can do about it." He didn't have a father to talk to, but talking to Quentin somehow felt like it. He'd disappointed the older man horrifically, and he was ashamed of himself. Quentin deserved better.

"You see it, so what have you done about it?"

"I told her I loved her at the start of the race yesterday. I said I was in love with her."

"And?"

"She wouldn't listen. She wanted to put her head down and complete the race without talking about it. And then her parents and brother had that engagement dinner last night and it was…awful. I hate what I've done."

Quentin nodded. "What you've done is lay bare what had apparently been right under the surface."

"Not that it does me much good," Jordan said. "And I don't deserve anyone's pity. I tried a shortcut, a sure thing to a job that I thought would take me to a better life, only to realize the life I had here was pretty great. I roped my best friend into playing along only to realize she's more than just my best friend."

"And now?"

"Now I've built a trap of my own devising. I can't stay here because you're probably going to fire me. I'm obviously not going to Virginia. And I've sliced a big hole in the best relationship I've ever had."

"Maybe you should come to Virginia after all," Quentin said.

"You can't seriously want me there."

"You're not going to pretend to be engaged again, are you?"

"No. Making that mistake once in a lifetime is too often for me."

"Then come to Virginia and start over," Quentin suggested.

Jordan shook his head. "Thank you. That's an offer I would have jumped at before I realized some important things this summer. You've been nothing but kind and decent, but I can't accept your offer that I didn't get fairly."

"What if we forgot that part?" Quentin said. He didn't meet Jordan's eyes. He was looking over Jordan's shoulder and Jordan didn't blame him. How could Quentin still be so kind after the way he'd lied?

"No, but thanks. I don't want to leave Christmas Island. It's funny—I thought I had it bad here with my poor upbringing, but now I realize I'm the luckiest person alive to have the friends I do and live on this magical island."

"What about Violet?"

Jordan slumped forward and put his head in his hands. "I'm going to spend every day for as long as it takes begging her to forgive me and convincing her that she's the love of my life and I can't live without her."

"You'll be busy," Quentin said.

"I'll have time on my hands since I wouldn't blame you at all for firing me."

"You're not losing your job here," Quentin said.

Jordan looked up. Quentin was still looking over his shoulder. "That's kinder of you than I deserve."

"Stop talking about what you deserve. You've earned a second chance with your excellent job performance all these years. I don't know if you'll get a second chance with Violet, but I believe you're about to find out."

Quentin pointed behind Jordan, and Jordan knew without turning around that Violet was standing right behind his chair.

CHAPTER TWENTY-SIX

JORDAN ROSE FROM his chair so quickly it teetered and almost tipped over, but Violet steadied it. She'd overheard the conversation beginning with Quentin renewing the offer to come to Virginia and then Jordan turning him down.

She'd heard what Jordan said about her.

Jordan stood before her, his hands open as if he was ready to catch something. Quentin smiled at her behind Jordan's back and walked away down the length of the porch.

She swallowed. "You didn't answer my texts."

"I'm sorry. I was…"

"I know. I came up here to tell you we couldn't do this any longer. The pretending had to be over."

Jordan nodded.

"Jillian Shelley came to my boutique a little while ago and offered to host our wedding for us, free of charge, in Virginia or here. She said—" Violet had to break off because sobs threatened her words. "She said she didn't have any children of her own and she wanted to do this for us. It broke my heart."

Jordan reached for her hands, but she clasped them together. She wasn't ready for his touch. Not yet.

"Did you mean everything you said to Quentin Shelley?" she asked.

"Everything."

"You turned down the job in Virginia even though he was still going to take you despite our lies."

"My lies," Jordan said. "You were blameless in this."

"I went along with it."

"Because you cared about me and you're the best friend in the world."

Violet crossed her arms. "I hated every minute of it."

"You did?" he asked, and then he nodded. "I'm sure you did. I'm sorry."

"I would do anything to help you, but I hated being the person who was going to help you right off this island."

She let her arms fall to her sides.

"I'm not leaving now," he said. "You helped me see what I have here. What we have here."

"What do we have, Jordan?"

"I told you yesterday that I was in love with you, and it's true. I've never loved anyone like I love you. I can offer you a lifetime of friendship behind us and a lifetime of love ahead of us."

He reached for her left hand where she still wore the engagement ring. He ran his finger over the ring and then curled his hand around hers.

"I left it on after the dinner last night," she said. She'd wanted to take it off, but somehow she couldn't.

He kissed her hand. "Would you consider leaving it on?"

"There's no point in pretending any longer," Violet said. "I heard you tell the truth to Quentin, and I was proud of you. That's the Jordan I know and—"

Jordan got down on one knee on the porch floor. "Violet, I love you and I never want to spend a day apart from you. Will you marry me?"

She'd heard what he'd said to Quentin, but she didn't need that confirmation. Jordan had always been an open book to her, as she had to him. Until recently when they'd tangled themselves up in knots. Those wrinkles were gone now, and all she could see was her life-long love in front of her with hope in his eyes and his ring on her finger.

"Yes," she said. "I love you, too, Jordan. I have for a long time, and the shock of knowing I could lose you brought it all to the surface. I don't ever want to spend a day apart from you either."

Jordan rose to his feet and pulled her close. She loved the feel of his arms around her, not just the warm hug of a friend, but the embrace of someone she loved and was going to build a life with.

She pulled back and kissed him with her eyes closed, enjoying the warm morning breeze on her face and Jordan's familiar scent in her senses. This was perfection.

When she opened her eyes, Jordan was smiling at her. "Do you think our friends will believe us this time?"

She laughed. "I'm sure they will. But I have to tell my family the whole truth from the beginning."

"Will they be angry?"

"Maybe a little at first, but as long as I assure them the tale will have a happy ending, I think we'll be just fine."

"It does have a happy ending," Jordan said.

"And an even better beginning," Violet agreed.

They held hands and walked into the hotel lobby where Quentin and Jillian Shelley waited with Violet's brother.

"I think I'm catching on," Ryan said, "but I needed some backstory from the Shelleys. Promise me this is the real thing and you're happy," he said to Violet.

She laughed. "It's the real thing and I'm happy."

"Good," he replied. "I don't want to take a swing at Jordan, and more importantly, I already said you two were perfect for each other and I hate being wrong."

"You're not wrong," Jordan said.

"Welcome to the family," Ryan said, extending a hand. "Again."

"This time for real," Jordan said.

"I just want to say congratulations," Jillian said. She came forward and hugged Violet. "I'm sorry I won't have the pleasure of seeing you in Virginia, but I do love visiting this island and my offer of helping with your wedding still stands."

"A wedding," Violet said, turning to Jordan. "This time, we have to be serious about actually planning one."

"Tomorrow works for me," Jordan said.

Violet laughed. "Being in the clothing business, of course I've considered what I might want in a wedding dress someday, but I'm going to need a little time to find the perfect dress."

"So, next week?" Jordan asked.

Violet smiled and hugged Jordan, already imagining walking down the aisle with a fabulous train behind her and her true love waiting in front of her.

* * * * *

Don't miss the next book in Amie Denman's Return to Christmas Island miniseries, coming December 2023 from Harlequin Heartwarming.

Get 3 FREE REWARDS!

We'll send you 2 FREE Books plus a FREE Mystery Gift.

THE NORA ROBERTS COLLECTION

40% OFF!

Get to the heart of happily-ever-after in these Nora Roberts classics! Immerse yourself in the beauty of love by picking up this incredible collection written by, legendary author, Nora Roberts!

YES! Please send me the **Nora Roberts Collection**. Each book in this collection is 40% off the retail price! There are a total of 4 shipments in this collection. The shipments are yours for the low, members-only discount price of $23.96 U.S./$31.16 CDN. each, plus $1.99 U.S./$4.99 CDN. for shipping and handling. If I do not cancel, I will continue to receive four books a month for three more months. I'll pay just $23.96 U.S./$31.16 CDN., plus $1.99 U.S./$4.99 CDN. for shipping and handling per shipment.* I can always return a shipment and cancel at any time.

☐ 274 2595   ☐ 474 2595

Name (please print)

Address   Apt. #

City   State/Province   Zip/Postal Code

Mail to the Harlequin Reader Service:
IN U.S.A.: P.O. Box 1341, Buffalo, NY 14240-8531
IN CANADA: P.O. Box 603, Fort Erie, Ontario L2A 5X3

NORA2022

#483 TO TRUST A HERO
Heroes of Dunbar Mountain • by Alexis Morgan

Freelance writer Max Volkov recently helped solve a mystery in Dunbar, Washington, and now he's staying in town to write about it! But B and B owner Rikki Bruce is perplexed by another mystery—why is she so drawn to Max?

#484 WHEN LOVE COMES CALLING
by Syndi Powell

It's love at first sight for Brian Redmond when he meets Vivi Carmack. Vivi feels the same but knows romance is no match for her recent streak of bad luck. Now Brian must prove they can overcome anything—together.

#485 HER HOMETOWN COWBOY
Coronado, Arizona • by LeAnne Bristow

Noah Sterling is determined to save his ranch without anyone's assistance. But then he meets Abbie Houghton, who's in town searching for her sister. Accepting help has never been his strong suit...but this city girl might just be his weakness!

#486 WINNING OVER THE RANCHER
Heroes of the Rockies • by Viv Royce

Big-city marketing specialist Lily Richards comes to Boulder County, Colorado, to help the community after a devastating storm. But convincing grumpy rancher Cade Williams to accept her advice is harder than she expected...

HWCNM0723